CW00850546

English Department
Rivington & Blackrod
High School

THE INFINITE RIVER

To
Joe
Hope you
like my book.
Best wishes.

THE INFINITE RIVER

Book I of Tales from the Other Place

Michael R. Jones

Book Guild Publishing
Sussex, England

First published in Great Britain in 2011 by
The Book Guild Ltd
Pavilion View
19 New Road
Brighton, BN1 1UF

Typeset in Palatino by Ellipsis Digital Limited, Glasgow

Printed in Great Britain by
CPI Antony Rowe

A catalogue record for this book is available from The British Library.

ISBN 978 1 84624 606 7

The Geography of the Universe

Take heed, oh please, dear traveller,
For these distances are vast,
Impossible, impassable,
Your shoes will never last.
But come and take a load off,
Have a rest and stop a while
To consider for a moment
Just how tiny is a mile.
And while you're sitting thinking
Spare a thought for anyone
That would dare to cross the fullness
Of this grand continuum.
For one soul to truly witness
Every sight there is to see,
They would have to cross
The openness of all eternity.
Yet to know the endless wonders
And to touch the endless dreams,
Makes the fabric of reality
Rip cleanly at the seams,
Because it kills the concept
That our universe is endless,
Which has become the thinking
Of the brainy and the brainless.
But listen, please, dear traveller,

Take heart and don't despair.
There's a river through the cosmos
And a drifting planet where
Every thought and every vision
Dreamt up by the human race
Will be watching, growing,
Living, waiting
In
The Other Place.

Taken from *The Codex Imaginarium,*
by The Mysterious Wandering Gump

Prologue

Let your mind wander through the swirling mists of the cosmos. Allow yourself to glide, faster than the speed of light, past the many millions of stars and solar systems. Race effortlessly through the glassy eye of the Helix Nebula, then soar gracefully between the Pillars of Creation where countless suns are born. Dance for a while on the edge of the Galactic Horizon and then, only then, can you journey onwards into the blissful, majestic unknown. Here a wide band of light comes into view. Look how it snakes endlessly through the universe, but don't pause too long. This is The Other Place, and it won't make much sense to you, not yet. Keep moving. Rush down through the strange atmosphere and bewilderingly obscure landscape until you can just make out a bright-red structure gleaming in the light of an alien dawn. You can tell, even from this height, that it is mind-bendingly big, and you can hear, even from this distance, that the strange beings inside the ruby coliseum, the Googoldome, are far from happy.

'Silence, silence!'

Captain Calefaction, the supreme ruler of The Other Place, slammed his gavel down onto the hard diamonite desk repeatedly. He could feel his heart, which beat at a temperature of absolute zero, pounding in his super-cooled carbon chest. The trial of Lazarus Brown was not going well. Despite having a heart that was the coldest object in the known universe, the Captain was not a cruel man. The accused may have been a vengeful life-hating tyrant but he was, after all, his half-brother, and it was the Captain's place to assign punishment for the prisoner's crimes. He had opted for banishment rather than death and the crowd was not pleased. There were over ten million of them and they had travelled from all along The Other Place to see justice done. Apparently this was not it.

The Captain gazed down at the hated figure in the centre of the arena floor. From the staggering heights of the Captain's Table he looked as insignificant as a single cell. How misleading. That small dot was responsible for more death and pain than any other entity in history. Close to, the view was not much more revealing: Lazarus Brown was a worn-down skeleton of a man. His pinstripe suit hung off his emaciated frame as if it were draped over a wire hanger. His skin looked pale and pasty as if he had not seen natural light for some time and his hair was ragged and tatty like that of a beggar. His demeanour on the other hand was poised and graceful. His eyes were sharp, alert and dangerously intelligent. They blazed out at the world through the spherical walls of his transparent prison, an unbreakabubble. The Captain could almost feel the vinegar sting of their sharp bitterness.

Captain Calefaction gave a deep sigh then held up a large golden key. He displayed it briefly to the baying masses before allowing it to fly from his open palm. It arced high above the arena floor and stabbed into thin air like a dart in a board. Seconds later it started to spin rapidly, pulling and distorting space around it as if it were drilling a hole in reality itself. Still the crowd jeered and hollered, even as a wide black vortex rippled into existence and the unbreakabubble began to float towards it.

Lazarus looked eerily calm in his spherical prison. He stared vacantly into the rift, and something caught his attention. No one can know what he saw through that window into the universe, but whatever it was, it both surprised and excited him. Suddenly he began to sing. His voice filled the Googoldome. It smashed logic with its volume and drowned out the heckling crowd. His song was incredibly discordant and painful to hear. It was as if there were tones within tones, each one overlapping in both key and pitch. Suddenly the unbreakabubble shattered into a thousand pieces, discomfort turned into anarchy and ten million beings panicked.

As the glass prison exploded around him Lazarus Brown was thrown tumbling through the air. The open mouth of the screaming rift tried to suck him into oblivion but somehow he remained a calm epicentre in a world of chaos. He casually shot a white-hot tendril of energy from his hand. It wrapped itself around the key and anchored him to the centre of the raging vortex. By now the spectators had started a mass exodus. Crawling, flying, oozing, running, transmigrating, galloping and rolling, they all fled in terror. Still Lazarus Brown remained calm. He was almost smiling. He spoke. There was no effort in his voice, but it was so loud it seemed to bypass the ears and directly assault the brain.

'Behold your true leader as he is forced out into the void. I may have been cruel but beneath me those of you who survived would have been stronger, better. Now I must leave you under the pitiful care of my older, weaker brother, soft and snivelling, ready to be beaten into submission once more. Oh, and brother . . .' Lazarus Brown focused all of his terrible attention on the Captain, who felt as though his frozen heart would stop completely, '. . . tell The Gump I'll see him soon.'

Without warning a burst of energy leapt from the crackling portal and sliced through the tether holding Lazarus in place. Still smiling, he was pulled away into oblivion. The key was torn from its mooring point and followed the Technomancer into the void. The Googoldome was silent.

High at the back of the towering stands, unseen by anyone, The Mysterious Wandering Gump listened to the cosmos. There was a jarring chord in the symphony of the infinite – something was not quite right. It would seem that sooner or later this world was going to need a hero after all.

Chapter One

Fifteen Years Later

A fish is a fish when it swims in the sea,
And most fish have done this throughout history.
But as soon as it wiggles on land, can't you see,
There's no end to the things that it thinks it can be?

> Taken from *The Evolution of Thought*
> by The Mysterious Wandering Gump

Greenery Frankincense Jackson was a normal boy with a weird name. His mum was a rather unimaginative hippy. All her friends had called their children names like Tree or Leaf or Shrub. She had a lot of friends who had gone on to have a lot of children and consequently when Greenery was born all the good names had been taken. As for Frankincense . . . well, some parents just don't know how cruel they're being. At least he could shorten it though, so most of his friends called him Frank.

This was an odd morning for Greenery Jackson. For one, he was sitting up a tree with a hole in his pants. His nest of bright-orange hair looked like the world's spikiest, furriest fruit and his maroon school blazer was getting increasingly dirty.

The reason for his current predicament was staring up at him from ground level, growling and drooling heavily as it sized him up – Mongo, Mrs Wilson's boxer dog. Mongo had decided several weeks ago that he needed a new toy. Perhaps his current ones had lost their squeak or maybe he had solved the mysteries of his shiny rubber bone and was looking for a new challenge. Either way he had made it his mission to stop Greenery Jackson passing in front of his house. This had made the fifteen-minute walk to and from school a lot more interesting.

It said a lot about the type of person Greenery Jackson was that he actually enjoyed this new challenge and had revelled in finding different ways to outsmart his slobbering nemesis. These included: a modified dog whistle that acted as a canine attack alarm, bringing the other neighbourhood dogs running, distracting Mongo long enough for Greenery to escape; and a scent bomb made of crushed garlic and chilli oil which had sent Mongo fleeing with his tail between his legs.

Greenery had been lucky enough to get to school completely unmolested yesterday but that was because he had passed by Mrs Wilson's house at the same time the postman was being licked. Not by Mrs Wilson, by Mongo.

He had decided, however, that today would be the day he called Mongo's bluff. When the slack-faced hound had come barking and growling out of Mrs Wilson's driveway, Greenery had stood his ground. He even bent down to stroke the furry mess. He was hoping that a bond could be made between himself and the dog, creating a lasting relationship that would assure him safe passage from now on. This was not to be the case.

There was barking and snapping and fierce dribbling, all of which ended with a definite bite on the bum. It was lucky Greenery's school trousers were so baggy or else he would have been in considerable pain. Now, sitting up a rather pleasant silver birch tree with a cold draught blowing where it shouldn't, he was really regretting his decision.

'Come on, think, think,' he muttered to himself as he ran through the options available to him. Suddenly a spark of inspiration ignited his memory and awoke his cerebral cortex. He started to giggle to himself as his devious little plan took shape.

He wrestled two packets of pepper, rescued from the school canteen, out of his pocket. He hadn't needed them yesterday as, for once, the spaghetti bolognaise was surprisingly edible. Next he took from his school bag the piece of chalk that Mr Howcroft had thrown at his head last Tuesday for asking why light was invisible. He poured one packet of pepper into the other and using the loose pencil sharpener blade he had in his pencil case he scraped some chalk shavings into the same packet.

He climbed gently down the tree, making sure he was just out of reach of Mongo, who was looking as though he had acquired a taste for school uniforms. Hanging upside down he sprinkled his concoction into the dog's upturned snout. The effect was immediate.

The funniest thing about watching a dog sneeze repeatedly is the fact that they can't wipe their itchy nose and stand up at the same time. Snuffling, wheezing and staggering all over the pavement, Mongo beat a very wonky retreat. Greenery leapt from his safe haven and legged it down the street as fast

7

as he could. He was still chuckling to himself when he reached the gate of St Augustine's Secondary School just in time for the bell.

Greenery grabbed his jeans from his locker, and apart from the long, dog-related, discussion with his form teacher about why he was wearing them, it was a rather uneventful day. That was, until just after lunch. He was sitting in class staring through the window at the rainy vista of Littleton Bay. The small town had been his home for the past twelve years, which was in fact his whole life, and he was very fond of it. He was also listening intently to his teacher talk about precipitation.

Her name was Mrs Forecast. She was a small woman who was nearly as wide as she was tall. Today she was wearing a vertically striped jumper that made her look like a middle-aged beach ball. She was drawing a complicated diagram on the board involving evaporation, clouds and wind currents. It was the water cycle.

'Greenery Jackson, are you listening to me?' Mrs Forecast was a new teacher and didn't know how silly a question this was. Greenery always listened. He listened to teachers like a microphone listens to music. He was interested in everything. He couldn't help it. He wanted to know. His favourite words were 'Why?' 'What?' and 'How?'

'Yes, Miss, of course I am.'

'Well, you've done nothing but stare out of the window the entire time I've been talking. Is there something out there more interesting than my class?'

Greenery sighed deeply. He could see where this was going. Teachers didn't like him for some reason but he couldn't help it. He was a very honest boy, sometimes too honest.

'I've been looking out of the window, Miss, because right there for everyone to see is a working model of the water cycle. If you tilt your head this way, towards the beach, Miss, you can actually see where all the clouds are forming due to evaporation. An onshore breeze is pushing them this way, causing them to rise and their temperature to fall, condensing the water vapour and making it rain right on the playground. I've been looking out of the window because it is much more detailed and beautiful than your diagram, especially since on your diagram the clouds are moving against the wind, Miss.'

The class stared at him open-mouthed and silent. Even Greenery's best mate, Sam, looked shocked. All that could be heard was Mrs Forecast drawing in breath like a low pressure sucks in air. As she did so, she turned a rather pleasant shade of purple which reminded Greenery of red onions, his favourite pizza topping.

'You cheeky little boy! How dare you talk to me like that! I am your superior . . .'

'But you asked me.'

'I asked you nothing.'

'Yes you did.'

'Are you arguing with me, young man?'

'No, Miss Forecast, I'm correcting you.'

That was the last straw. Mrs Forecast actually stamped her foot like a little girl and went from purple to red. A kind of pepperoni colour, thought Greenery.

'I want you out of my sight now! Go to the headmaster's office and tell him what you've done.'

Greenery stood up. 'I'd just like to say, Miss, that being interested in the world and finding it more attractive than a

9

diagram is not a crime and I think you're wrong to punish me. Oh and you've spelt precipitation wrong, Miss.'

'GET OUT!!!'

'Fair enough.'

Mr Johnson was not a new teacher. He was an old, old man who had spent his life around the young. This had made him somewhat understanding of the oddities of youth. He sat in his cosy little office with a fire burning and Take-That the cat curled up in front of it. In the corner stood an old wooden carving of a Native American that always made Greenery feel good. He somehow felt reassured by it, as if it were a totem of justice.

'Ah! Greenery. Here again are we? Now what did you do this time may I ask?'

'I corrected Mrs Forecast's spelling and tried to point out to her the beauty of nature.'

'I see ... and how exactly did you attempt to do this ... hmm?'

'By showing her a real-life example of the diagram she had drawn incorrectly on the board, Sir.'

'I see and I imagine she did not take too kindly to this?'

'She did not.'

'And she sent you here.'

'Yes she did.'

'And here you came.'

'I did ... Yes.'

'And here you are.'

'Am I? Yes.'

If Mr Johnson had one fault it was stating the obvious repeatedly while his old, old brain tried to think of an appropriate response.

10

'Well, here's the thing, young Mr Jackson, I can't just ignore the fact you've been sent to me by a teacher. However, knowing you as I do, I hardly think it would be appropriate to punish you for simply . . . being you. So, you will go up to the attic and you will clean out the store cupboard at the end of the upper east corner. I seem to remember young boys like attics. You can take your time. I'm sure there are lots of things you'll find interesting and as far as Mrs Forecast is concerned that will look like an appropriate punishment.' Mr Johnson sat back in his chair and his eyes glazed over a little as a distant memory popped in to say hello. 'I used to love attics when I was a boy . . . dusty, poky. A real Aladdin's cave of wonders, some of them. Once, in my grandfather's attic I found a stuffed American bald eagle in which a family of mice had made a rather nifty home. As I recall, the entrance they used was right up the eagle's . . .'

'I'll just be going then, shall I, Sir?'

'. . . Bottom . . . What? Go where, young man?'

'The attic, Sir, to clean it out.'

If Mr Johnson had one fault it was that his old, old brain was, well, old and his memory was about as much use as a skateboard is to a man with one leg.

'Oh yes, off you go then. Here's the key to the store cupboard.'

With the key in hand Greenery turned around and plodded off in the direction of the creepy creaky stairs that went all the way up to the attic. Truth be told he was overjoyed at the thought of spending an afternoon all by himself rummaging around through past treasures.

The store cupboard at the end of the upper east corner

loomed large above Greenery. He knew exactly where it was. All the boys did. It was legendary.

The story went that hundreds of years ago it was the place where confiscated items were kept when they were taken away for good; a treasure trove of forbidden articles and weapons of mass distraction. One day, however, after years and years of juvenile contraband being forced into its bulging wooden shell, it had been sealed for ever.

Now, armed with the key, Greenery had what every boy in school coveted, the answer to what lay inside the cupboard of confined confiscations. He approached it carefully, placed the key in the big heavy lock and turned it. Click, Clonk, Clang. He reverentially opened the sturdy oak door to feast his eyes upon . . .

'Paperwork?' he shouted in disgust. 'Paperwork? Oh nuts!'

It was boring work and the afternoon crept on immeasurably slowly as he rummaged half-heartedly through phone bills, class reports and old essays.

The first hour seemed to last a week, the second, a month. Then after aeons of tedious work Greenery's hand brushed against something hard and cold in the messy pile of boring old junk. As soon as he touched it, it erupted vertically through the detritus of paper, sending sheets of the stuff high into the air only to fall down around him again like snowflakes.

When the air had cleared Greenery was left staring at a large key. It seemed to radiate a light of its own from deep within and lit up the dusty attic like a beacon of hope. It hovered three feet off the ground perfectly still and silent.

Now that's more like it, he thought.

*

In his office Mr Johnson was having trouble concentrating. Something was bothering him. An impressionable young thought was desperately trying to be noticed through the fog that was his tired old brain.

Take-That the cat yawned, stretched out lazily and opened one beady eye to stare at Mr Johnson. He could tell that something was bothering the old man.

Their eyes met briefly. In that second the fog cleared and the interloping memory in Mr Johnson's crusty brain was revealed in all its horror. His face turned a deathly shade of white. The cat continued to stare.

'My God! What have I done?'

He stood up, hobbled out of his office and trundled down the corridor moving faster than he had in years, shouting about 'keys', 'mistakes' and something being 'too early'.

Greenery stared open-mouthed at the key as it hung motionless in mid-air. He walked around it carefully, studying it from all directions. It was roughly twenty centimetres long with about half its length given up to a luminous turquoise handle. The end that went into a lock was bright shining gold. On its side was a switch that had two settings: 'Dormant' and 'Active'. The switch was set to dormant. He reached out slowly, half expecting to feel nothing, thinking that this must be a hallucination of some kind, but when his hand closed around it, he gasped with shock . It was real! Solid and cold. He quickly let go again, then stared in disbelief. Not knowing what else to do, he pushed the key gently with the tip of his finger. It drifted away slightly before returning to a perfectly stationary hover.

Greenery's constant and intense curiosity got the better of him. With a burning desire to find out what would happen he grabbed the key and flicked the switch on its side from dormant to active. It shot instantly from his hand like a greyhound out of the traps. He let out a rather embarrassingly girly yelp but the key made no sound whatsoever.

'Uh, oh.'

He had no choice: he ran as fast as he could after the accelerating projectile.

As he jumped over old boxes and tried to avoid piles of memorabilia he started to wonder if he had perhaps made a mistake. This thought was cut short, however, when the key embedded itself up to its turquoise handle in the solid brick wall at the other end of the school attic.

He slowed his pace to an out-of-breath stagger and walked carefully up to the point of impact. It wasn't until he reached out, to see if he could pull it from the wall, that the key started to turn of its own accord. Slowly at first and with a slight grinding noise but gaining in speed until after a few seconds it was spinning madly like the end of a drill. Hot brick dust flew from the twisting dibble and the grinding noise rose in pitch until it became an ear-splitting note just inside his hearing range. At the same time, a section of brickwork about the size and shape of a door removed itself from the wall, moving towards Greenery as if it were being unscrewed. The key's unrelenting screaming reached exactly the right pitch to smash all the glass nearby. The small attic windows, glass cupboard doors and a few picture frames stored away for safekeeping exploded in a shower of fractured reflections.

As the last of the glass tinkled musically to the floor, the section of wall came to a halt. Greenery watched in disbelief as the bricks began to dissolve like aspirin in water. He almost turned and ran but once again curiosity got the better of him. He watched open-mouthed as each new brick melted away and more was revealed of a dark vortex spinning threateningly behind it. It looked like the black holes Greenery had seen in countless science-fiction films. Now fear took over and he finally turned to run, but couldn't. The ominous rift was tugging at him, pulling him towards it with a force like gravity, impossible to resist. When most of the bricks had gone, Greenery realised he was helpless.

As he struggled desperately, looking for anything to hold on to, anything to save him, he decided there was only one option. The key! It was still hanging effortlessly in space and shining with that bizarre incandescence. He reached out for it, thinking he could hold on to it for support, but as he grabbed the cold metal whatever force was keeping it afloat suddenly stopped. It lay in his hand like a dead fish.

The brick doorway had entirely vanished and with nothing to hold on to Greenery was powerless.

'HEEEEEelp!'

He was sucked into the void with terrifying speed and was gone long before the attic door burst inwards.

Mr Johnson stood framed in the rotting doorway panting and sweating. He looked around at the scene of devastation, shattered glass, messes of paper and a boring blank brick wall. A very surprised-looking rocking horse met his gaze but Greenery Frankincense Jackson was nowhere to be seen.

He sank slowly to his knees and whispered despairingly to himself:

'His father's going to kill me.'

Chapter Two

Entrance Fee

If anything were possible
And anything is.
I'd like to think that any drink
Can also learn to fizz.

Taken from *Mind over Matter*
by The Mysterious Wandering Gump

Greenery scrabbled frantically in mid-air, desperately trying to claw his way back to the solid attic floor but it was useless.

'HELP!'

Try as he might there was nothing to hold on to.

'HELP ME!'

No friction of any kind he could push or pull against.

'PLEASE SOMEONE HELP!'

There was no one to help.

He reached out for his shrinking world one last time then cried out in fear as it winked out of existence.

'NO!!'

He was left floating helplessly in the cold, empty silence of the void.

The blackness surrounding him was absolute but it wasn't

dark. He could see his hand in front of his face as clear as day as if a light were shining on him from an unknown source. There was also a feeling of speed, of movement, but he found it impossible to tell which direction he was travelling in.

Greenery hugged the key close to his chest. It felt real and reassuringly solid in this place of nothingness. Realising it was probably his only ticket home, he shoved it deep into his pocket and, as he did so, he noticed a speck on the infinite horizon. A dot of light growing, a feeling of gravity returning, fast and heavy and unable to stop.

Greenery's feet skidded along the grassy turf. He stumbled, tripped and came to a painful halt on the damp ground.

He lay on his back, breathing hard but refusing to panic, and tried to take stock of his situation. He was alive and in one piece even though he felt a little bruised from his clumsy landing. He was obviously not in the attic any more, but where was he? He stood up slowly and carefully, brushed himself off and looked around.

The first thing he noticed was the colour. He was standing in a small grassy clearing in the middle of a kaleidoscopic forest. The entire spectrum was laid out before him, from dusty saffron and amber through cobalt blue and aquamarine to the brightest magenta. This mind-blowing array of tone and shade came from the plants and flowers of staggering beauty that surrounded him.

Next to register in his tormented conscious were the sounds. Tweets, flutes, snuffles and chirrups radiated from the hidden denizens of the rainbow undergrowth. It was clear that wherever he was it was teeming with life.

There was another sound too, on the edge of hearing, only getting closer. It sounded like . . . footsteps?

'RUN!'

Greenery turned to see where the shouting was coming from.

In the distance there was a strange-looking man carrying a bag and sprinting towards him. His head looked too big for his body and he was completely bald except for a blue tuft of hair in the centre of his scalp. There was something wrong with the vision though. Greenery rubbed his eyes and looked again. His perspective had been way out before. The stranger wasn't a long way off; he was just very small. He was still running towards Greenery and he looked terrified.

'RUN!!'

The petrified midget was only waist high but even with such short legs he was moving fast. As he shot past in a screaming blur, Greenery managed to grab hold of his wrist and tackle him to the ground.

'Aarghh! Get off, get off me!'

'Wait, please, just wait a minute! Can you tell me where I am?'

'Get off me, you flipping loony. Let go. Run!'

'What are you talking about? Run from what?'

'Those.'

Greenery turned to see where the frightened maniac was pointing.

Coming over the rise of a small bluff was a pack of horse-like shadows; dark, gangly creatures that moved like a speeding mist. It was impossible to tell how many there were as their bodies constantly morphed into and through each other. Their breath steamed out from between sharp white teeth as they powered onwards.

'Now run, you flipping idiot, run!'

Greenery didn't need telling again. Whatever those things were they looked dangerous. He ran as fast as he could after the abbreviated man who was already moving with surprising speed.

'We can't . . . outrun them,' he shouted breathlessly over his shoulder at Greenery. 'We need . . . to hide.'

'A tree . . .! What about a tree?'

'No good . . . they'll have it down in seconds.'

'Well, I don't know . . .' Greenery risked a peek over his shoulder and was sorry he had. 'They're gaining on us!'

Suddenly a neon-pink bird leapt out of a small bush and dashed across their path. It was the size of a large dog and with four spindly legs it moved like one too. The blue-tufted stranger let out a cry of joy and turned sharply to follow it.

'This way!' he shouted as he did so.

Greenery followed him between the many stems of a short bush with large tartan leaves. He emerged on the other side just in time to see the bird and the midget retreating down a hole in the ground. Without any hesitation he leapt into the den, praying the swarm of nasties hadn't seen him.

It was cramped and dark in the burrow but he managed to wriggle himself around so he could peep out of the top and through the tartan thicket. The swarm was not far behind them. Within seconds they were outside Greenery's hiding place and much to his dismay they stopped dead in their tracks. Now they were closer he could see how the plant life wilted and died at their slightest touch. They had left a monochrome wake behind them, the flora robbed of both colour and life.

They began sniffing the air and tasting it with their long forked tongues.

'It won't be long before they find us, you know,' whispered the little man.

'Well, what do we do then?'

'We need to make it to water. They can't cross water.'

'Is that possible?'

'It might be, if you're willing to fight.'

'Me? Why me? Why can't we both fight?'

'Because, young man, I am going to be the weapon.'

'What?'

'Have you ever heard of a Punster?'

'What? No.'

'Well, listen up. My name is Night Light . . . pleased to meet you . . . and I am a Punster or a Pun Monster, if you will.'

'Sorry . . . what on earth are you talking abou-'

'Listen, boy, we don't have very long, so shut up, listen and let me explain. I'm a shape shifter but I can only change into things that are some kind of pun or play on words. Don't ask me why. I am what I am, as the saying goes. Now in a moment I'm going to turn into a vampire bat which is a very powerful weapon. It won't kill them, nothing will, but it might slow them down enough to give us a chance. OK?'

Greenery felt his head begin to spin. He was sure this was some kind of hallucination. He must have banged his head back in the school and this was all a crazy dream or something. He had little choice however so he decided to play along for now.

21

'Er . . . OK.'

'Good.'

Night Light closed his eyes and puffed out his cheeks. With a noise like a minotaur juggling he turned a small section of the universe inside out and disappeared. In his place was a well-used cricket bat wearing a bow tie and a cloak. Its furry handle was the same blue as the Punster's tuft of hair. If Greenery hadn't been so scared he would have burst out laughing.

'That's a vampire bat?'

'Yes. Now pick me up and head out of the hole, run the way the bird was heading.' It was strange how Night Light's voice came from deep within the wooden bat. 'It's not too far to the river. When we get there, dive in and swim across. They won't follow. If any of them get too close to you, clobber them . . . GO!'

Greenery took three deep breaths to steady his nerves then, with a sudden rush of adrenalin, ran for it.

The second he burst from his hiding place the dark creatures spotted him. They let out a terrible whinny and began to gallop after him. Everything in their path died instantly.

Greenery was running so fast he thought his legs were going to fall off. Even so, the shadows were gaining on him. They were so close now he could feel their warm breath on the back of his neck. One of the equine demons surged forward with a burst of hatred and tried to sink its venomous fangs deep into Greenery's exposed neck. He swung the vampire bat wildly over his shoulder and the second the weapon made contact with the dark, solid mist, it withered away to almost nothing. It was as if the life force had been sucked right out of it. The entire swarm let out a scream of agony and shrank back momentarily. Greenery managed to gain some ground, but only a little. The injured beast returned to full strength almost immediately and the enraged herd advanced once more.

A bright reflection through the undergrowth, a shimmer of light on water caught Greenery's eye. He put his head down and powered onwards.

They came at him again and again but somehow he managed to fend them off until eventually he made it. He came to the water's edge and barrelled straight in without even breaking his stride.

It was as if the black misty mass had hit a solid brick wall. They slammed against an invisible power again and again, but however much they screamed and snarled, they were unable to cross the water.

Greenery swam across to the opposite bank and for the second time in seven minutes lay on his back, breathing hard. This time, however, he found it much harder to fend off the rising panic.

The vampire bat rolled out of his hand and one mini big-bang later Night Light was standing next to him dripping over the boy's school uniform.

'Where am I? And what the hell were those things?' Greenery blurted out, almost in a scream.

'Oh, not from around here, are you? All right, calm down, lad, I can see you've had a bit of a shock. Come on, sit up here and I'll explain it all to you.'

Greenery sat down on a nearby fallen tree. Even though he felt like he was losing his soggy and bedraggled mind, he managed to listen to Night Light.

'Those horrible things are Night-Mares, a feral population of female horses made completely out of darkness. I was trying to trade with them. I turned into one of them but they spotted me as a fake and turned on me.'

'Night-Mares?'

'Yep. Well, that's their common name. Technically, according to the genetic records, they're Traceys.'

'I don't need to know *whose* they are; I want to know *what* they are.'

'That *is* what they are. They are Traceys. That thing there . . .' he pointed to the brooding swarm '. . . is a herd of Dark Traceys. They were discovered by the great explorer Sir Algernon Ridgley Thinkathought. He named them after his wife, Lady Tracey Thinkathought.'

'He can't have liked his wife very much to name such rancid things after her.'

'On the contrary,' said Night Light, 'he loved her dearly. Problem was he had no imagination, so he named everything after her. There are currently two lost kingdoms of Tracey, the River Tracey, there's Tracey Day and three hundred different kinds of flora and fauna, all with the distinguished title of . . .'

'Tracey?'

'Oi! He was a great man. He also invented the Tracey.'

'Of course he did, silly me. Listen, I think I've had a bang on the head or something but can you please tell me where I am?'

'Well, it's a bit of a relative term, "where", isn't it?'

'No . . . it isn't.'

'Yes it is,' said Night Light, picking up a small stone and

placing it in his bag. 'I would say the stone is in my bag but you would say "the stone is in *your* bag". You see? Relative.'

'Yes, but the stone is still in the same place.'

'Ah yes but . . . it's . . . What?'

'Look, can you tell me where I am or not?'

'Well, where you are is hard. What it's called is easy. Welcome to The Other Place.'

'The Other Place?'

'Yep. Or The River as most of us locals call it. Now looking at you I'd guess you were human, right? Male?'

'Er . . . yes.'

'I thought so. Not seen one of you in a while. You got a name?'

'What? . . . Oh yes, Greenery Jackson.'

'Nice to meet you, Greenery Jackson. OK, this is how it works: your species, like so many others, has a tendency to make stuff up, to fantasise if you will. Now we live in an infinite universe, right?'

'I think so.'

'Trust me, we do. And whenever one of you brainboxes dreams up something new, physics dictates that in an infinite universe it has to exist somewhere. Follow me?'

'I think so.'

'Good. Well, that place is here.'

'What?'

'This is the place where things like Traceys and Punsters exist. We have to be somewhere, and so we are here. In fact, everything exists here. It has to, or else your little bit of the cosmos would be very cluttered indeed.'

'What, everything?'

'Yep!'

'Talking carrots?'

'Yep, everything.'

'Flying saucers?'

'Both kinds, small plates and spaceships.'

'The Loch Ness monster?'

'Er, no, anything that exists in your world doesn't need to exist here, does it?'

'OK, well how about a blue giraffe that wears roller-skates?'

'Yes!'

'So where do the roller-skates come from?'

'They come with the giraffe. Look, everything exists here. Everything! It has to. Now you can spend all day coming up with ridiculous things and I won't have seen them all, but trust me they exist. Get used to it. Now, how did you get here, young man?

'Well,' said Greenery, reaching into his sodden pocket, 'I found this key and it just made a hole that I sort of fell through.'

As he spoke he started to fumble through the contents of his pocket. There was the usual stuff – a Lego brick, a conker, half a piece of string and twenty-three pence but no key. 'It's gone!' he moaned, 'I put it in my pocket, I know I did.'

'Would you say that key was your most valuable possession?' asked Night Light.

'Well, this conker is a fifteener but yes I suppose it was.'

'It's been taxed then.'

'What?'

'Taxed! Like a toll over a bridge or a road tax. The powers that be take your most valuable possession on entering The Other Place. It's basically your entrance fee. Can't be helped,

I'm afraid. Well, you can't get back home without it so I guess you'll be staying here. See you around, kiddo.' With a little wave and a nod, Night Light started to wander off into the woods.

'Whoa, whoa, whoa!' shouted Greenery, running after him. 'Are you just going to leave me then, like this, all alone in the middle of a forest?'

'No, course not.'

'Oh good.'

'This is a jungle. See ya.'

'No wait. I need help. Please, how can I get my key back?'

'You'll have to go to the Central Collections Office and petition them. If you're very lucky they might let you earn it back.'

'Will you please help me? I don't know this world at all and I could use a guide.'

Night Light turned and sighed deeply. 'I tell you what. I'll take you as far as Big Tree; I'm on my way there anyway. It's market day tomorrow. You'll be able to get transport from there.'

'Transport to where? Where do I need to go?'

'You need to go to the capital city of course; you need to go to Tracey.'

'Of course I do, silly me.'

Chapter Three

The Road to Big Tree

When the caterpillar turned into a butterfly,
   Did it know what it was doing or did it think that it would die?
   Did it dream of metamorphosis all that time?
   Was there method in its madness was there rhythm in its rhyme?

Taken from *The Evolution of Thought*
by The Mysterious Wandering Gump

Mr Johnson had made his way back to his office and was rummaging around in his desk drawers. Even though he was desperate to find what he was looking for he was moving slowly and quietly so as not to wake the sleeping cat.

When his wrist caught on a heavy paperweight and knocked it over, the lazy feline shifted groggily in his sleep. Mr Johnson froze in mid-search and looked as though he was going to have a heart attack. Eventually the cat settled down again and Mr Johnson continued with his hunt. A moment later his face lit up and he scurried out of the office clutching his prize.

What Mr Johnson did when he returned to the attic would have surprised even his oldest friends. He held out in front of him what looked like a small compass with a digital readout. He flicked a switch on its side and a ray of red light flickered from a tiny hole in the front of the gizmo. It spread out in a fanlike shape and began to spiral its way around every square inch of the attic. After a minute or two the task was complete. The strange red beam retracted back inside Mr Johnson's thingamabob and a message flashed up on the screen.

RETRO ACTIVE SCAN COMPLETE.
GATEWAY ACTIVATION POSITIVE POST 1032 SECONDS.
KEY PRESENCE ===== NEGATIVE.

Mr Johnson sighed deeply and placed the little machine back in his pocket. 'Oh well,' he thought, 'time to wake up the cat.'

The sun was shining and it was a warm summer's day. Greenery's shirt and jeans were drying quite quickly but his school blazer was still heavy with water. He carried it in one hand and put his tie in the pocket.

As he followed along behind Night Light, Greenery stared around him in disbelief. He found himself losing track of new and wondrous sights.

There was a small grove of ultraviolet trees all of which were connected via their upper branches and then became one single bush higher up. Several simian-looking creatures were sunning themselves in its glow. There were trees that walked past them, some that floated, and one that was playing football against a team of bright-yellow flowers using its own fruit as the ball.

There were countless creatures. Some that flew, some that

walked and some that disappeared and reappeared at random. He saw a group of snakes, each with its tail in its mouth, forming a wheel and rolling along like a train. There were beetles as big as badgers being ridden by bright-blue spiders. And at one point, something colossal passed overhead.

One of its massive feet came down about twenty metres away from them. Greenery craned his head upwards but all he could see was a gigantic hairy leg disappearing into the clouds.

Night Light told him they were in the Jungle of Bungle and that it was a national park kept in honour of an old ruler of The Other Place. Captain Bungle the First.

Apparently he was a very peaceful ruler who loved nature and his jungle had been kept mostly wild for centuries.

After about an hour or so, Night Light stopped abruptly and put his little pack down on the ground.

'This should do!' he said, rubbing his hands together. 'I'll be back in a little while. You wait here. If you're hungry, those flowers over there will taste like anything you want and the sap from that tree is delicious.'

'Where are you going?' asked Greenery.

'I'm going to get us some transport to Big Tree, my fine young friend.'

'You're just going to leave me here?'

'Oh you'll be all right. Listen, it's a long way off, is Big Tree, and if we want to get there before nightfall we have to move quickly.'

'Well, what's the quickest way to get there?'

'The quickest way is to leave yesterday but it's too late for that. I do, however, know a much faster way than walking.'

He winked at Greenery, popped his little patch of universe inside out and turned into a large plastic dog.

'I give up,' said Greenery. 'What are you now?'

'I, young man, am a Tupper-Were-Wolf. Not only can I keep your sandwiches fresh for days, I also have an excellent sense of smell.'

With a couple of quick sniffs he pointed himself in the desired direction and bounded off into the thick colourful foliage.

Alone and still for the first time since his arrival, Greenery noticed he *was* feeling a little hungry. He wandered over to the flowers Night Light had told him about, plucked a petal from one and gingerly took a small experimental bite. It tasted exactly like warm steak pie with gravy. The more he chewed it, the more real this illusion became to him. Another bite and he could taste roast potatoes, carrots and sweetcorn.

He ate three petals and felt quite full, but still wanted more. He went back and picked another one, which became waffles and cream, drizzled with maple syrup. It was delicious.

Not knowing how long it would be before he had the chance to eat again, he pocketed several more then went over to the tree with the allegedly delicious sap. It was oozing out of a hole in the bark and looked a lot like jet-black honey.

He scooped some up onto his finger and licked it. It was cold, refreshing and tasted exactly like qwebur berries. Qwebur berry is a taste that can only be described as a mix between mustard and chocolate, with a dash of tuna fish. It's an acquired taste and one that for some inexplicable reason Greenery relished.

Thirst quenched and hunger sated, he sat down on the floor

to await the return of his guide. It was strange but somehow tasting something had made this place more real than just sight alone. Perhaps he wasn't dreaming after all.

Greenery was just coming to terms with his adjusted sense of reality when he heard a buzzing sound in the distance, something like a swarm of bees, only deeper and angrier. Obviously, he assumed the worst. The things he had seen so far meant this noise could be made by any manner of beastie, one that might just as easily turn him in to a golf club as eat him. He was frantically looking for somewhere to hide when he heard a friendly voice call out.

'It's all right, big fella. It's me! Don't panic.'

Greenery looked up and saw two bizarre animals coming towards him through the jungle. They were basically very large fish, except that where their lower fins should have been they had wheels, one at the front and one at the back. They were speeding towards Greenery, weaving madly through the tree trunks and looking every bit as if they were going to run him over.

The buzzing noise that had frightened Greenery was made by some kind of organic engine near the gills.

When the leading fish was practically on top of him, they both pulled up abruptly and skidded to a halt.

Pop! And there was Night Light.

'Greenery Jackson, I'd like you to meet my mate Dave. He's a Motor Pike.'

''Lo,' said Dave, the fish on wheels.

'Err, hello.'

'Climb on then,' said Dave. Greenery did as he was told.

'Dave is a lot stronger than me,' said Night Light. 'I might look like a Motor Pike but I'm still just a small Punster and I'm not carrying you all the way to Big Tree, you big lump.'

'Can he breathe?'

'Not as such, no.'

'Well, how does he survive then?'

'In your world, don't you have creatures that live in the sea but breathe air?'

'Yes we do. Quite a few, as a matter of fact.'

'Well, this is the same only reversed. As long as he gets back in the water every now and again to breathe, he'll be all right.'

'Oh, OK. How long can you hold your breath for, Dave, if you don't mind me asking?'

'Three weeks,' said Dave, the fish on wheels.

'Right-ho, let's be off then,' said Night Light, popping back into his previous fishy form.

There was hardly any feeling of acceleration. One minute they were still and the next they were moving. They were moving very fast indeed.

Dave seemed to like getting as close to the trees as possible and enjoyed really sharp turns. There isn't much to hold on to on a fish; they're not really designed to be ridden by humans. With a bit of coaxing from Dave, Greenery wrapped his legs around the main bulk of the body, grabbed the barbells near Dave's mouth and pulled them up like reins.

It was fair to say that for the first twenty minutes or so Greenery was terrified. He thought he was going to die at least eighty-seven times, but as the journey progressed he learnt to trust Dave and anticipate his movements. After about half an hour, he was actually enjoying himself.

Eventually they came out of the thick colourful foliage and onto a wide track that served as a basic road. On the opposite side of the rough highway was a vast open plain of tall purple grass. It looked beautiful swaying in the gentle breeze.

If Greenery thought they were moving fast before, it was nothing compared to the speed they reached when Dave really opened up. Tears streamed into his eyes and the world blurred as they sped away to Big Tree.

Back in Littleton Bay it was the end of the school day. Mrs Gloria Jackson stood outside in the playground watching the stampede of chatting kids as they streamed out of the door.

Usually she let Greenery walk home from school along the beach with some of his friends but today she had finished work at Bent's Garden Centre early and felt like she should come and pick him up. It was strange actually – she felt a need to be here, a sudden drive. As if her son's safety depended on it.

'Hi, Mrs Jackson!'

'Oh hi, Sam. Is Greenery with you?'

'No. I haven't seen him all afternoon, sorry.' This was technically true and there didn't seem much point getting Greenery into even more trouble.

The minutes and the children passed and still there was no sign of Greenery.

Eventually, when the playground was quiet, Mr Johnson came out of the school door. He did not lock it as was usual but came straight over to Gloria instead.

'Is everything all right, Mr Johnson? I can't seem to find Greenery. Did he leave early?'

'Mrs Jackson, won't you come inside?' he said solemnly. 'We need to talk. I'm afraid there's been an accident.'

'There it is!' shouted Night Light, pulling up alongside Dave and Greenery as they raced along.

'What is?' yelled Greenery in return.

'Big Tree, you dafty. Look!'

Greenery had been riding for the past hour with his head buried deep in Dave's flanks. This way his eyes didn't stream so much and he found he could doze a little. At Night Light's prompting he looked up ahead of them. He nearly fell off his fish when he saw Big Tree.

The trees here were slightly larger and marvellously grander than the ones back home but the tree on the horizon dwarfed them all, like an oak tree dwarfs grass. It was ginormous.

In the Big Tree visitor's guide, it will tell you that Big Tree's big tree is two point one kilometres in diameter. The top branches are one hundred and seven kilometres high. So high in fact that they are in space. Fortunately all their nutrients come from the ground and don't need oxygen to thrive at that altitude. The four main branches from the trunk are the lowest at six thousand metres, just below the layer of cloud cover. One of the Big Tree's big leaves weighs as much as a fully grown Feathered Tracey.

Five hours after first arriving in The Other Place Greenery Jackson fell off his Motor Pike at the foot of Big Tree, exhausted and thirsty. He wondered what bizarre experience could possibly befall him next.

'Right,' said Dave, 'pay up.'

'Oh yes, I believe I owe you one musical interlude,' said Night Light.

He put his sack down on the ground and took a deep breath. Pop! Where he had been standing there was now a group of five rubbery musicians. They started to play a tune that Greenery didn't recognise. It was good though. Dave began to sway slightly in time and then as the music gripped him he began racing round in small circles. He even jumped up like a dolphin at one point. After the music was done, so was Dave, apparently. He bid them both a fond farewell and with a quick wheelie was gone, speeding off back down the track. Pop!

'Don't tell me,' said Greenery, 'That was an elastic band, wasn't it?'

'You catch on quick you do. They love the sound of an authentic elastic band do the Motor Pikes. In fact, they'll do just about anything for a tune. I had to play him one before we left and one on arrival. Job done, I'd say. Let's go shall we?'

Night Light and Greenery wandered over to the lift station. Night Light pulled a velvet cord that hung down from above and Greenery heard a bell ring high up in the tree. He looked up to see a large flat platform swing out above them hanging from a sturdy wooden joist. It began to descend slowly on a complex system of pulleys. When it reached the ground they climbed on and it began to rise again. 'Even the lowest branches of the tree are far too high to be reached every day,' explained Night Light as they ascended, 'so it was decided long ago that the town should be much nearer to the ground.'

'So where is it then?'

'See for yourself.'

The lift reached the end of its steady climb and Greenery realised just how miraculous this place was. The entire town, streets, buildings, bridges and stairs, was carved into the face of the trunk in intricate detail. The brickwork was etched onto the side of buildings. Gates and doors were adorned with elaborate carvings and every cobble had been sculpted with the finest care.

The streets rose in a gentle spiral around the trunk, weaving above and below each other. In some places they passed right through the centre of the tree. It was stunning.

'Welcome,' said the lift operator as they reached street level.

'How do?' replied Night Light. 'Know any lodgings nearby with vacancies?'

'The Acorn has, I think. Three levels up on Knott Street. You'll be looked after and fed well. It's market day tomorrow so I'd get a good night's sleep if I were you. You'll want to be up early.'

They made their way carefully through the streets of Big Tree. Having a vertical town on one side and plummeting death on the other took some getting used to.

Most of the inhabitants looked remarkably normal, just people getting on with their daily lives. However, there were a few that were far more interesting. Now and again he would glimpse multicoloured rainbow people or tiny little beings. Some looked a lot more like monkeys than humans. I guess that's what happens if you live in a tree long enough, thought Greenery.

They reached The Acorn just as the sun was turning the evening sky bright orange. With some bargaining and fumbling around in his bag, Night Light assured Greenery he had secured them lodgings.

After a hearty fish supper (Greenery couldn't help wondering whether it was Motor Pike or not), they climbed upstairs and were rewarded with two ridiculously comfy beds. Seven point six minutes later Greenery was fast asleep.

Chapter Four

Lazarus Who?

A crystal is a rock that grows like a flower.
A hero is a person with a bit more power.
Taken from *Cosmic Geology*
by The Mysterious Wandering Gump

The Djinditsu stood motionless in the high branches, scanning the busy marketplace for the human. Her animal senses were sharp and a foreign scent in the air told her that he was close. From this vantage point she could see the whole square but there were so many traders and merchants here this time of year that it was impossible to pick out one individual.

Suddenly two shapes in the crowd, far too big and way too ugly to be local, caught her attention. If she couldn't tell who they were by looking, then their accompanying stench told her everything she needed to know. They were Violents and they too were here for the boy. If she had any chance of protecting him she must find him before they did.

For the first time since his arrival Greenery was without his guide. Early that morning Night Light had gone off with three pence, which, he assured Greenery, was enough to buy a ticket to Tracey. They were planning to meet later back at The Acorn, leaving Greenery some free time to explore the marketplace.

Its stalls were a riot of colour, each one filled with wonders he didn't understand. It occurred to Greenery that he might not have another opportunity to get a souvenir. If he ever wanted people to believe him about this place he would need proof. He didn't have much to bargain with. Still, anything 'otherworldly' would do.

One stallholder in particular caught his attention. He could have been Mr Johnson's brother, although Greenery doubted Mr Johnson's brother ever walked around wearing an old suit of armour. His bright-blue eyes shone out at the world between a fuzzy white handlebar moustache and an equally bright, low-cut fringe. He was selling a collection of what looked like snow globes, except inside each one the scene was alive with real people and real weather. There were lots of different ones to choose from.

One was a typical winter scene, although the people inside had given up with the snowman and were having a snow-ball fight. Another looked like some kind of assault course. Little soldiers were running up and down it while a burly sergeant major pointed frantically and shouted at the slower ones. Greenery's favourite, however, contained a beach scene – the waves were crashing down on a sandy shore and tiny people were surfing and sunbathing. It reminded him of home in the summer. He picked it up and handed it to the stall-holder.

'How much is this, please?'

'Ah you have a good eye, young man, but is that really what you're looking for?

'What do you mean?'

'Oh it's a pleasant scene. I've sold dozens of them today but how about something special? How about this one?'

The stallholder bent down and unwrapped a most peculiar-looking snow globe. He held it out for Greenery to inspect.

There was a small ramshackle hut built at the entrance to a cave. Several shiny and artificial-looking trees lined the decaying road that led up to this entrance and the whole scene was on the shoreline of a strange bright-red lake. Greenery felt drawn to it somehow – the more he looked at it the more mesmerised he became by its strange beauty.

As he looked into the globe, a tiny figure came out of the hut and stared back up at him, right into his eyes. Greenery couldn't turn away. He had no idea how long the moment lasted but he felt like he was being judged, as if the man in the snow globe could see something deep inside him. Eventually the miniature man shrugged and wandered back into his hut. The spell was broken.

Greenery had to have it.

'Wow! How much is that one?'

'Well now,' said the man in tarnished armour, 'that all depends on what you've got.'

Greenery turned out the contents of his pockets.

'I'm afraid all I've got is this manky bit of string, a Lego brick and twenty pence, but this conker is a fifteener. It's really, really hard.'

'Twenty pence, you say?'

'Yes.'

'Sterling?'

'Erm, yes.

'Bit of advice, my boy, keep that kind of information to yourself. Not everyone is as honest as I am. Two pence will be sufficient and enough for me to close up for the day.'

Greenery completed the transaction and was about to thank the stallholder when a shadow fell across the old man's face. Looking terrified he scurried away and pretended to deal with another customer. Greenery placed his new trinket in his blazer pocket and looked round to see what had scared the old man so much. He was instantly sorry he had.

Towering over Greenery was a snarling savage with muscles like basketballs. His face and most of his torso were wet and dripping where the skin had been completely eaten away. The meaty tissue that was exposed looked slightly green, as if it were rotting, and his cold eyes peered out at the world through a fleshy pulpy mess of a head.

The snarling savage smiled.

A dusty, filthy-smelling sack was shoved over Greenery's head from behind and the world went black.

'Damn!'

The Violents had got to him first. They were moving fast but the Djinditsu could easily keep up with them. She was not hampered by the busy throng of the marketplace and skipped silently from rooftop to rooftop. She would make her move when it was quiet. It didn't do to upset the public by killing in front of them. Too many awkward questions.

Greenery screamed and kicked and wriggled and squirmed but all to no avail. Whoever was carrying him was immensely strong. The bag over his head prevented him from seeing anything but he felt like he was being carried fast. He felt himself bumped and jostled painfully as strangers were knocked aside by his fleeing kidnappers.

After what seemed like an age he was placed on the floor and the bag was untied. He tried to run but in front of him was an intricately carved wall. It was a dead end. With no other choice he turned to face his assailants.

One he recognised from the stall, repulsive and oozing; the other was equally terrifying.

He was some kind of robot with living skin stretched awkwardly over the top of his misshapen metal body. The skin was pulled way too tight, causing sharp corners of machinery to rip through painful-looking wounds. Each man held a large club and stared menacingly at Greenery.

The Djinditsu watched silently from above as the Violents stopped and placed the boy on the floor. Good instincts, she thought as he tried to run. When he turned to face his captors she saw his face clearly for the first time. Humans, it would seem, were not as ugly as she had been led to believe, although his hair was a ridiculous orange colour and stood out at all angles.

The dripping, slimy one spoke first.

'Where is the key?'

'What?' asked Greenery.

'The key, where is it?'

'The key? I don't have it. I've been told it's been collected. Tax or something. I'm on my way to Tracey to get it back from Central Collections.' The words tumbled out of his mouth in fear. His legs were shaking and he was finding it harder and harder to stay conscious.

'Then we're going to Central Collections,' said the other one, the android.

'Er yes, I just told you that. I'm on my way there now.'

'*We* are going to Central Collections. I don't think *you*'ll be able to make it.

'Why not?'

'You'll be dead.'

The robotic grotesque moved forward with his club raised to strike. As he did so a sleek figure dropped from the branches high above and landed in perfect silence between the monsters and the schoolboy.

Even before it landed, the elegant shape had pulled two curved daggers from small sheaths it wore on its belt. Greenery stood frozen with terror, watching the creature spin and twist away from the kidnappers' blows in a strangely graceful arc. It leapt high into the air and threw both daggers. Each one embedded deep into a different foe.

They were knocked back momentarily but recovered quickly. The creature took this opportunity to draw a huge broad sword from some webbing on its back. All three fought fast and hard, clubs and muscle against steel and speed.

Whatever the shape was, it was not only fast but strong. It lifted the decomposing ogre in one hand and threw him against his comrade. They collapsed in a pile on the floor and suddenly the dancing fighter was on top of them. With a final flourish it drove its sword straight down, pinning both kidnappers to the solid wooden floor.

The fight was over and the Djinditsu froze, crouched upon

the tangled duo like a cat ready to pounce. Greenery saw the creature clearly for the first time and realised it wasn't just an it, it was a girl, and her posture wasn't her only feline attribute. Her tight muscular frame was covered from head to toe in short black fur. Her face, however, was bald and a delicate mix of cat, bear and human features. Her small pointy ears were pierced and she wore leather clothes that reminded him of tribal warriors he had seen on documentaries. She was slightly taller than Greenery but he had no idea how old she was.

She climbed slowly off the Violents, breathing hard and staring at Greenery with a peculiar look on her face that he couldn't read. As she stalked him Greenery once again became very aware of the dead end behind him.

'So you *did* have the key then?' she asked. 'You're the one who came through?'

'Yes, I did. I'm sorry, who are you? . . . Who are they? . . . Look, I'm really confused; I don't know what's going on.'

'Here,' she said, handing him a small bottle. 'My name is Towelyn.'

'Greenery.'

'I'm on your side, Greenery, don't worry. Drink this, sit down and calm yourself. I have business to attend to.'

Greenery sat heavily on the floor. He drank the warm liquid and felt calmed and energised at the same time.

He turned to watch Towelyn as she approached the bloody, tangled duo. The cyborg was clearly dead. Blood and other, less organic, fluids, were pouring from a huge gash in his side. The other was not so lucky.

'Who sent you?' she asked the fallen Violent.

No response.

She kicked him fast and hard, making his body slam against the long blade that was already pinning him to the floor.

He let out a long low moan.

'Who sent you? How do you know about the key?'

Nothing.

She kicked his body against the sharp sword edge again and again. She was about to go for a third time when he spoke.

'Stop please . . . There is a prophecy . . . an old tale that an Outworlder would travel to The River and bring back the key.'

'Everyone knows that. How did you know the carrier would be here?'

'We know because a pack of Night-Mares saw him yesterday; they heard him speak of the key. They can travel in your dreams at the speed of thought and my master chose to send them to me . . .'

Blood was pouring from his wounds but the flesh head wouldn't stop talking. With great effort he raised his arm and pointed at Greenery. Coughing up blood as he spoke he spat the words out in defiance of death.

'He is the boy from the prophecy. The key is back in The Other Place and we will use it to restore our great leader to power, the power that is his by right and by blood. All hail the Technomancer!'

As the thug called out to the heavens he grabbed a dagger from his friend's belt and plunged it fatally into his own heart.

'It is a sign. *He* will return,' he whispered, as his life faded away.

'We have to go!' said Towelyn, turning to Greenery. She was very focused and businesslike. 'If they're using Night-

Mares to communicate, then his leaders already know the key is in Tracey; we have to beat them to it. Come with me.'

'No way!' yelled Greenery. 'I'm not going anywhere with you until you tell me what's going on.'

'You must come! They will not stop hunting you.'

'Answer me!'

Towelyn gave Greenery a long appraising look before softening a little.

'I'm sorry. I will answer your questions. You have a right to know and I suppose you must be very scared, but please, we can't stay here. Even if they were alone in Big Tree I have just killed two people and would rather not be caught chatting over their bodies. Now please walk calmly away with me.'

With that she pulled her broadsword from the two dead bodies and politely gestured to the end of the alleyway, back towards the busy market.

They walked in silence for a little while. Greenery felt numb and confused. His bright new world had suddenly turned cold and menacing. Everywhere he looked now he saw monsters not wonders.

Greenery got the impression Towelyn was being quiet on purpose, to give him time to calm down and reflect. The slow sedate pace of her walk was helping and the drink she had given him was still having a euphoric effect. Eventually they came to rest on a whittled bench in the middle of a quiet plaza.

'Are you feeling any better?' she asked as they sat down.

'Yes thanks.'

'Would you like some more dragon's milk? It's very nourishing.'

'Dragon's . . .? Er, no thank you. I'm feeling fine now but please tell me what's going on?'

'Those two men belong to a cult called the Violents. Years ago their leader, a terrible man, Lazarus Brown, was banished from this world.'

'Why?'

'He killed hundreds of thousands in a mad quest for power. He was desperate to become the Captain but he was . . .'

'The Captain?'

'It's what we call our ruler. What you would call a king I suppose. Anyway Lazarus believed it was his birthright to be Captain. But he was beaten, eventually, by a great ruler. Captain Calefaction led a charge on Lazarus' stronghold and defeated him in a great battle.'

'Wow! What happened then?'

'Well, even though he knew it would be the right thing to do, the Captain couldn't find it in his heart to execute his brother.'

'They were brothers?'

'Half-brothers, yes. So he created the key, your key, and he sent Lazarus Brown away to a place he could never return from. Unfortunately it went a little wrong. The key was meant to stay here but as you know it didn't.

'Anyway some of his followers have passed down a prophecy that someone from that place would bring the key back here and that with it they could return the Technomancer.'

'So where is Lazarus? If the key made it all the way to Earth, where I found it, then surely Lazarus did too. But then why didn't he use it to come home?'

'I don't know. I'm not sure the Violents know but they

believe the prophecy is true and they are desperate to take the key and return Lazarus Brown to power.'

'Well, we'll have to get to it before they do!'

Towelyn smiled and ruffled Greenery's hair.

'You don't have to protect The Other Place, Greenery; that's *my* job. I'm a Djinditsu; it's what we do. That's why I was following you and your friend and why I know about all this.'

'I'm not bothered about protecting anything; I want to go home.'

'Oh, I see.'

'No wait! That came out wrong. I don't want that Lazarus bloke getting his hands on the key. Even after I've used it. I just meant, well . . . you know . . . I'm a kid. There's not much I can do.'

'You're human, right?'

'Yeah.'

'Well then, you can do more than you realise. Come on, let's find your friend and get moving. It's still a long way to Tracey.'

Chapter Five

Tracey

There once was a man who sat on a wall.

He watched the workers work and he watched the tired fall.

He watched them reap the corn and he watched them bake the bread

And he watched them till he understood the thoughts within his head.

Taken from *The Idiot's Guide to Humans*
by The Mysterious Wandering Gump

Back at The Acorn, Night Light was waiting patiently. As Greenery approached he flourished a shining silver ticket.

'Here we go, transport as promised.' He noticed Towelyn and looked at her suspiciously.

'Who's this then?'

'Her name is Towelyn. She's coming with me to Tracey.'

'But I only got you one ticket.'

'I don't need a ticket,' said Towelyn. 'The Djinditsu are given free transport by the Big Treeites in return for the protection we offer.'

'You're a Djinditsu?' asked Night Light open-mouthed. 'I've

never seen one before. Well, why didn't you say so, Madam? Oh you're in good company, boy. You can't go far wrong with a Djinditsu at your side. Let's go, I'll come and see you off.'

They walked up some stairs and along many winding paths for a kilometre or so. It was quite steep and hard-going. When they were almost at the top of the town they turned sharply down a small passageway that led almost right into the centre of the tree. At the end of this narrow alleyway was a man in a smart burgundy uniform. His cap had the words 'Tree Barge' embroidered on it in gold lettering. As they approached him he opened a door to a small circular chamber, not much wider than a large person. He doffed his cap and smiled politely at Towelyn.

'They're with me,' she said as she stepped inside alone and thanked the man.

He shut the door to the little room and it closed with a sucking noise. After a couple of minutes the man opened the same door again and the chamber was empty.

'Next please.'

'OK, what's this?' asked Greenery.

'Capillary travel,' said Night Light. 'This dried capillary goes all the way up to the top of the tree, which as you will remember goes into space, a vacuum. By opening and closing airtight seals they can suck you up the tube to anywhere in the tree. We are going to the Tree Barge port. Relax, it's fun! You go next.'

Greenery handed in his ticket and nervously stepped inside the chamber. As he entered he looked up and was indeed standing at the bottom of a towering chimney. He barely had time to regret his decision before the door sucked itself shut. Immediately he felt air tugging at him. His spiky hair stood up even further and his shoelaces flew upwards. Slowly his feet came off the ground and then, as his stomach was left wondering what it had done wrong to be left behind, he rocketed up the smooth wooden pipe.

'Aaaaaaaaaaaaarrrrrrrrggghhhhh!!!!'

At first it was just a vertical flight, then he heard noises like valves opening and closing and he was sent down a tunnel to his left, then right, then upwards again. After a couple of chicanes he flew from the end of the capillary which came out through the floor in a large round room. Greenery was spat out of the end, five metres into the air, and landed with a bump on the heavily cushioned floor. As he sat there woozy and giggling slightly, a door opened in the wall and Towelyn stuck her head in.

'Come on, lazybones, can't sit around there all day. We've got to get your friend up next.'

Greenery sat with Towelyn in a comfy waiting room just off the arrival chamber. There were squishy chairs and plush magazines. *Leaf Surfer* looked interesting. Soft music and running water could be heard from somewhere.

Once Night Light had arrived, the three of them set off down another corridor. As they walked, the sound of water grew louder and louder until they emerged into a cavernous space. It was lit with softly glowing moss that grew in intricate patterns on the wall. Around the edge of the cavern was a carved wooden quay. which surrounded a huge amber lake. Tied up at the pier was a large covered gondola with a paddle wheel at the stern and several passengers already on board, making themselves comfortable.

'How is this possible?'

'Well,' said Night Light, 'the Big Tree is more like a bush than a tree. This is its central trunk but it has smaller ones scattered all over. The upper branches are all connected in one enormous shrub that spreads for thousands of kilometres. We are now thirty-seven kilometres up. This is a river of sap and you two are going to sail on it all the way to Tracey.'

'Oh,' was all Greenery could manage as he struggled to contemplate the thought, 'I guess this is goodbye then.'

He was surprised at how sad he felt leaving Night Light. He had grown accustomed to the little Punster very quickly and knew he was going to miss him. Still at least he wasn't alone. That would be much worse. He looked at Towelyn, his fleecy guardian angel, and smiled. As he turned to go Night Light reached out and hugged him fiercely round the waist.

'See you around, fella,' said Night Light. 'Thanks for helping me out yesterday. I reckon I'd have been done for if you hadn't fought off those horrible things.'

'Let's hope you're just as useful if we have to fight off the Violents again,' said Towelyn.

'Violents? Why would you be fighting them off? Are they after you?'

'They're after my key, Night Light. They need it to bring back their leader apparently.'

Night Light stared, open-mouthed at Greenery as if he was seeing him for the first time. He blinked a couple of times then tried to speak.

'Wait ... You mean *your* key ... Well, *the* key ... It's ... But ...'

'Are you all right?' asked Towelyn, looking concerned.

'Your key is *the* key?' Night Light finally managed.

'It's the key of Captain California.'

'Calefaction,' Towelyn corrected.

'Yeah, *him*.'

'Well, why didn't you say so, son? That means you're . . . Wait . . . He said this would happen.'

'Who did?' asked Greenery.

'The Gump . . . never mind. You're a living legend, a would-be hero on a noble quest. You've got to get that key back. If the Violents get it, we're all in deep trouble.'

'We could use some help,' said Towelyn, sounding rather hopeful.

'Madam, I would be honoured to accompany you.'

'You're coming with us?' asked Greenery, almost jumping for joy.

'If you'll have me, lad.'

'Course we will!' Greenery knelt down to the same level as the Punster and squeezed him till he nearly popped. 'Thanks, Night Light.'

'Come on, let's get on board before they go without us,' he said, looking embarrassed. 'You'll have to buy me another ticket, then you can tell me all about how you two met.'

Mr Johnson stood in front of the whole school. He had called a special assembly that morning.

'Settle down, please! Settle down. Thank you.'

The room came to a hush and Mr Johnson solemnly walked out in front of the children. He looked tired, sad and especially old that morning.

'It is with a heavy heart that I have called the school together for this unusual assembly. I'm afraid I have some grave news.

Greenery Jackson, one of our beloved pupils, a dear, sweet, special boy, has passed away. He was taken from us yesterday in a tragic accident. I know he was very dear to a lot of you. Today's morning lessons have been cancelled. You can all go back to your form rooms and your teachers will be there should you need to talk about anything. That is all.'

The school was silent with shock. As they left the sports hall in single file, Mr Johnson made his way back to his office. He sat down heavily on his old leather chair and opened a drawer in his desk. He removed a half-full bottle of purple-and-yellow striped liquid, then took the tiniest possible sip. He replaced the bottle and sat back in his chair with his eyes closed, humming to himself.

'Your attention please – we are now making our final approach to Tracey,' said a monotone voice through loudspeakers.

Greenery, Towelyn and Night Light had been sitting up on deck since leaving Big Tree and had been enjoying the ride. It had been a very pleasant journey, apart from the entertainment. On the small stage a man was playing music by stroking different size frogs, each one a different colour. He was being accompanied by his singing hair. The sound was like a set of bagpipes being squashed through a mangle.

'The last leg of our journey will be somewhat faster than the previous part,' continued the announcement. 'So we do ask that all passengers return to their seats and apply the crash helmet, life jacket and safety harness found in the stowage box beneath. Thank you.'

As soon as the loudspeaker fell silent the boat began to pick up speed. Greenery began strapping himself in.

'What do they mean, somewhat faster?'

'Well, we're about forty-eight kilometres from Tracey as the crow flies but we're still sixteen kilometres higher than the port so the last bit of our journey is very much downhill.'

Greenery double-checked his harness and swallowed deeply.

'You'll be fine, kiddo. The boats are so well made these days; they hardly ever smash anymore.'

By now the barge had really picked up speed. It was hard to tell how fast they were going because they were still in an enclosed branch, but by the wind on his face Greenery knew it was *very* fast! Suddenly the whole ship lurched down an almost vertical waterfall. What had been a quiet river became raging rapids and the boat was tossed around like a matchstick riding a tsunami.

'Would you like a drink, Sir?' said a calm voice from behind him.

Greenery turned to see a serene waiter harnessed to a track in the ceiling. It kept him vertical yet allowed him movement among the tables.

'We're going to die!' screamed Greenery.

'Any nuts or other snacks?'

'Aaaaarrrgghhhhhh!!!'

'Very well, Sir, thank you for travelling Tree Barge.' And with that the waiter moved off. Amazingly one or two people actually gave orders, though hardly anyone managed to finish without pouring their drinks all over themselves.

Slowly, gradually, the sap returned to its graceful pace and the boat sailed peacefully into a giant hall similar to the one they had left behind in Big Tree. This one, however, had no jetty or walkways around the edge.

'Are we there yet?' asked Greenery.

'Not quite,' replied Towelyn with a wry smile.

A large shutter came down and sealed the tunnel entrance behind them. With a metallic grinding noise from somewhere deep within the tree, the entire mass of sap started to revolve, slowly at first and then faster and faster, until the whole cavern became a huge swirling plughole. As Greenery stared into the centre of the whirlpool he realised they were being flushed away. The barge began its decreasing circular path around the cavern, getting faster and faster until it reached the centre. Just as Greenery thought he was going to be sick, the ship fell several metres onto a blanket of squishy orange moss and came to rest rocking gently from side to side. Workers immediately extended gangplanks and people started to disembark, chatting happily to each other, laughing and planning the day's business. Apparently this was all perfectly normal to those who travelled by Tree Barge.

Ten minutes later the three of them emerged from the base of the tree that grew in the centre of Tracey, the capital city. It was strange, thought Greenery, to enter one tree and leave from another without ever seeing daylight. He turned back to look at the tree they had come from. It was about one-fifth the size of Big Tree but was still enormous. High up in the distance he could see the branch they had sailed through to get here. Several others also spanned out from this hub in other directions.

The tree itself was growing from the centre of a perfectly circular island which was in the centre of a perfectly circular lake. On the outer shore of this lake was the busy city.

Four bridges spanned the gap between the two shores. Each

one was the shape of a letter – U, E, D and F. They started walking along the graceful curve of the D-shaped bridge.

'What do the letters stand for?'

'They're the compass points, Greenery,' said Towelyn.

'No they're not. The compass points are North, South, East and West.'

'Maybe where you come from, lad, but not here they're not,' said Night Light defensively.

'What do they stand for then?'

'Upstream, Ebb, Downstream and Flow.'

Greenery was about to ask more questions about the relevance of these names but was distracted by the cornucopia of incredible sights that opened up before him. In Big Tree most of the people had been human-looking or at least vaguely human-shaped but here the human form was very thin on the ground.

There were two giant ducks swimming in the lake with long swanlike necks and hundreds of tentacles instead of feathers. One of them noticed him staring, lifted its hat and shouted, 'Good afternoon.' Towelyn smiled and waved back.

Rolling along the bridge but going in the opposite direction Greenery noticed hundreds of multicoloured marbles. When one rolled over his foot the entire collection of balls formed up into the shape of a man, complete with face. 'I'm sorry,' it said with a voice like glass smashing, 'didn't see you there,' then it broke down again into its component parts and rolled away.

A convoy of small vehicles drove past – a fire engine, police car, ambulance, tow truck, bin lorry and a bus – each one like a large toy. They were all singing in harmony as they went about their business.

Between each bridge was a canal, all four of which spread out into the city. From the nearest canal came a large transparent tube that went into a glass building full of water, strange fish and Merpeople. There were desks inside with computers and what looked like paper, but Greenery assumed it must be waterproof somehow. Every so often someone would enter or exit the building using the pipe.

'What's that place?' Greenery asked.

'That, my boy, is the Embassy of the underwater kingdom of Atlantis,' answered Night Light. 'Beautiful place. I'll have to take you there some time. Might have to get you some gills first though.'

The Atlantis Embassy wasn't the only strange building. In fact, they were nearly all just as odd. There was one in the shape of a castle that was made of lime jelly. There was one that looked like a cloud and floated slightly above the street. Greenery noticed it was actually tied down. Probably to stop it blowing away, he thought. Some were monumental, some were just mental, and he could have sworn that one winked at him.

As they left the bridge and joined the hustle and bustle of the busy city, he was bumped into by creatures beyond description, as well as others more easily recognised. There were minotaurs and centaurs, griffins and sphinxes, angels and cherubs, basilisks and chimeras, and countless others. Tracey was a vast metropolis and every little bit of it was full of sublime, outrageous and simply ridiculous things. He loved it.

'Excuse me, is this the right way to Central Collections?' Night Light asked a passing Pygmy Monopod.

'Er yes, I believe it is. Straight down Avenue Road, turn left at the Dirigible Giggle Foundation, right at the Unicorn Hair Salon and you'll see it. It's just opposite Star-Books.'

'Right-ho, thanks.'

The Unicorn Hair Salon was exactly that. Inside, sitting on modified barber's chairs were a couple of glowing white horses each with a majestic ivory horn on their forehead. One was having a perm done and the other was looking at shoes in a magazine while she got her new do blow-dried.

As they rounded the corner the tax office came into sight. It was a four-sided pyramid made of dull grey metal about two hundred metres per side. It had no windows anywhere and just one tiny door at street level facing them. Coming out from this door was the longest queue Greenery had ever seen. Anywhere. Ever.

Greenery's heart sank to his shoes. He had come to have certain ideas about his adventure and had liked it when Night Light called it a quest. Standing in a queue for a week was not what he'd had in mind.

'Right, well it looks like we might as well get used to standing still,' said Night Light as he joined the line behind a lady who was attempting to train her chocolate mice. She wasn't doing very well. She couldn't quite resist eating one of them every now and again as a punishment.

'Oh how wrong you are,' replied Towelyn with a smug look on her face. 'You're with the Djinditsu now. We don't queue.' And with that she calmly sauntered along the line all the way to the front. When they reached the small entrance to the central tax facility, a life-size toy soldier blocked their way.

'Stop in the name of Captain Calefaction. Where exactly do

you three think you're going?' the plastic guard shouted in Towelyn's face.

'Central Collections.'

'Oh yes, and I suppose you horrible lot are so important that you think you can just wander in without a pass or without queuing up like every other soul that passes this way.'

'Yes we are and yes I think we can.'

'On whose say-so, little miss?'

'Mine!' She produced – from somewhere Greenery didn't realise it was possible to have pockets – a small leather wallet. Inside it was a shield-shaped badge and an official-looking piece of paper.

'You're a Djinditsu! Oh bloomin' heck . . . I mean excuse me, Miss. Certainly, Miss. In you go. And your fine gentlemen companions . . . er . . . I mean, not companions, you know just . . . er . . . well, friends. Well, in you go, Miss. Sorry, Miss . . . er . . . Ma'am.'

'Thank you,' Towelyn said. Smiling coquettishly, she slinked past the guard, followed by Greenery and Night Light who were both desperately trying not to laugh.

The inside of the tax office was quite dimly lit. Glowing orbs hung motionless in the air and gave off a soft radiant light. The entire building was basically one large room with each floor jutting out like a shelf from the slanted walls into a central chamber. Stairs and passageways crisscrossed the empty space between floors and walls. There were no windows anywhere and everything was made of the same matt grey metal as the outside.

As Greenery's eyes grew accustomed to the semi-darkness he saw pieces of paper flying around everywhere from room to room and floor to floor. It wasn't until one passed by him that he saw it was being carried by a small green beetle.

'Filing bug,' explained Towelyn when she saw the confused look on his face.

'Okey-dokey, artichokey. Where is the office of Central Collections?' asked Night Light.

'Top floor,' said Greenery.

Towelyn and Night Light turned to look at him.

'And how do you know that, young fella-me-lad?'

'Cause it's on this sign here. I read it.'

'Clever clogs!'

'All right then,' said Towelyn, 'it's a long climb. We'd better start moving.'

Chapter Six

Central Collections

If you could fly like a bird would you dream of running?

If you could swim like a fish would you wish that you could dance?

If you could taste music would you long to hear some drumming?

Would you want to live forever if you really had the chance?

Taken from *The Codex Imaginarium*
by The Mysterious Wandering Gump

Mr Johnson had insisted on accompanying Gloria Jackson to Littleton Bay General Hospital. She could not be expected to identify the body of her son alone.

Sobbing quietly into a handkerchief she followed him down the long quiet corridors that led to the morgue. A stiff, waxy-looking pathologist greeted them solemnly at the door and led them both inside. Lying on a gurney in the middle of the room was the body of her twelve-year-old son.

'He lost so much blood, so quickly; there was nothing anyone could have done,' said the pathologist. 'We still don't know what made all that glass shatter. It could have been atmospheric pressure changes but we may never know. I'm sorry.'

'That's him . . . Excuse me!' Mrs Jackson practically ran from the room.

'Thank you, Doctor,' said Mr Johnson and followed her.

The pathologist sighed deeply and covered up the young body. He turned off the lights and left.

In the silent dark laboratory the body on the gurney started to glow green. The eerie light shone right through the thin white blanket covering the small cadaver. A thick lime gas began escaping from under the covers and falling to the floor. It seemed to be a lot heavier than the surrounding air.

As more and more gas poured from the gurney onto the floor, the body dissolved away slowly into nothingness. Lights twinkled on and off inside the gaseous mass and the small emerald cloud began swirling around the room. Eventually the tiny nebula coalesced to form a small solid shape.

Take-That the cat shook himself off once. Nudged the door open and left the now-empty room to go and find the headmaster.

Greenery and Night Light were out of breath following the long climb up the inside of the pyramid. They stood outside the door to Central Collections panting heavily and staring at Towelyn who was, as always, calm and composed. After taking a moment to get his breath back Greenery knocked on the door.

'ENTER!' boomed an amplified voice. They entered into a large empty hall. At one end of the room was a raised platform. It looked a lot like a theatre with a proscenium arch but had only one entrance right in the middle of the back wall. The colour theme was of course grey.

'STATE YOUR REQUEST!' demanded the empty stage.

'I came here yesterday through some kind of portal . . . You took a large gold and turquoise key from me. I need it back . . . Please. I'm from Earth. I want to go home . . .'

'SILENCE,' interrupted the voice. 'WAIT!'

They waited . . .

'NO!'

'What do you mean no? You can't just say no! I need it. It's mine. I have to get home, you . . .'

'SILENCE!' . . . Mutter mutter mutter mutter . . . 'OK you tell him zen! . . . Why do I have to go? . . . What? OK, OK, I'll tell him . . . Oh it iz ztill on . . . Shhh! . . . WAIT THERE.'

The door at the back of the stage opened and an odd little character emerged. He was basically a ball with arms and legs; his head and torso made one perfect sphere. It looked though as if someone had over-inflated him with helium. His feet just about touched the ground, but it was an effort. He propelled himself forward by stretching down and using his tiptoes to push himself along. After a clumsy entrance and taking a moment or two to reach the trio of travellers and make sure he was facing the right way, the balloon man spoke.

'Greetings. I am ze Under-Zecretary of Zentral Collections. My name is Buoyant.'

Greenery noticed he spoke with a strong French accent, which he thought odd as he was sure Monsieur Buoyant was about as French as Colonel Sanders. 'We know ze key of which you zpeak. Of course we do! It iz legendary. But we need to know: what do you offer in return?'

Greenery's heart sank a little. He knew he didn't have much to bargain with.

'I have a Lego brick, some string, a well-used conker and fifteen pence in sterling.'

'Fifteen pence iz a handsome amount. What colour iz your brick?'

'Yellow.'

'It iz not enough!' the Under-Secretary shouted, losing control of his buoyancy and floating off the ground a little. His skinny legs waggled frantically until he touched down gently again.

'It's all I have.'

'Neverzeless it iz inzufficient. A legendary artefact zuch as ze key of Captain Calefaction requirez anozer item of equal value in its place. You must bring uz . . . ze Tear of ze Cyclops.'

'No! That's not fair! It's on the Faraday Plate!' shouted Night Light as even Towelyn gasped in shock.

'Yet zis iz what we ask.'

'It's too far away!' protested the Punster.

'You will have help. We will provide you with a Cecephelophopus to take you. We know who you are, Outworlder, and we too have heard ze prophecy. If we give you back ze key you might lose it to ze Violents and Lazaruz Brown will return. It iz a big chance to take, zo we ask of you ze impossible. Go to ze shores of Macadamia and bring us back ze Tear of ze Cyclops. Zen and only zen may you have your key.'

'But . . .'

'GO!'

With his last shout the collections officer lost all altitude control and floated away. As the three friends left his room he was bouncing gently against the ceiling with his arms and legs waving madly and shouting something in French.

Outside, back in the corridor, they were met by a small car. It was a Citroën 2cv. and was similar to the other vehicles Greenery had seen on the bridge earlier.

'Good afternoon, Ladies and Gentleman. If you would be so kind as to follow me I will take you to your Cecephelophopus.' With that he drove off.

'What's a Cecephelophopus?' asked Greenery.

'You'll see,' Towelyn and Night Light said in unison.

They followed the little car onto a spiral ramp at the back of the building and started to walk casually downwards. They stayed on the ramp all the way to the ground floor and then continued spiralling down several floors beneath. The pyramid shape continued down as well as up so that each progressively lower floor became larger than the one above it. As they walked, Greenery, as usual, had questions.

'What's the Tear of the Cyclops?'

'The Cyclops were once a proud and noble people,' said Towelyn. 'They were numerous and had a great empire in the land of Macadamia. But in the reign of Lazarus Brown they were hunted and butchered.'

'Why?'

'Because once removed, the eye of a Cyclops can be used to see anywhere or anything, but only once. Then it is useless. Seeing through Cyclops' eyes gave Lazarus a great strategic advantage over his enemies. Unfortunately as a disposable commodity they did not last long. The Cyclops were wiped out.'

'Terrible shame it was! Awful!' added Night Light.

Towelyn nodded. She looked genuinely sad but continued anyway.

'Just before the last Cyclops was killed it shed one tear. The only time a Cyclops has ever been known to cry. One of Lazarus Brown's generals collected that tear in a glass vial and took it to the safest place he could think of. He wanted to give it to his leader on his next tour of Macadamia.'

'Where? Where did he take it?'

'He placed it in the centre of The Eternal Abyss. It is said that it's impossible to remove the Tear from its resting place unless you have the codeword.'

'What's the codeword?'

'No one knows. Lazarus was caught and banished before he had a chance to recover the Tear.'

'So how do we get it then?'

'I don't know.'

'Well, why would anybody want to? What's so special about a tiny drop of salt water?'

'Because,' said Towelyn, 'the Tear of a Cyclops will give anyone who drinks it the power to see anything they want to, whenever they want to. Oh! . . . It looks like our four-wheeled friend is turning.'

They were now ten floors below ground level. The little car took an exit ramp from the main roadway and led them to a wide-open space like an aircraft hangar. There in the middle of the floor were three of the strangest creatures Greenery had seen so far.

Apart from two massive wings a fully grown Cecephelo-phopus is very similar in shape to a giant octopus. They are roughly twice as big as an elephant with a similar-shaped head and they can change colour at will, which they do constantly. These colours dance across their skin in funky moving patterns, and can form any picture the animal so wishes, earning them the nickname 'Disco Beasts'.

The Cecephelophopus uses the same means of propulsion as an octopus – jet propulsion. But instead of squirting water behind it, it fires air very fast from its body. In the air no creature can match an adult Cecephelophopus for speed, grace and agility.

Two spherical men who looked like smaller versions of the Central Collections Under-Secretary were finishing strapping three saddles onto the back of the closest Cecephelophopus. The large animal strained under the tight harness and somehow looked quite angry.

It is a credit to the nature of Greenery Frankincense Jackson that he had not gone mad on his journey so far. Most people would have probably flipped out around about the time they saw their first Motor Pike. To anyone of a less curious disposition three waiting Cecephelophopi could have easily tipped them over the edge. However, Greenery's inquisitive nature and desire to learn took precedence over everything else.

He started running around the Disco Beast looking at it from every angle. He was dazzled by the flamboyant display of bright colours and dancing patterns. When the Cecephelophopus' skin changed from a green-and-red maze complete with Pacman-like figures zooming around it, to a smiling and winking picture of his own face, Greenery looked so happy Towelyn thought he might pass out.

'It's amazing! It's beautiful! How does it move?'

'It flies.'

'Wow! Let's get on, I want to ride it. Let's go!'

'Come on then,' she said with a smile in her voice.

The two harness fasteners had finished their work and were leaning a small stepladder up to three seats tethered firmly to the animal's back. As he climbed on board Greenery's hand brushed the skin of the Disco Beast.

It didn't feel at all like he expected it to. It was incredibly smooth with a layer of very, very fine, very short downy hair and it was warm. It felt as if the Disco Beast were the world's largest novelty hot-water bottle cover.

They sat down in the comfortable leather chairs, with their legs spread out in front of them. Towelyn was in front holding the reins that were strapped to the protruding wing-like ears. Greenery was in the middle and Night Light was at the back just in front of a large storage trunk.

'Have you flown one of these before?' he asked Towelyn, leaning out from behind Greenery.

'Not as such, no; but I'm told it's quite easy. Pull both reins together you go higher; pull left you go left and pull right you go right. To go lower I squeeze my legs together. Easy!'

'And what about speed control?'

'There is no speed control with a Cecephelophopus. It's either fast or stop. Right, let's go!'

By now, the two mini versions of the Under-Secretary had removed the ladder. On Towelyn's command they started running around the Cecephelophopus, shouting loudly and waving brightly coloured flags. With a strange elephant-like trumpeting, the Disco Beast rolled over so that all of its tentacles radiated out from its body with its face pointing

70

skywards. The three passengers were also facing vertically upwards.

A noise like a quiet vacuum cleaner started somewhere within the animal. As the noise rose in intensity it also rose in pitch and volume until it sounded like a small jet engine.

'What's happening?' shouted Greenery.

'It's warming up,' yelled Towelyn over the noise, 'it's breathing in, filling its lungs. When that's done it will start to breathe out from its second mouth and we'll be off.'

The last word of her sentence hung in the air. She might as well have been shouting in a library. The loud noise of the intake of breath had cut off sharply and the hangar was silent.

'Uh oh!' sang Night Light.

WOOOOOOOOOOOOOOOSH!

The Cecephelophopus went from stationary to full speed instantly. Now that it was breathing in both directions it moved with absolute silence. Apart from the three screaming maniacs strapped to its back.

As Towelyn fought to gain control of the reins the animal whizzed around the confined space of the sub-basement with phenomenal speed and aerial dexterity. It looped, turned, twisted and spun in unbelievably tight circles around the room. Finally Towelyn managed to gain some steering ability. At the same time she spotted the exit tunnel leading diagonally upwards and headed for it at breakneck speed.

Outside the cold grey tax pyramid the queue was still slowly and quietly winding its way towards the entrance. The spot-light shards of an early-evening sun caught a lady Rhinocerfox flirting unsuccessfully with a Rapture-Reacher; and a Five-Horned Gabbermouth telling tales to the restless.

71

The calm and tranquillity of the meandering line was shattered instantly when a Cecephelophopus with pink and green flashing polka dots came hurtling around the side of the huge building. It zoomed low over the queue, knocking off several hats and one removable head. All that could be heard as the Disco Beast passed by was an ear-piercing scream in perfect three-part harmony.

Chapter Seven

Flights of Fancy

Looking down from above, the world is small.
  Looking out through your eyes you will never see it all.
  Looking in from without, space is full,
  But all that you can see are the shadows in your skull.
                              Taken from *The Perception Machine*
                              by The Mysterious Wandering Gump

Way up high, above the crazy confines of Tracey and far removed from any risk of collision, it was astonishingly peaceful. The Cecephelophopus moved through the sky in perfect silence with the grace and power of an angel. Greenery was admiring the view.

The landscape below was breathtaking. They were flying over patchwork fields in an incredible array of colours and in some places you could even see the stitching. Delicate rivers of every hue traced the contours of the land like life-giving veins.

They flew over a lake made of vegetable soup where boats were trawling for carrots. From this height you could just make out the edge of the bowl that surrounded the chunky lagoon and the port that had built up around the spoon. He saw towns and villages dotted everywhere. Little pockets of life in an incredible variety of forms.

On they flew over giant craggy cliffs that plummeted down to a leafy gorge at least as big as the Grand Canyon. There was no river at the bottom though. Night Light said it had been made by the migratory route of the tiny Forever Snail which would crawl back and forth along the same three-hundred-kilometre stretch of land forever, looking for its lost mate.

They flew over a wood of conifer trees. It wasn't until the Cecephelophopus swooped down to take a bite of one that Greenery realised the whole forest was on the move. Every tree was marching in unison to some evergreen destination.

At times the Disco Beast was just as enchanting as the land-scape. It was constantly changing pattern and colour. At one point the whole animal started to fizz like static on a TV screen except it was bright orange and luminous purple. Greenery became so hypnotised by this that he started to zone out. The static didn't last long, however, and was soon replaced with pictures that matched the floor below. It was like riding a transparent flying carpet.

He sat on the back of the magnificent Cecephelophopus and thought to himself how incredibly lucky he was to be here and to see all that he had seen.

As the evening rolled by, the ever-changing scenery revealed more and more wonders but as night began to fall the temperature began to drop.

The two funny little men that had prepared the Cecephelophopus for them had strapped a large travelling trunk behind the back seat. When Greenery's teeth began to chatter Night Light rummaged around inside the case until he found three large fur coats. With these handed out everybody was a lot more comfortable.

'It's getting colder because we're travelling Ebbwards,' Towelyn shouted back over her shoulder. 'The land of Macadamia is on the fringes of the Faraday Plate. '

'Is it much further?' asked Greenery.

'About another three days' flying, I'd say.'

'Three days! Even at this speed?'

'Roughly.'

'Well, I can't stay up here all that time. I need more food and I need to . . . Well, you know. Not now, but I will.'

'We'll land shortly and make camp. The Disco Beast needs to rest anyway and we all need sleep. Night Light!'

'Yes, Ma'am?'

'What else do we have in that trunk back there?'

'Let's see now,' he muttered, turning around and rummaging through it.

As he did so the Cecephelophopus changed colour again. It became a dark royal blue with silver stars all over that twinkled against the night sky.

'Oh here's a list of what's inside. We have: the three Sasquatch coats that we're wearing, three Yeti-hide exposure suits, six ration packs containing qwebur berry juice, sliced spaghe-tree with minced dodo and fresh treacle drops. Oh that's good news: there are three bubble-hats so we can sleep comfortably, two emergency glow-worms, both dormant, and a pen.'

'What's the pen for?' asked Greenery.

'You never know when you might need a pen.'

'Fair enough.'

'That looks like a good place to camp,' Towelyn chipped in, 'down there just next to that hotel.'

They circled around the small field Towelyn had pointed to, getting lower all the time. The open space was roughly the size of a football pitch and was surrounded by a thick wood of Do-nut Trees. At one end was a large white inn with a thatched roof.

They were quite close to the ground now and going relatively slowly. Just as Greenery began to think the landing would be quiet and uneventful the Cecephelophopus accelerated again. This time, however, it was heading straight down.

When it was about two metres away from turning them all into a very large and colourful stain, it pulled out of the dive and rose vertically about twenty metres. Then, pointing straight up, it stopped dead in the air and spread its entire body as wide as it could, creating a betentacled parachute. The Disco Beast and its passengers drifted slowly to earth and landed with only the slightest bump.

'Textbook!' said Night Light, unhooking the small ladder that was attached to the lid of the travelling trunk.

'Are we going to sleep in the inn?' asked Greenery.

Both Night Light and Towelyn looked at him like he was crazy.

'We've got bubble-hats,' Night Light said. looking slightly confused.

'Oh. That's good, is it?'

'Why would anyone sleep in a bed when they've got a bubble-hat?'

'I don't know. Why would they?'

'They wouldn't.'

'Oh well, I'm glad we cleared that up then.'

'They would, however,' Towelyn said, waking both Greenery and Night Light from their confusion, 'go inside said hotel and order a great big meal. Particularly if they had been travelling all day and were starving.'

'Amen to that, Ma'am.'

'What about the Cecephelophopus?'

'It'll be fine. They imprint on their owner until passed on to the next. If someone tries to steal a Cecephelophopus, the first thing you know about it is when you stand in what's left of them. Come on – food!' With that she trudged off to the pub.

The sign above the door read: 'The Splintered Winter'. It was an odd name for a pub perhaps, but quite apt. As the three travellers entered, the first thing they noticed was the heat. After travelling for so long, so high up, they were all rather chilled.

Inside, though, it was warm and snugly. The soft yellow lights, low ceiling and wooden-beamed roof all conspired to give a traditional warm welcome.

This effect was spoiled somewhat by the falling snow and the frost-covered tables at either end of the long room. All the customers but one were sitting in the warm sunny part of the room.

The barman was a mild-mannered, kindly looking soul. He would have looked at home behind the bar in The Red Lion in Littleton Bay were it not for the massive antlers growing from his scalp. He noticed the three weary travellers and each of their questioning looks. With a deep sigh he began to explain the strange weather phenomenon as though he had done this a million times before, which of course he had.

'It's a localised seasonal variance,' he said in a tired but friendly voice. 'Winter follows summer; summer follows winter and so on. Come back in six months' time and the middle of the room will be cold and the edges will be warm. Come back in three months' time and it will be an even split – winter over there, summer over there. Now what can I get you folks on this fine evening?'

'Three hot Yaba roots, please, and some menus,' answered Towelyn.

They sat down at a table in a cosy corner, as far away from the chill of winter as possible while they waited for the land-lord to fetch their drinks.

'I think we should give him a name,' said Greenery.

'I'm sure he's already got a name,' said Towelyn. 'Probably a family, maybe some kids.'

'No, not the barman, the Disco Beast.'

'You mean the Cecephelophopus?' said Night Light, joining in.

'Yes. Why not?'

'Well, no reason I suppose, Mr Man. All right, what do you want to call him?

'Tim . . . No, that's boring . . . er . . . Fahnghorn . . . No, that's just stupid.'

'Bublufermerious?' said Night Light.

'No, that's *really* stupid. How about Sky Painter?'

'I used to have an Uncle Bublufermerious. Nice man.'

'Sheba,' said Towelyn. 'It was my mother's name.'

The other two stared at her looking like confused goldfish.
'You did know she's a female, didn't you?' she queried.
'No,' they both said together.
'Oh! Well, she is.'
'OK then,' said Greenery as the barman came over. 'Sheba.'
The Yaba root as it turned out was the root of a plant heated up. With a metal straw you could pierce its hard skin and suck the juice out, which was warm, nourishing and tasted a bit like earthy hot chocolate.

As Greenery looked over the menu he overheard the conversation of two dark figures on a nearby table. He couldn't make out exactly what they looked like but they smelt of onions.

'It's a dark time, aright.'
'Yerp.'
'Strange things a happenin'.'
'Aye.'
'Portents and the like.'
'Yerp.'
'It's them there Violents.'
'S'wat I heard too.'
'They're no better than they shouldn't be, but they've not been this active for manys a year now. I reckons it's that prophecy.'
'What? That one The Mysterious Wandering Gump made about that young Outworlder fella and the key needed to bring back old Lazarus "mad as blue peanut butter" Brown?'
'That's the one.'
'Know what I heard?'
'What?'

'I heard from old Mother Dodykins that he's here, some-where along The River. That young lad has arrived.'

'No!'

'That's what I heard. She heard it from her son-in-law who trades on market day in Big Tree. Said there were all kinds of commotion this morning. They found two dead bodies. In a right mess they were.'

'I should not like to be that young fellow. What with all them lot after me.'

'Did all right though, didn't he? Killed two of 'em.'

'Well, two yeah but what about the Armies of Sorrow? The Mysterious Wandering Gump also predicted that he would defeat the Armies of Sorrow.'

'Oh yeah, I'd forgotten on that. They reckon the Armies of Sorrow killed thousands.'

'S'right.'

'Could be millions!'

'Nar!'

'Yar!'

'Nar!'

'Yar!'

'When I says Nar! I means Nar!!'

'Ahr.'

'Are we ready to order here?'

Greenery was snatched back to the conversation at his own table by the waiter's interruption. Confused and worried he stared up at him blankly.

'I'll have what she's having, please,' he mumbled in a small voice. It made no difference anyway. He didn't know what any of the food on the menu was.

The rest of the meal passed in a kind of vague blur. His food came and went. It was passable. There was conversation but he couldn't remember it. All he kept thinking was 'The Armies of Sorrow'. Now he had to defeat a whole army? It sounded terrifying.

Another thought kept nagging at him, deep in the back of his mind. Why? Why did he have to learn all this stuff from an overheard conversation in a pub? Why had his so-called friends not told him? Did they really think he was that weak? Couldn't they just be honest?

The evening came to an end. Somebody paid with something but Greenery couldn't remember who or how. They said their goodbyes to the barman and trudged back across the clearing to where they had landed. When they got back to camp Greenery was woken from his misery by the severe lack of Cecephelophopus.

'Where is it? It's gone. You said she would be OK,' shouted Greenery, running around the edge of the clearing in a panic and waving his arms around.

'Relax,' said Towelyn in a voice so calm she practically purred. 'She'll be here.'

She smiled back at Greenery's confused expression and walked purposefully off to the treeline. She beckoned Greenery to come and join her.

'Now I want you to repeat after me. Cecephelophopus cecephecomeheremust.'

'Cecephelophopus cecephecomeheremust?'

'Good. Now cup your hands and shout that into the woods.'

Feeling ridiculous, Greenery did as he was told.

'Cecephelophopus cecephecomeheremust!' After a moment's

silence a strange trumpeting came echoing back from somewhere nearby.

As Greenery slumped down on the grass feeling wretched,
a tree next to him began to uncoil its twisted boughs. He
watched them slithering around with no idea what was
happening but as parts of the tree started to change colour
he realised he was looking right at Sheba. She had rolled over
so that her tentacles were furthest from the ground and had
contorted them into strange, angular branch like formations.
She had changed colour, shape and texture to match the
surrounding trees perfectly.

'See,' said Towelyn rather smugly as Night Light began
unloading the camp from Sheba's travelling trunk. 'She's
imprinted on you. You can call her whenever you want. They
have excellent hearing and can locate any sound they hear
with almost pinpoint accuracy.'

It didn't take much time for Night Light to get a fire started.
He simply changed himself into a flame-thrower, a man who
juggles fire but keeps burning himself and discarding the flames.

When they had a nice cosy pyre burning and Towelyn had
warmed up some more Yaba root for them all, Greenery
decided he had to say something. He couldn't get the oniony
strangers' conversation out of his head. It made him feel sick
to think about facing an entire army.

'Towelyn?'

'Yes, Greenery.'

'Who are the Armies of Sorrow?'

The atmosphere in the camp changed immediately. Without
looking up, Towelyn put her drink down on the floor then
slowly turned to face him.

82

'Pardon me?'

'The Armies of Sorrow, I heard some people talking about them in the pub.'

'You don't have to worry about that right now. Why don't you try and get some sleep?'

Towelyn obviously thought this was an end to the conversation. Greenery had other ideas.

'Oh, OK, sure! I just overheard two strangers saying that I have to fight a bunch of blokes who killed millions of people. But you're right. Why worry about it? I'm sure I'll have a lovely restful night. Nothing to worry about except certain death! Come on, Towelyn, I'm not an idiot; just tell me the truth! . . . Please?'

She waited until he had finished then, without taking her eyes from his, answered very slowly. 'The Armies of Sorrow is not a *who*? It's a *what*.'

'What?'

'Exactly. It's a weapon, a kind of gun, invented by one of the Violents. It was designed so that one man could take on an entire army. You point it at a large group of people and pull the trigger like any other gun. This gun, however, fires emotion not bullets. Whoever is in the path of the wave instantly feels intense sorrow and depression. When turned up to full power one shot from the Armies of Sorrow can make an entire regiment take their own lives. You don't have to lift a finger. Your enemies kill themselves.'

'That's awful!'

'Yes it is. It's horrible and I didn't tell you about it because to be honest I'd forgotten about it. When Lazarus Brown was at the height of his power these kinds of atrocities were happening every day. All good people were scared and a lot of us died. I can't tell you everything that happened because we are talking about years of history here. But I can promise you that if you have any other questions I will answer them quickly and honestly as I believe I have done since we met. OK?'

'Yes, OK.'

Greenery sat in silence for a moment or two prodding the campfire with a stick. Towelyn could tell he still had something on his mind but chose to stay silent. 'I'm sorry I shouted,' said Greenery eventually, 'but I'm scared. I'm in a strange place facing strange dangers and every time I think I know what's happening something else comes along and I feel just as useless as I was when I first arrived.'

'That's OK. You *are* useless,' she smiled, 'but that's what we're here for, to look after the clueless wonder. Speaking of which, I think it's bedtime.'

'Indeed it is!' shouted Night Light from the depths of the sturdy crate. He clambered out holding three metallic objects and threw one each to Towelyn and Greenery.

'This, my young fellow-me-lad, is a bubble-hat and I guarantee you've never been as comfortable in your life. Go on! Put it on!'

Greenery put it on. As soon as the circular hat touched his head it shrank to a snug fit. Next a large clear bubble began to grow from the top of the strange headgear downwards, over and around him. The dry, soapy matter spread slowly down his body and Greenery could feel a slight tingling where it passed over his skin. Within seconds he was completely enveloped in a large warm bubble that floated ever so gently above the ground. Tendrils of soapy matter from his bubble connected to Towelyn's and Night Light's, all three came together and anchored themselves firmly to a sturdy-looking tree. Within moments he was asleep. He had never been as comfortable in his life.

Chapter Eight

The Dawn of the Violents

'My watch is broken,
but it's right twice a day,'
Is the sort of thing
An optimist might say.
'I know they're only scuffed,
But I need new shoes.'
Is one example of
Some pessimistic views.

Taken from Homo Sapiens Are Only Human
by The Mysterious Wandering Gump

Morning broke, but after some emergency tinkering by the Temporal Technicians the rest of the day continued as the rest of the day should.

Greenery awoke to find Towelyn and Night Light huddled round the campfire. Night Light was frying something that looked like Blu-Tack but smelt delicious and Towelyn had a nice warm Yaba root all ready for him. After a pleasant breakfast they climbed on board Sheba and were whisked skywards once more.

In Littleton Bay the sun rose to find Mrs Jackson sitting on a seafront bench opposite the old abandoned theatre. She was oblivious to the biting wind as she stared at the white peaks of the cold grey waves. She had been there all night. The vacant, tear-streaked expression on her face only hinted at the pain raging inside.

Mr Johnson had also been awake all night. He had been chasing mice round the basement of St Augustine's and was carrying a bag of dead rodents home for his cat. He was hoping this would make amends for the fiasco in the attic the other day.

As the day began in Tracey, life was happening as life usually does. The town crier was standing in the middle of the main square blubbering like a baby and announcing the day's news between sobs. The tree barge had already deposited its first load of commuters and tourists, who had all gone scurrying about their business. And the streets and thoroughfares were filling up with the universal misfits that inhabited The Other Place.

In the town hall Mayor Fanacapan Schnigwiggler was about to sign a treaty that would ensure great trade routes with the six-fingered Mitten People of Mollusc, thus enabling the towns-folk of Tracey to buy fantastically made woollen garments for the upcoming winter months.

Outside Central Collections the enormous queue was already forming. Most of its longest-standing members had taken to camping out overnight so as not to lose their places. Bleary-eyed and somewhat sleepy pleasantries were being exchanged when a female Budgericar pointed at the sky and screamed.

She honked her horn and flapped her doors frantically until all along the line people were pointing, screaming and finally running for their lives. Out of the sky swooped an enormous beast.

It was bigger than a Mega Whale, uglier than a Scrumple-toad and more ferocious than a Snarling Gjammerhammer. It could be called a Dragon in so much as it had claws and wings and hundreds of razor-sharp teeth but there the similarity ended. Its body was segmented like an insect's and it had some kind of exoskeleton, yet the skin looked very fleshy and soft with sporadic tufts of bright-pink fur. It smelt of death.

Riding on its colossal orange back were hundreds of crea-tures, swarming over it like an infestation, each one more grotesque and deformed than the last. They shouted and cheered while their beast of burden descended onto the square outside the tax office, crushing several smaller buildings. The mighty monster gave a cry of fury as rope ladders were thrown from its haunches and the hideous passengers started to flow down them.

They surrounded the square, the pyramid and several onlookers who had not managed to run in time. On and on they came marching from the back of the great worm until they were in position. The Violents had landed.

They stood motionless yet there was a sense of tension and threat about them. It felt to the terrified few who had been trapped, as though each one was a coiled spring or a mouse-trap ready to snap and kill at the slightest provocation. In unison the Violents turned and gave a strange form of salute as the last member of their clan slowly left the back of the beast.

He was at least three metres tall and made of burgundy marble with white veins running throughout his body. The smooth polished rock looked clean and bright in contrast with the dirty, oozing, dripping and sweating of his followers.

He strutted slowly around the square with an air of disdain for all that he saw, as if he owned it and it was his to save or destroy as he saw fit. His name was Ignatius Trump.

He strolled up to the toy soldier on guard duty and spoke to him in a voice as sharp as mustard and cold as ice.

'Yesterday a Djinditsu and a human were here.' He pronounced the word 'human' like one might say cockroach.

'Yes, Sir ... Y ... y ... yes they were,' replied the terrified guard, shaking as he spoke.

'That was not a question. Where did they go?'

'Central Collections, Sir.'

'And afterwards?'

'I don't know where, Sir, I'm sorry. They flew out of here on a Cecephelophopus. Don't know where they were heading though, Sir.'

'Thank you, you have been most helpful.' He reached out with both hands and pulled the little plastic man's head clean off. The guard fell to the floor instantly. He was dead.

'Unit one, ONWARDS!'

On his command a team of seventy Violents detached themselves from the main force and headed into the mighty metal pyramid. They swept through the building like a mini apocalypse. Everyone who came before them fell. If they didn't run or hide in time, they died. Eventually the tide of death stopped outside the door to Central Collections.

Walking behind his minions, with the same carefree manner

as before, came the shining stone giant. He punched his way through the reinforced metal door and into the domain of Monsieur Buoyant. Having heard the noise and commotion outside, the taxman had been desperately trying to flee but in his state of heightened emotion he found it increasingly difficult to control his buoyancy. When Death came strolling into his office the little man was found bobbing upside down against the ceiling, hysterical and terrified. To his credit he didn't tell them what they wanted to know straight away. He was brave and strong with a surprisingly high pain threshold. Of course in the end he gave in, he talked, but he should be remembered in this story as a hero. His was not a kind death.

The Violents cheered in victorious joy as Ignatius Trump strutted back into the centre of the courtyard. Clutched within his raised fist was a large gold and turquoise key. On its side was a switch that read 'Dormant' and 'Active'. An expectant hush descended over the loathsome crowd.

'Children of the Way! Our time has come. For so long Captain Calefaction has sat on the chair of office instead of our rightful leader, our true Captain, Lazarus Brown! But now we have the means and the will to return him to his rightful seat and restore order to The Other Place!'

He decisively flicked the switch to 'Active' . . . Nothing happened. Again . . . Nothing. He flicked the switch for a third time only to be rewarded with a big fat nothing.

The outpouring of rage that escaped from his mouth could be heard all over Tracey. The last echoes of his frustration died away and he looked up with hatred in his cold stony eyes. He called for his second-in-command.

The order was barely a whisper yet it carried so much hate within it that all who heard it shrank away.

'Despatch the surfers. Bring me Greenery Jackson.'

Greenery was feeling great. They had been flying all morning in glorious sunshine and Sheba was feeling playful. Now and again as the mood took her she would loop, swoop, tumble and fall around the clouds like a fish darting through a coral reef. It was very exciting and made a change from the monotony of yesterday's flight.

The view as ever was fantastic and, even though it was very cold now, they were wearing their Yeti-hide travelling suits which kept them toasty warm.

Towelyn was up front steering and Night Light was trying to explain to Greenery the multi-phasic geometry of past life, single-souled telephone communications.

'So, lad, once your past medium has joined chakras with their modern-day medium soul twin, they basically just mix the astral tariffs and you and your past self can have about five minutes of talk time before the rifts close . . . What's that?'

'I don't know, I didn't understand any of that. What's what?'

'That noise.'

'Oh that, that's you talking gibberish again.'

'No shut up! . . . That buzzing noise.'

'If it's a low throbbing buzzy sound it could be my brain. You've probably caused permanent damage with all that mumbo-jumbo.'

'No, stop messing about, boy. Can't you hear it? It's getting louder.'

Thud! . . . Thud! . . . Thud! Thud! Thud!

Whatever hit them was small and fast. The impact in the side of the Disco Beast was felt by all three of them.

'What was that?' shouted Greenery.

'Trouble!'

Thud! . . . Thud! Thud!

Another volley of something smacked into Sheba's side. She cried out in pain and descended. At almost exactly the same time, the sky turned black as out of the clouds above them came a huge swarm of metallic-green insects. They looked like newts or small salamanders but each one had four wings on its back and a horn on the end of its nose. Dragon Flies. They blocked out the sun with their numbers.

Panicked and scared the Cecephelophopus managed a burst of speed the likes of which they had not felt before. The already rushing scenery below became a blur as the Disco Beast began to stampede. This gave them enough distance to see exactly what was attacking them.

On top of the swarm of Dragon Flies were two Reptilimans. They were surfing on large boards and riding the swarm like a monstrous wave. They seemed to be controlling its direction and speed by moving their body weight. Their thick scaly tails acted as extra legs and gave them excellent balance.

Sheba was hurtling away from them like a demented rocket ship, but with a slight forward shift of their body weight the Reptilimans led the mass of insects in an accelerated charge.

Like a tide breaking on a cliff face the wave of Dragon Flies crashed relentlessly into the travellers, the only difference being that cliffs don't bleed. The Disco Beast, having the largest surface area, took the worst beating. She was covered with gashes and puncture wounds where thousands of creatures had bitten, stung and flown straight through her skin. She was managing to stay airborne but only just. Her entire body was the dark blue and purple of a violent bruise.

Greenery moved fast and managed to hide inside the travelling trunk. He took a couple of hits but nothing too serious. As he closed the lid he caught sight of Night Light who was slumped forward and seemed to be hurt quite badly.

Towelyn was at the front of Sheba so she had fractionally longer to react to the onslaught. As the cloud descended upon her, she sprang to her feet and jumped.

With the balance and grace of a ballet dancer's pet cat she ran against the swarm, using each tiny Dragon as a stepping stone. She leapt from one to another with incredible speed and superhuman skill. She had one aim in mind, one goal and the look on her face said it all – murder. Onwards she went battling against the tide of angry creatures until she was only a metre away from one of their attackers.

Taking only a fraction of a second to prepare, she launched herself at the nearest lizard. She drew her sword in mid-flight and even before she had landed behind him, on his own surfboard, she had neatly and cleanly removed his head from his body. As his remains tumbled somewhat eloquently to ground, whatever control he had on the throng of insects faltered and they seemed to lose focus momentarily until his partner regained it.

Now Towelyn was standing on one board parallel to the Reptiliman on the other. He was too far away to reach her but unlike his dead accomplice he looked prepared and ready to fight. He was carrying a bow and had a quiver full of arrows on his back. Towelyn watched tensely as he took one and notched it into his bow, then as the insects pitched and rolled violently she noticed his weakness.

His attention was split between her and controlling the swarm. He was having to work twice as hard without his partner and was obviously struggling. She turned to face him.

With her sword held in both hands and swung back over her right shoulder, she looked like a baseball player ready to swing.

He took the shot. The arrow left his bow straight and true but his aim was not perfect. She swung at the bolt and her aim was deadly. The deflected arrow rebounded to bury itself in the lizard man's head, right up to the fletching.

As he fell to oblivion, all control over the mighty cloud of insects died with him and there was a dark explosion of living shrapnel as the swarm scattered in every direction. Towelyn was left with nothing to stand on while the pounding inflicted upon Sheba had proved too much for the battered Disco Beast. All of them began falling to their deaths.

As Towelyn fell there was no panic. The Djinditsu are trained from birth to assess, react and respond. The trouble was there was nothing to respond to. No lifeline, no last-ditch attempt, only air, empty space and the hard solid ground rushing to meet her.

From his hiding place inside the trunk Greenery had no idea what was going on but as his stomach lurched and he rose up against the lid of the case he knew he was in trouble. He forced the lid open against the rushing air and instantly felt sick with fear.

Sheba was clearly in trouble. Her skin had turned pasty white and slimy, as if it were leaking. She was bleeding profusely from hundreds of gashes all over her body, and worst of all there was no movement, no sign of life, just a limp form falling through space. Night Light was nowhere to be seen.

Suddenly Greenery lost his hold on the travelling trunk and was forced from the bogus safety of his hiding place. He began flailing wildly for a handhold, for some purchase upon the large case that he so desperately needed to believe was his sanctuary. As the contents came loose he grabbed the only thing within reach and then Sheba was gone. He was a lone dot in the sky, falling to his death. He looked down at what he'd grabbed and noticed he was holding a bubble-hat.

Without thinking or knowing exactly what he was doing he rammed it on his head. The bubble that encased him took away the deafening sound of rushing air and from his silent cocoon he could feel his descent slowing. He could still feel his heart rate pounding but it seemed for the moment, as he floated gently to earth, that he, at least, was safe.

Towelyn had convinced herself she was fine, that she was OK with this death, but as the ground continued to accelerate towards her a lifetime of conditioning was beginning to falter and she found herself petrified. To be unable to move or act as she sped towards her end was her ultimate fear.

Seeyoulatersolongfarewell seeyoulatersolongfarewell seeyoulatersolongfarewell . . .

A noise on the edge of hearing was growing louder. It sounded like an engine but with a strange voice-like quality to it.

Seeyoulatersolongfarewell seeyoulatersolongfarewell. . . .

From somewhere above her, a small plane with an open cockpit and a blue tuft of hair on top of its double-decker wings swooped down and caught her deftly in a comfy leather seat. There was no one flying the plane yet its movements were fluid and practised as it sped off towards the gently bobbing figure of Greenery in the distance. Too shaken up to fully appreciate what was happening, Towelyn sat in stunned silence and let the small craft take her where it wanted.

Greenery was slowly recovering from the shock of falling. Even though it had only been a few seconds it felt like forever. His heart was still pounding as a noise outside of the bubble caught his attention.

Seeyoulatersolongfarewell seeyoulatersolongfarewell seeyoulatersolongfarewell . . .

He turned to see Towelyn slumped in the front seat of a small aeroplane. As they came closer he could pick out the engine noise more clearly. It sounded like a series of goodbyes strung together and joined up. When he saw the tuft of blue hair he knew exactly who and what was flying towards him. When it was directly below him he ripped the bubble-hat from his head and fell into the rear passenger seat of the Bye-Plane, laughing so hard he could hardly breathe.

He stopped suddenly. With a feeling like one of those mini Dragons had flown straight through his chest and punctured his heart he remembered about his Disco Beast. He leant over the side of the Bye-Plane and saw far below the wide shape of Sheba spread out to slow her descent. She was using her body as a parachute to fall slowly to earth.

'We have to go after her!'

'We can't.'

'What do you mean, Towelyn? We have to. She's hurt.'

'Greenery, we can't!' she said, looking just as hurt as Greenery felt.

'Why not!'

'Because the Violents are still after us. Besides there's nothing we can do to help her, we can't treat her or move her and if we stay with her we will be hunted down and killed. She might be all right. Cecephelophopi heal quickly. She can find a place to hide and recover on her own. She's better off without us.'

'But it's so unfair.'

'Listen, folks, I hate to make things worse but we're still in trouble here.'

Night Light's voice came from somewhere on the dashboard. It was quite disturbing.

'May I remind you that I am only a little fellow and even though I look like a plane I'm still just me. I can't carry you two much longer. We have to land right now.'

'If we land they will find us,' said Towelyn.

'If we don't I'm gonna drop you. Sorry, love, it's that simple.'

'What's that over there?' They both turned to look where Greenery was pointing. In the distance winking as it caught the afternoon sun was a large, transparent city, floating along in the gentle breeze.

'That,' replied Towelyn, 'is our salvation. Can you make it, Night Light?'

'Let's find out.' With a spurt of speed came the roar of the engine. Now Night Light was travelling at full speed he seemed to make a different noise. Goodbye-goodbye-goodbye-goodbye-goodbyeeeeeeeee!

*

Gloria Jackson was disturbed from her grief by the sound of breaking glass tinkling behind her. She turned to look at the old theatre across the road but with so many small windows it was difficult to spot any new breakages. She looked back out to sea, staring vacantly at the horizon as she had been now for close to twenty-four hours.

Her mind seemed to have shut down; any thoughts about life were just too painful. She almost didn't register any kind of shock or surprise when a winged lizard landed on the bench next to her. She stared at it without reacting. It looked like a tiny dragon.

The little creature sniffed the air before flying off towards the beach. I've been sitting here too long, she thought. I'm starting to see things. She stood up slowly and shuffled home, lost in a world of pain. It was time to arrange the funeral.

Night Light touched down awkwardly and skidded to a halt on a wide boulevard in the middle of the shining city. There was a strange ethereal quality to the place. The roads, buildings and vehicles looked too delicate to be real. They were completely transparent but visible because they shone elegantly round the edges where they caught the light.

When Greenery stepped off the Bye-Plane he was surprised at how solid everything felt. He had half expected to fall right through the floor and was clutching his bubble-hat tightly just in case.

Pop! Night Light stood before him, back in his normal diminutive shape. He was struggling to breathe and had a dark bruise above his left eye. He caught Greenery watching him and looking concerned.

'I'm all right, lad.' he panted. 'Don't look so worried! ...
Just a bit tired after carting you two lumps all the way over
here.' He pointed at his forehead. 'One of them insect jobbies
caught me a good'n on the head, knocked me out of it for a
bit. I came to just as I fell off Sheba's back. I'm OK though.'
He reached up as high as he could and gave Greenery a friendly
pat just below the shoulder. 'Good thinking, sonny, with that
bubble-hat. Gave me time to save meself and Towelyn.' He
turned around to check on the Djinditsu but was surprised
to see that she wasn't there. 'Oh! Now where do you think
she's wandered off to?'

They quickly scanned the area but could see no sign of her.
It was only then, they noticed a small crowd of locals had
gathered around and were watching them intently. They
seemed harmless enough, just confused and very curious.

Every one of them was a good deal taller than Greenery
and very, very thin. They were see-through like everything
else but, whereas the buildings looked completely clear, the
people had a blue tinge to their translucency and looked more
liquid than solid.

'Where are we, Night Light?'

'Well now. I'm not so sure. I reckon we're still pretty high
up and it looks as though we're floating along in the general
direction we need to be but apart from that, I've got to be
honest, I've no idea.'

Greenery looked down through the street and to the ground
far below. It was true the floating city was travelling fairly
quickly and roughly in the right direction. He knew this
because he could still make out the course of a chocolate river
they had been following before they were attacked.

By now they were surrounded by a much larger group of strangers and as Towelyn was still nowhere to be seen he thought he should attempt to make contact. He picked someone at random and tried to be as friendly as he could.

'Hello.'

'Lo.'

'Don't be afraid, we come in peace. We mean you no harm.'

'We mean you no harm.'

'Oh well that's nice. I'm glad. Thank you.'

'Thank you.'

'You're welcome.'

'Well come.'

'Oh I see. You're just repeating me, aren't you?'

'Am I?'

'You were.'

'I was.'

'Oh well, you don't seem to be any more.'

'I'm not.'

'Why?'

'I'm bored.'

'Oh!'

With a shrug of his shoulders the stranger wandered off slowly. Greenery turned to Night Light and gave him a 'well I tried' kind of a shrug. Night Light looked back and shook his head.

'Oh! OK clever-clogs. Let's see you do better then,' said Greenery.

'I, boy, am a diplomat, a businessman and an entrepreneur; people are my speciality. Watch and learn.' Night Light cleared his throat and addressed the crowd in a large jolly voice.

'Greetings, people of . . . er . . . here. My companion and I are not here to cause you any problems or danger. We are simply weary travellers who have stumbled upon hard times on the journey of our life. If you could all spare us some time we would like some information . . .'

'Travellers!' interrupted a tall local.

'Er . . . yes we would like to ask you . . .'

'Journey!' he shouted out again.

'Yes and we need your help to get going . . .'

'How?' came his third interjection.

'How what?'

'Not how what, just how?'

'Just how?'

'Yes.'

'Sorry!'

'No need for sorry. Just go.'

'Go where?'

'We don't know. It's your journey.'

'But how?'

'That's what I want to know.'

'What?'

'No. How?'

'Well, what I mean is, we would like a little help to start . . .'

'I'm bored.'

'Me too.'

'And me.'

Five or six of the strangers gave Night Light a look usually reserved for the kind of person that likes to play the banjo with their ear and sing to their shoes. They wandered off quietly.

Night Light turned to Greenery

'Don't say a word.'

'Idiot,' mumbled Greenery, shaking his head at the floor.

'Ah! There you are!'

They turned to see Towelyn walking toward them holding hands with one of the locals. This one, however, was taller than the others and looked a lot bluer. It was difficult to tell if he was thinner than his kinsmen or if this was just an illusion caused by his increased height.

'What do you mean "here we are"? We're not the ones that went wandering off.'

'Oh yes, well in that case, here I am!'

'This lot are barmy,' said Night Light. 'We can't get any sense out of them at all. Where are we anyway? In all my days of travelling I've never met any of these lot.'

'You don't get up in the sky much then, do you?'

'Well no, actually. I try and avoid heights since my cousin got eaten by a Legal Eagle. Poor old Cook Book. We were both soaring along as a flight of stairs when all of a sudden we heard something behind us. Cook Book reacted too late. Woof . . . he was gone. He never had a chance. There is danger in the sky, danger! And a small Punster makes easy pickings for a big scary bird in a wig.'

As with most of Night Light's little digressions there followed a couple of stunned, silent seconds. Towelyn was the first to regain her composure.

'OK. Well, these good people are the Vapours and they're not barmy; they simply don't meet strangers that often. They are not used to communicating vocally.'

'How do they normally communicate then?' asked Greenery.

'They manipulate the water vapour in the air into shapes and patterns. It's a visual language. It's quite beautiful and expressive actually. They use the same technology, only on a much larger scale, to build their cities. They can make the water droplets in the air completely solid yet somehow stay as light as a gas. It's very clever.'

'You like this bunch of wackos, don't you?'

'Yes, Night Light, I do! Last time I was in a Vapour village it was after a particularly hard battle. They looked after me and nursed me back to health. I have a great respect for them, and they are not wackos!'

'Well, how do we talk to them then?' Greenery could see Towelyn was not her usual placid self. Maybe, he thought, the fall had shaken her up more than she was letting on. He tried to keep her calm by showing an interest in a subject she obviously cared about. 'It must be possible if you lived with them.'

'You just have to be very direct and to the point. They get confused very easily with words. As I said, it's not their natural way of communicating.'

Towelyn turned to her tall companion and made a couple of gestures towards Night Light and Greenery.

'Those two, my friends. Us three stay together. Same journey.'

'Yes,' was all he said. He smiled at them all and left without another word or gesture.

'That's the leader. His name is Henry 2 Oscar. Whoever is the tallest Vapour in the village automatically assumes responsibility for the rest. Kind of like a big brother in a lot of ways.'

'Erm, I don't want to cause a fuss or anything but what are

we going to do next and how will we get to Macadamia?'
Greenery was still being quite tentative. He was worried about
upsetting Towelyn.

'Well, we're in luck actually. It's Rivali.'

'What?'

'Rivali, or the Festival of Flights, as it's also called. It's the
time of year when all the airborne nations gather together to
celebrate life in the sky. This year they are gathering above
the Hawking Plate, which means, luckily for us, they have to
pass over the Faraday Plate. Henry 2 Oscar has agreed on a
slight diversion and we will be over Macadamia in a few days.
In the meantime we can stay here.'

'Where?' asked Night Light.

'Harriet 2 Olive and Hubert 2 Orville are the best molecule
manipulators in the village. Even as we speak they are making
a house for us to stay in, and do you know what they want
in return? Nothing. You see, Night Light, these barmy wackos
are quite possibly the kindest, most generous race you will
ever have the good fortune to meet.'

The house that was created for them was luxurious. It had
a large and expansive ground floor and then three slightly
smaller upper floors, which meant instead of a bedroom they
each had an entire level to themselves. Better still, each one
had a balcony so they could sit out and watch the world float
by beneath them.

The Vapours had the ability to make the water in the air
take any form they wished. Even though the walls and floor
were as solid as granite, Greenery's bed, which was made out
of the same substance, was as soft and fluffy as . . . well, as a
cloud. In accordance with the travellers' wishes they made

some areas of the house opaque. Privacy was a new concept to the Vapours.

In the days that passed Greenery was completely content. They wanted for nothing. They were given food, drink and entertainment. In the evenings the Vapours loved to dance to a kind of music that was more soulful than any Greenery had heard before.

They danced with their bodies but also with the clouds, manipulating them to flow through and around each other in time with the enchanting music, forming intricate shapes and patterns in the dusky twilight. It was a simple life, drifting along in the sky. He saw a lot more of the Vapours and learnt how to talk to them in a simple straightforward way. Night Light, however, had a lot more trouble with this. He couldn't get the hang of using one word where three sounded so much nicer.

The native language of the Vapours was impossible for any of them to speak but Greenery enjoyed watching their conversations. The complex imagery they produced in their hands was captivating and the way the shapes morphed from one to another so quickly was quite hypnotic.

On the fourth day Greenery and Night Light were sitting on his balcony watching The Other Place drift by below when the land disappeared. Was it the edge of the world? An impossibly massive cliff that extended as far as the eye could see dropped down vertically to an open expanse of swirling, frothy fluid far, far below. It looked like liquid mother-of-pearl, only with a metallic tinge to it that made it almost transparent. When Greenery stared into the depths of the strange plasma he was sure that he could make out the night sky deep within the abyss. It made no sense.

'Night Light, what's that?'

'That, my boy, was the edge of the Socrates Plate. We should enter the air space above the Faraday Plate very soon. That's the Plate that Macadamia is on.'

'What do you mean, plate?'

'Land mass. Floating on The River down there.'

'That's a river? It looks more like a weird ocean to me.'

'No, lad, it's not an ocean and it's not a river; it's The River. The Infinite River. We should be over land again by nightfall.'

'What do you mean The River? What's a plate? Look, will you please tell me where and what this place is?'

Night Light gave a 'here we go' kind of sigh and put his drink down.

'Do you remember when we first met I told you *where* is hard. Well, that's because it's so closely linked with *what*. Now, *what* isn't that easy either but I'll try.' He leant forward so he was face to face with Greenery, 'You can't think of The Other Place as a planet, Greenery, not in the way you're used to anyway. You see, this whole place exists in a constant state of motion caused by . . .'

'Night Light! Greenery! Your dinner's ready.'

'. . . Ooh food. Come on, lad, let's eat.'

'No wait, Night Light, don't go! Night Light!'

On the fifth day Greenery, Towelyn and Night Light were all woken early by a large crowd of Vapours. The sun was just rising and peeking between two massive clouds in a golden sky. Below them was land once more but it looked cold and barren.

'It seems we are here,' said Towelyn after speaking briefly with Henry 2 Oscar.

'Where?' asked Greenery.

Towelyn looked slightly puzzled before replying.

'Macadamia of course.'

In his floating, tranquil state Greenery had forgotten all about his quest. He had also forgotten about the Violents. With his arrival at Macadamia it all came flooding back to him with a shock like a faceful of cold soup.

'Oh well,' he said, trying to shake off the feeling of dread, 'I suppose we should get our feet back on the ground.'

Chapter Nine

Macadamia

They call themselves the human race,
So where's the finish line?
Are they racing one another?
Or just racing Father Time?
> Taken from *The Idiot's Guide to Humans*
> by The Mysterious Wandering Gump

Greenery looked down from the floating city to the land below. From this height there wasn't much to see. Directly below he could make out some small hills covered in snow. Ebb-wards there were some small hills covered in snow. Flow-wards there were some small hills covered in snow and, if he squinted Downstream and strained his eyes, he could just make out some small hills covered in snow.

'Nice.'

'Well, young fella-me-lad, it might not be much to look at but we're not here for the scenery, are we. Now let's get a wriggle on. The sooner we get going the sooner we can go getting on about getting home.'

This last sentence actually caused a few of the Vapours to shudder and move away from Night Light a little, as one might move away from someone who dribbles on your shoe while they talk to you. If Night Light noticed, he chose not to show it.

'How exactly do we get a wriggle on then?' asked Greenery.

'Ah . . . yes . . . well . . . I . . . er.'

'Follow me,' said Towelyn, making no attempt to hide her laughter.

Across the square from their temporary accommodation was a floating chariot. It was large enough to hold all three of them with plenty of room left over. In front of the cart and ready to tow it were two vaguely equine creatures with five legs. They were made of the same organic water substance as the Vapours. Henry 2 Oscar jumped into the front of the carriage, grabbed the reins and they were off.

As they bobbed along through the streets, people came out of their houses and shops to wave at them. Some created visual messages of goodbye, a ship sailing away or two figures parting. Even though Greenery couldn't understand them completely, the meaning was both obvious and touching. After a short journey they came to the Ebb-wards-most edge of the city.

The cart pulled up and everyone disembarked but there was still no obvious way down to the ground. A group of six Vapours were waiting for them right on the edge of the city. Greenery was a little worried they might expect him to jump.

They were all nearly as tall as Henry 2 Oscar yet they were unlike any of the other locals in one obvious respect; each had a different coloured tinge to their translucency. They were standing in a straight line facing the chariot with a gap for Henry 2 Oscar to fill. When he was in place they stood in order of colour – red, orange, yellow, green, blue, indigo and violet. They turned as one to face the open sky. They held hands and began to hum.

From each individual flowed a mass of water vapour matching the colour of its creator. This matter poured into the open sky then mingled with the other streams to form a perfect rainbow. The three travellers stood transfixed as the Vapours kept on ploughing the sky, each one forging a wide furrow of colour into open space.

It's exactly like a rainbow from back home, thought Greenery. Except this one is curly and solid with railings down the side.

When the helter-skelter was complete Henry 2 Oscar detached himself from the others and came over to the trio.

'Rainbow slide is done. You go now. Your stay was our pleasure. Goodbye.'

'Thank you, goodbye,' was all that Towelyn said as the three of them stepped onto the solid rainbow. There didn't seem much else to say.

Facing the multicoloured slide and looking down to earth, Greenery was suddenly very aware of just how high they were. But the Vapours had been extremely good to them and he had no reason to distrust them now.

The surface of the slide was quite soft and squishy. It gave a little under his feet as he jumped up and down to test it out.

'Ready?' said Towelyn.

Greenery and Night Light exchanged nervous glances and then nodded at her.

She extended her hand to Greenery and he took it gladly. Night Light followed suit and took his other.

'One, two, three, jump!'

They leapt as one onto the gentle slope of the main descent. All three landed on their bums and immediately sped off down the super slippery slide. After the first few metres they really began to pick up speed. The gradient grew gradually steeper and steeper until they were hurtling downwards like a toboggan on a multicoloured Cresta Run.

After a minute or so Greenery began to wonder exactly what provisions the vapours had made for slowing their descent safely. He had visions of flying off the end of the rainbow and hitting a solid wall face first.

'Erm . . .'

'Yes, lad, exactly: Erm.' Night Light had obviously been thinking the same thing.

They both looked at Towelyn. She didn't seem worried at all. She felt, rather than saw, the other two nervously looking at her and she turned to face them. She looked them both full in the face and laughed. She laughed. It was an infectious sound of pure joy. They couldn't help it – the other two joined in, surrendering themselves to the moment and feeling a rush of life surge through them.

'Race you!' was all she said as she let go of Greenery's hand, pressed her body flat to the slide and managed to gain some ground ahead of them. Greenery pulled his hand away from Night Light's, lay down as flat as he could make himself and tried to be as aerodynamic as possible.

'Oh ecky thump!' was all Night Light managed.

He lay back but his little pot belly seemed to be working as a windbreak. He wasn't as heavy as the other two, being so much shorter and so he picked up exactly no speed whatsoever. As the two leaders sped off down the slide all they could hear was a disgruntled 'Typical!'

As hard as he tried Greenery just couldn't catch up with Towelyn. She was used to being covered in fur and had kept her Yeti-hide exposure suit neat and sleek. He had somehow managed to get his all matted up. It was causing marginally more friction than hers and giving her the edge. He wondered momentarily if it was worth stripping off but the thought passed in a second and brought about another fit of the giggles.

Realising he couldn't beat her he decided to have some fun instead. He began spinning on his back, lying on his front and slowing himself down just so he could tease Night Light by speeding off again.

Laughing, tumbling and clowning around, they eventually came to the end of the slide. It was not, as Greenery had imagined, a flat brick wall. Instead the helter-skelter reached the floor and continued along at ground level.

Their momentum kept them sliding along on the perfectly flat plain for a good couple of hundred metres. By the time they came to a complete stop they were all level again and were sitting up chatting and laughing. They stopped within twenty centimetres of the end of the slide. Perfection.

Far, far away from Greenery, past Tracey, past the shores of Atlantis, past the Psychedelic Desert and even beyond the boundaries of the Nowhere Zone lie the extensive swamplands of Scumlumpia. This is a barren place where nothing grows apart from Slimeweed and Dung-Trees. Scarabstings and Spiderhogs are typical of the fauna of this dismal ecosystem and the ground underfoot is moist, sloppy mud, metres deep in some places. No birds fly over this place; no sane person comes here by choice.

In the centre of Scumlumpia lies the rotting carcass of Ben Nevis, the infamous Titan who brought about the fall of Captain Sowadaya Wantfromme. His corpse, the size of a mountain range, has been lying here, decomposing for decades. Slowly, with the passing of time its decaying stench has spread throughout the lands. Scumlumpia smells of death.

Inside the cadaver of Ben Nevis the Violents have made their home. The fortified entrance is through the mouth. Guards stand protected behind molars and canines and there is a small passageway between the two front teeth. On special occasions the top jaw can be winched open using giant pulleys operated by huge Eleph Ants. The city centre opens up onto a wide piazza that was once a working stomach and the twisted maze of streets surrounding the Plaza of Acid, as it's known, are the remains of the intestines and liver.

The palace of Ignatius Trump is located right in the Titan's heart. In his throne room, the left ventricle, Ignatius was restless.

'I cannot stand this silence. My surfers should have been back days ago. I should be crushing that small human's skull right now, instead of waiting. I hate waiting!'

'But, Sir, we are doing all we can. We have dispatched Slack Riders and Wind Trippers. There are Snoop Troopers in every major town and nobody has heard . . .'

A frantic pounding on the door interrupted the rambling underling. With a gesture from their leader two guards opened the throne room doors and a small snivelling wreck of a thing ran in panting.

'Excuse me Your ... er ... Ignatiusness, I think we may have made contact.'

'How?'

'Well, Sir, it's Derrick. He thinks he's found the mind of a passing Dragon Fly.'

'Take me to him. Now!'

On the highest peak of Ben Nevis, which happens to be his bent knee, Ignatius Trump's most skilled insectoid psychommunicator had been scanning the skies with his mind. He was looking for the remains of the swarm that had attacked Greenery. Just one Dragon Fly was enough. He had found one passing by a long way away and had successfully brought its path towards him. Just as the small monster landed on his shoulder a flap of skin used as an access panel to this lofty lookout point opened and his ruler stood before him.

'Ah, Derrick, you have done well, very well. Now do even better and tell me what happened.'

'Yes, Sir, certainly, Sir.' He clicked through various mandibles.

Insectoid psychommunicators tend to have a certain insect-like quality about them. Derrick was no different. The little bug on his shoulder clambered up towards his ear.

'Bzzzz buzz clik clik buzzzzzzzz.'

'I see. Go on.'

'Click buzz buzz clack click buzz click buzz.'

'Ooh, that's impressive.'

'Clack click click, buzz buzzzzzz buuuuuuuuuuzzzzzzzzzzzz!'

'Oh dear, yes that must have hurt.'

'Buzz!'

'Thank you. Goodbye.'

As the little fly flew away Derrick stood watching it with a dreamy, faraway look in his eyes, all six of them.

'Well!'

'What? Oh, it seems your Surfers are dead.'

'Dead?'

'Well, he's not entirely sure, what with being an insect and all, but one got an arrow through the brain and the other no longer has a head, so I wouldn't expect them back any time soon if I was you.'

'I see. Did he say what happened to our prey?'

'Yes he did.'

'Well!'

'Oh I see, yes, they got caught by a particularly dodgy pun and landed on a solid cloud.'

'Then they must almost be at the Tear of the Cyclops by now. Get me the fastest thought plane we have. I need to send a message to our frozen operatives in Macadamia.'

Without waiting for a reply he jumped back through the trapdoor the way he had come and was gone. Derrick tried to follow him but the flap of skin had been locked shut from inside. Feeling a little hard done by, Derrick began the long dangerous walk to the belly button, the next closest entrance to the citadel.

They had been walking through the deep snow for about half an hour. The white drifts were piling up and it was pretty hard-going. Night Light had transformed into a pair of snowshoes (large trainers made of snow). They didn't sink into the white powder as much, so it had made his way slightly easier.

'There it is!' Towelyn stopped and pointed off into the distance. 'The Eternal Abyss.'

It took them about another half-hour to reach their destination. There were no paths leading to it or markers to show its location; it simply rose up from the white blanket as if it had grown from the snow itself.

The Eternal Abyss was a large dome that rose to a height of around twenty metres and was completely transparent. It wasn't until he touched its smooth sides that Greenery realised it was in fact made from ice. Ice that was so smooth and blemish free it had the appearance of pure crystal.

There was a small arch-shaped entrance, no taller than Night Light on the side opposite to them. As they walked around to the doorway Greenery had time to study the weird abyss further.

There was a stone path about a metre wide that ran around the interior perimeter of the dome. On the inside of the path, the side away from the ice wall, there was another smaller dome. This one seemed to be made of a gas or mist, Greenery couldn't tell exactly which. Looking closer he realised it was radiating from a bottle in the centre. The strange fog poured from the top of a small vial and plumed out to make this dome within a dome.

The bottle itself stood on a vertical tower of small turtles. Between the inside edge of the gas dome and the tower of amphibious reptiles there was nothing. An ominous-looking hole was all that lay between them.

'I assume the Tear of the Cyclops is in that small bottle then?'

'Yep, nice innit?'

116

'Yes it's very pretty, but I don't see how it's impossible to get to it. All I need is a big stick with a hook on the end, or you could turn into something that flies and just fetch it for me, couldn't you?'

'Hah! Says you. People have been trying to get that for years. If it was that easy do you think something that powerful would still be there?'

'Oh, I don't know.'

'It's the interior dome that's the problem,' said Towelyn. 'The instant anything enters it, the top turtle will leap into the pit, taking the Cyclops Tear with it.'

'Oh. Well how deep is it?'

'It's bottomless.'

'Right OK, yes, very deep but how deep?'

'It's bottomless,' she repeated.

'It can't be. Nothing is bottomless.'

'Come here, clever-clogs,' Night Light called over, beckoning Greenery to the doorway. 'See that hole there? It's bottomless. If you could lean over the side and peer down it with a very powerful telescope, past the layers of dirt, past the rock strata, past the magma chambers and right on down, even through The River, do you know what you would see?'

'No.'

'Stars, lad. You would see stars. That hole opens up onto the vastness of the universe. It is truly bottomless.'

It took Greenery a couple of seconds to fully contemplate what Night Light had said but, as the wonder faded away, common sense as always took its place.

'So what are the turtles standing on?'

'No one knows. It might just be turtles all the way down.'

'Well, how am I supposed to get it, if it's impossible to get?'

'You have to use your imagination.'

'Well, what good will that do?'

'Excuse me, you're human, aren't you?'

'Yes.'

'So this place is made from the things that humans have imagined.'

'I know that. I mean at least I thought it was just the place where things we imagine are kept.'

'Yes it is but if something is thought of that has never been imagined before then it has to come into existence somewhere and that place is The Other Place.'

'You mean if I think of something that no one has ever thought of before it will just pop up right here.'

'Yes.'

'Well, what about all those things I mentioned to you when I first arrived, the talking carrots and the blue giraffe thingy?'

'What about them?'

'They didn't just pop into existence, did they? I know I was a bit shaken up but I'm pretty sure I would have noticed.'

'That's because someone had already thought of them first. If something already exists here you won't bring it into being again.'

'Oh I see.'

'Go on, try it. Think of something that's completely new.'

Greenery puffed out his cheeks and exhaled. A look of bewildered concentration crept slowly across his face.

'How about a squirrel with no nose that pinches other squirrels' nuts?'

'Is that supposed to be funny? Come on, lad, you're not even trying.'

'I am!'

'Come on then, impress me.'

'OK, OK. An orange dinosaur the size of a grain of sugar who speaks Chinese.'

'You mean Toby? He's been here longer than I have. Try again.'

'Greenery, you can do this. It's what you're here for.' Towelyn smiled encouragingly as she spoke. Greenery felt his spirits lift and tried again.

'A creature the size of an elephant that is made entirely of sequins, has lights on its head and communicates through song and dance.'

As Greenery spoke there was a slight change in the quality of the air. His breath hung in front of his face, like it does on a cold day. It seemed to briefly take the shape of the animal he had just described before it became a haze and evaporated away into nothingness.

'Nice one, lad. You did it.'

'Well done! You have just created a new species. A male and female Bedazzlephant will now go forth and thrive because of you.'

'What do you mean I did it? Where is it?'

'Well, it's not here, you big numpty.'

'This is a big place, Greenery,' Towelyn calmly explained. 'Things that are created can take shape anywhere. The thing you described might live in a hot climate but, even if it didn't, it is doubtful it would have appeared here.'

'Well, that doesn't help us get the Tear at all then.'

'We did say it was impossible.'

'It can't be impossible. There has to be a way.'

'That's the spirit but it's beyond me, boy. I haven't got the foggiest idea how you could get it.'

'Is it possible to teleport inside the second dome? That way you wouldn't break its surface and the turtle might not jump.'

'Theoretically you could transport yourself inside it but it's the turtle itself that's trained to jump as soon as you're within that second dome. It's got nothing to do with breaking the surface. So it wouldn't do you any good. It's still goodbye, bottle time.'

'Listen, you two,' said Towelyn. 'It looks like this might take a while. I'm not sure we're completely safe from the Violents. I'm going up to the top of that ridge to keep a look out while you two bright sparks put your heads together.'

As she jogged off to the vantage point about half a kilometre away she could hear their discussion growing more and more heated. Over the course of the next hour or so Greenery and Night Light battled with the problem. Greenery would keep coming up with ideas and each time Night Light would explain why it wouldn't work. Some of the more bizarre ideas included melting the outer shell and redirecting the gas that formed the interior dome, plugging up the hole with more turtles than it was possible to imagine, approaching the bottle from underneath, hypnotising the top turtle and finally, Greenery's favourite, throwing Night Light down the bottomless pit and going for a hot drink.

'Oh now you're just being mean. How would I get back out again?'

'That's it!'

'What, what's it?'

'The only way to get the bottle is to follow it down into the hole, catch it and get back out again.'

'Oh, well that's easy then, innit?'

'It is if you have the right equipment.'

'And how do we get that, imagination man? Is it just going to appear exactly where we need it to? Do you have any idea how big this place is? Is it just going to coincidentally pop up right before us?'

The smile that spread across Greenery's face could only have been bigger with the help of a bent coat hanger.

'Funny you should say that.'

He closed his eyes and concentrated. As his thoughts took shape in his mind the air around him thickened like before. Slowly his breath took on form, only this time instead of dispersing into the ether the haze continued to solidify. After about half a minute a solid form dropped out of thin air and landed on the floor next to Greenery's left foot. He bent down, picked it up, and presented it to Night Light.

Lying in the palm of his hand was a small simple ring. It was matt silver with three black bands around its circumference and a two-tone black and silver sheen to its edges.

'But how did . . . Where should it . . . What does . . . Eh?'

'May I present you with the coincidence ring.'

'What?'

'It's a ring that brings about remarkable coincidences for the owner.'

'Yes but how did it materialise here, exactly where we needed it to?'

'Just a coincidence I guess.' It seemed impossible but the non-coat-hanger-assisted grin spread even wider.

'Right,' said Greenery, rubbing his hands together in glee, 'let's get started.'

After a few minutes of imagining they had everything they needed. Greenery was holding a small gun-like device that he assured Night Light was a machine that created short wormholes in space. He had a grabbing device attached to his back that worked like a torch except it shone sticky light on its subject. He was also wearing a space suit. This had been very difficult to realise. As it turns out a lot of people have imagined a lot of different space suits. The only one Greenery could create that had not been thought of before was made out of wool from the space-faring Llama-moth, an animal which he had also had to invent. He looked like a woolly astronaut who had been kitted out by someone's insane grandma. He felt confident though and had only had to explain his idea to Night Light five times, which all in all, he thought, could have been worse.

'But listen, sonny, you can't expect a wormhole to deposit you exactly where you need it to.'

'Why not?'

'Because they are totally random phenomenunoms . . .' He shook his head and tried again: 'Phenominie, phnemomenera . . . Listen it's a big old universe, kiddo; I'd hate to see you get lost in it.'

'Yes, it would be an amazing coincidence if I popped out right back here, wouldn't it.'

'You're bloomin' right it woul . . . oh. Have you still got the ring on?'

'Yes, under my glove.'

'Sunshine, I think you're either a genius or you're completely bonkers. Come on then, let's do this.'

Greenery crawled through the small archway of the first outer dome. It was strange viewing the world from inside his suit. He felt somewhat detached, as though life was a programme he was viewing on a very large television. His breath was loud in his ears and it was difficult to move.

As he walked along the path around the perimeter of the pit, the turtle on top of the pile turned to follow him with its beady suspicious eyes. Having walked the full circle and made sure the distance between the path and the centre was the same all the way round, about nine metres, he stopped and faced his prize. He was feeling quite nervous; in fact, if he was honest with himself he was terrified. He looked down into the pit. Its vertical walls and perfectly cylindrical shape made it look like the world's biggest wishing well. It looked dark, it looked dangerous and above all it looked deep. With one last preparatory breath he turned on his head light, bent his legs and leapt towards the Tear of the Cyclops.

The second his feet left the stone path the turtle flopped off the back of its brother and fell. Greenery could have sworn that it winked at him as it did so.

The speed was incredible. Rock was zooming past him at an alarming rate but what was even stranger was the deafening silence. There should have been a whooshing of air or a scream from a loved one but all he could hear was his own breath echoing inside his helmet and becoming somewhat laboured as he fought with his own fear.

He looked down. The bottle was no longer with the turtle.

The reptile was about a metre below him and the Tear was another metre below that. He curled himself into a ball and tried to fall as fast as possible.

He was tempted to close his eyes. The constant rushing of the cliff face so close to his own was making him feel sick and the tower of turtles wasn't helping either. Each one was smiling and winking; some even waved a flipper as he shot past. He kept his eyes open, however, as he was scared of losing sight of the small glass vial. If he didn't reach it before this hole opened out he could lose it in the raging flow of The River beneath.

He was now level with the hurtling turtle. Face to face it looked quite peaceful, as though it was enjoying the ride. Their eyes met. The turtle smiled at Greenery then stuck out its tongue and blew a raspberry, spitting reptilian saliva all over his visor. Just as Greenery was about to swat the little beast away his world went bright orange. The rock had turned to magma.

He was now falling through the centre of a fiery waterfall. His suit was obviously working fine as the heat that should have been stripping the flesh from his bones only registered with him as a cosy warmth. He looked over again at his falling companion expecting to see him roasting in agony but the little fellow seemed to be in his element. He was now lying on his back, flippers behind his head, and enjoying the earth-melting temperature like he was sunbathing on a beach. His little sunglasses only added to this impression.

Greenery looked for the bottle containing the Tear of the Cyclops and was devastated to see that the distance between him and it had grown in the time he had been distracted. It was now roughly between two and three metres below him and well out of reach.

For the next few minutes he tried everything he could think of to increase his rate of descent and catch his quarry. He curled into a tight ball, tried streamlining his body and falling head first, he even tried flapping his arms like a bird. All of this was completely in vain; if anything, he only increased the gap he was trying to shorten.

The glow from the molten rock was starting to fade, which meant the temperature was falling. Greenery looked down and could see below him the surface of The River. It was a long way off but approaching fast. Its strange pearlescent quality radiated an ethereal light up into the vertical shaft, making it easy to see how fast and strong the current was flowing. If the bottle hit the surface before he did he knew he would lose it forever.

Suddenly he remembered about his sticky light invention. He had been so caught up in the drama of the moment he had completely forgotten about it. He quickly grabbed it from his back, took aim and fired.

It worked! The beam of light grabbed hold of the bottle and held it fast. Greenery pressed a button and his tractor beam began to draw the bottle closer. It was agonisingly slow though. He wasn't sure if it would reach him in time. At the last second the bottle came within his reach. He grabbed it and pulled it to his chest just as he hit the surface of the strange flowing plasma.

The impact wasn't as hard as he had expected. Whatever The River was made of it was a lot less dense than water. The current grabbed him immediately. He was tumbled and thrown around in a crazy world of strange colours and confused turtles. He solved the mystery of what the tower of amphibians had been standing on when he slammed into the shell of the big mother turtle. She seemed completely unfazed by his presence and continued swimming along without a care in the world. Greenery could hear a loud rasping noise in his ears and it took him a few seconds to realise it was his own voice, screaming in fear and confusion as he lost all sense of direction.

Luckily his downwards momentum had kept him moving deeper and deeper into the depths of The River. Within a couple of minutes he emerged through the bottom layer and surfaced into the vastness of space.

Stillness. The immense beauty of the galactic landscape was breathtaking.

Greenery floated in awe beneath the underside of The Other Place. Only centimetres above him was The River. Its metallic surface looked like a huge pool of translucent mercury. Through its many layers he could see the shadow of the Faraday Plate and a round patch of brightness nearby where light from above spilled through The Eternal Abyss to meet him. He reached up and brushed his fingertips through the flowing energy; it moved around his hand with a glittering effect like sunlight on water.

Beneath him he caught sight of several star turtles that had also been carried out through the bottom of The River. He watched them swim off through space and wondered how big they would get and what worlds might be created around them.

An alarm within his helmet brought him back to the here

and now. He looked at a dial on his wrist and saw that his breathable air was getting low. He knew there had been forty minutes' worth in his tank so he must have been falling for longer than he realised.

He took his wormhole gun from its holster and, wishing he could stay longer, fired it into open space. A thin blue beam billowed from the end of his pistol and opened up a swirling blue-and-white vortex. It seemed to sit on the edge of space as if it were resting on a pane of glass. What little light there was seemed to bend around it and at the same time be drawn in towards its centre.

The pull from the wormhole's gravity well sucked him through head-first. His world went white. There was rushing, falling and flying, then he hit the wall of reality at a speed he couldn't even guess. Nanoseconds later he blipped back into real Space–Time. He should have been back in Macadamia; instead he was floating in the empty reaches of space.

'This is not good,' he said to himself.

Alone in space with no reference point and very little air he desperately wanted to fire the gun again but it was recharging. For now there was nothing he could do but float and worry.

As he hung there drifting in total isolation his angle of rotation brought him around to see what was behind him.

Greenery's eyes spread wide in wonder as The Other Place came fully into view. He was a long way from it, possibly hundreds of light years, but it filled his vision. The River cut through eternity like a wide ribbon of light. It stretched away to the limitless horizon in both directions, weaving past planets, flowing through nebula and arcing gracefully around the many wonders of the cosmos.

All along its surface were countless floating islands, the Plates. They ranged in size dramatically from colossal continents to tiny spots of rock. From this distance Greenery could see how the Plates were drifting ever onwards along The River, floating towards some unimaginable destination. That's why Night Light couldn't tell Greenery where they were – he didn't know.

'No wonder they call their leader Captain,' he mumbled inside his helmet.

He hung there motionless, watching the Plates drift smoothly along the astral conveyor belt, hypnotised by the majesty of this cosmic geography. Who knows how long he would have stayed there were it not for another small beeping noise.

His gun had recharged. With a small prayer to whatever power was responsible for the view he had witnessed, he fired his wormhole pistol into empty space. If it didn't take him back to Macadamia this time, he was dead. The gun caused a portal to open up directly in front of him and he was sucked beyond Space–Time once more.

Chapter Ten

Back with a Bump

A broken heart cannot be fixed
By paper and string and glue and sticks.

Taken from *Unusual Truths*
by The Mysterious Wandering Gump

The Eden Orchard of Eternal Rest was packed full. It was a sunny day and the cliff-top view over Littleton Bay was glorious. You could just about hear the waves breaking on the smooth sandy beach below. It was some small comfort for Mrs Gloria Jackson to see how many people had turned up at her son's funeral to say goodbye. She was grateful to them all. Greenery's best friend, Sam, was there of course, sitting right on the front row next to Mrs Jackson. Sam's eyes were red and puffy from crying but right now Sam was being strong and brave for Gloria's sake.

It was her idea to have the funeral here, a gorgeous plot of land overlooking the sea. After Greenery was buried, an apple tree would be planted on the site and a small brass plaque commemorating his life placed nearby. She thought the growth of the tree was a nice way to mark the passing of time and somewhere nice to sit and remember her son.

The school band started playing 'Amazing Grace' as the cardboard coffin began the journey to its final resting place. All of the coffins used here were made of a strong industrial type of cardboard. It was more ecologically friendly and also helped to promote the growth of the trees. Mrs Jackson had been particularly fond of this idea as she was one of those people who liked things to be as natural and harmonious with nature as possible. She was a hippy after all.

As the coffin came close to the freshly dug grave, one of the pallbearers caught his foot around a root from a nearby tree. He slid on a muddy bit of loose turf, his leg buckled and he fell over in a heap. The other three men were completely unprepared for the shift in weight. The coffin slipped, twisted then fell out of their grasp. If it had been a sturdy wooden coffin this might have been an embarrassing moment for all concerned but Gloria Jackson would never have learnt the truth. As it turned out cardboard coffins do not react well to being dropped, particularly when they contain something heavy.

There were gasps from neighbours, cries from friends and a huge scream from Mrs Jackson.

When everybody had calmed themselves down again and the funeral director had stopped apologising, the truth was spotted by everyone. Lying on the floor with its head sticking out of a gaping wound in the cardboard coffin was a crash test dummy the same weight and size as a twelve-year-old boy.

Mrs Jackson looked up at Mr Hatton the funeral director with eyes as cold and hard as an eagle. The blue of her iris looked like steel.

'Where's my son?'

'I . . . he . . . well, it's your . . . I don't know,' was all he managed.

'*Where* is my son?' Her voice was as cold as her eyes, yet there was a note of tension in it, a note of pain that made it almost unbearable to hear.

'I don't know, honestly I don't. Mr Charters took delivery of your son, Mrs Jackson, I don't know where his body is, I . . . I'm sorry.'

Gloria Jackson didn't even look back. She walked away from the funeral and mourners as if they didn't exist. She moved silently through the crowd and to her the world appeared like a fog. All she cared about now was Greenery. She walked across the orchard to her small blue Mini Cooper and sped off towards Charters, Hutton and Hatton, the funeral directors on the High Street.

Mr Charters was a tall, thin, kindly man. He had taken over the family business after the death of his farther because he had seen how much comfort his dad had been to those he served. Mr Charters believed his was a worthwhile profession, and he was good at, and proud of, his job. He was just sitting down at his desk to attend to some paperwork when the front door flew open and a lady with a face like thunder burst in.

'What have you done with my boy?' she said through clenched teeth. Mr Charters could tell she was finding it diffi-cult to stay in control of herself.

'I'm sorry, I don't know who your boy is, Madam, but I assure you we are here to help.'

'My boy is Greenery Jackson. You have taken his body some-where. I need to know where and why.'

'Mrs Jackson, we have done nothing with your son's remains. Mr Hatton has taken him to the Eden Orchard of Eternal Rest. Perhaps there was some delay in getting him there. If you like I could . . .'

'Hatton is there, the hearse is there, the coffin is there but my son was not inside it. WHERE IS HE!?'

'Mrs Jackson, I don't really understand what is happening here but let me try and help you. Who did you speak to when you first came in here?'

It took a huge amount of willpower on her behalf but Gloria Jackson tried her hardest to calm down and looked Mr Charters in the eye. The genuine look of compassion on his face did what words could not have done and helped her trust him.

'I spoke to a girl, a youngish girl, blonde.'

'That would be my sister, Michelle. Let me go and get her for you.'

He left through some dark red velvet curtains and returned a moment later with Michelle. She also seemed eager to help.

'Hello, Mrs Jackson. I remember exactly when we took possession of your son's remains because it was a little odd. I was the last to leave on Saturday night. I locked up and there were only two bodies in the chapel. I was the first here on Monday morning and there were three bodies there.' She paused and looked at her brother, who nodded at her for reassurance.

'Your son was already in his coffin, Mrs Jackson. It was a closed casket service and so no one has checked inside since. We never take delivery of any remains without several checks and double checks; there's lots of paperwork too. I'm afraid we must have all assumed one of the other two had dealt with it. Nobody thought it was a break-in as nothing was broken. There were no signs of anything being tampered with. The only strange thing was that there was a lot of cat hair around the place. I noticed 'cause it set off my allergies. Does that help at all?'

'Where do you take your deliveries from?'

'They come to us straight from the coroners,' said Mr Charters. 'Mrs Jackson, if you'd like to take a seat here, Michelle will make you a drink while I phone the police. I think that is the only proper thing to do.' He turned around to usher his sister out of the room and when he turned back again all he was faced with was a breeze as the front door hung open. In the distance the sound of a small car screaming away could be heard quite clearly.

Night Light was just starting to get worried. It had been a while since Greenery jumped down the hole and he knew the boy's oxygen must be running out. A noise in the distance made him look over towards Towelyn's lookout point but he couldn't see her. He assumed she must be below the peak of the bluff and just out of sight.

He turned back to the ice dome and nearly fell over in shock. Greenery was standing right behind him holding his helmet under one arm. His eyes were open and staring but he didn't seem to be looking at anything Night Light could see.

'Greenery? Are you OK, lad? You look a little . . . elsewhere.'

'It's too much, Night Light. It's . . . wonderful!'

'You saw it, didn't you? The River,' said Night Light in a voice as soft as velvet.

'I saw The River. I saw the Plates that float on top of it; there's so many. I saw it all but I couldn't see the end of it, Night Light. I looked. I looked so hard but I don't think it has an end.'

'Come on, lad, you've had a bit of a shock. Did you get the Cyclops Tear?'

'What? Oh yes, yes sorry,' Greenery shook his head hard as if trying to dislodge something deep inside. 'It's here, look.'

'You got it? Ah! Let's see, let me see it.'

Greenery held up the small glass bottle in front of the Punster's face.

'My word, would you look at that! You clever little devil you. I can't believe you pulled it off.'

'Me neither.'

'That means we can get your key back, Greenery. You can go home. Greenery!'

'What? Oh yeah home. Yeah, it does.' His smile started to return and his eyes focused on Night Light for the first time. 'I can go home!'

The memory of Littleton Bay seemed to bring Greenery round. In an instant he became his old self again and picked up Night Light. He spun the Punster round several times, cheering and laughing as he did so. Night Light objected strongly but Greenery could tell he was secretly enjoying it.

They were on their third chorus of the world famous 'We did it!' chant, accompanied by the equally infamous, bum-wiggling 'We did it!' dance, when Towelyn came sprinting up to them. She looked tense.

'We have to go.'

'Look, look! He got it. He's got the Tear.'

'Good, we have to leave now.'

'Why? I've only just got back.'

'Snowlar Bears.'

The smile and most of the colour drained away from Night Light's face in a heartbeat. 'How long?' he asked in a tight voice, far more serious than Greenery was used to hearing.

'Judging by their current speed and distance I'd say about ten minutes.'

'Right, let's go.'

'What? What is it?'

'There's no time to explain, Greenery, but if you value your life start moving now.' Greenery had never seen Towelyn so tense. If he didn't know her better he would have thought she was scared. They picked up all of their gear and started running away from The Eternal Abyss.

It was hard-going through the knee-deep snow. Towelyn seemed to move effortlessly as always. Night Light had turned back into a pair of snowshoes and so was able to keep up with her relatively easily. Greenery on the other hand was struggling.

His space suit was thick and heavy. Great clogs of wet snow became tangled in the Llama-moth fur and weighed him down even more. It wasn't long at all before he was exhausted.

'Wait, please wait,' he panted. 'I can't keep this up. I'm sorry, I'm not as fit as you two. I eat burgers and chips and only do PE twice a week. Stop please.'

Towelyn turned around with a grim look on her face. She looked at Greenery who shrugged apologetically and with a heavy sigh she scanned the horizon. Greenery turned to see what she was looking at but couldn't pick out any details in the ice-white wilderness. He was dismayed to see how little distance they had put between the pit and themselves.

'This isn't going to work,' said Towelyn. 'We can't outrun them.'

'We could always hide,' said Night Light, who had changed back into his usual shape.

'That's not a bad idea,' she said.

As quickly as they could, all three of them dug a hole about waist-deep in the snow.

'Get in.'

'What about you?' asked Greenery.

'There's no point in me hiding they've already seen me. Beside if they stop to look for me that means they will be looking for you as well. If they find me easily they may just assume I am on my own. Their information can only be sketchy at best. And anyway, someone has to cover you up.'

'What is it we're hiding from, Towelyn?'

'Greenery, you either hide now or you die – it's that simple.'

'I'll hide.'

'Good choice.'

Greenery and Night Light climbed into the small hole. Towelyn threw Greenery's Yeti-hide exposure suit over them both and covered it in snow. As soon as the camouflage was complete she turned and ran. Without the other two slowing her down she moved with the speed and grace of a March hare. She leapt through the air and then barrelled on through the snow for a few steps before leaping again. In this way she covered much more ground than simply ploughing forward.

Cramped, curled and closeted within his damp hiding place,

Greenery could hear Night Light's heavy breathing and his own heart beating loud in his chest.

'Night Light,' he whispered. 'Night Light!'

'What?'

'I need to know what we're hiding from.'

'We are hiding from an enemy that can't be stopped and can't be beaten. We are hiding from death. Now shut up and lie low.'

'I'm sorry, Night Light, but I have to know.'

He sat up slightly and lifted one sleeve of his makeshift ceiling the smallest possible amount. He pushed his eye up to the tiny crack and watched the Snowlar Bears descend upon him.

There were two of them. Big bear-like creatures, horrific and fierce that seemed to be made from the snow itself. They moved forward with terrific speed yet their legs hardly moved and their feet never left the ground. Instead, each one flowed across the surface of the snow like a wave. The powder rose before them took shape and form, then fell behind, leaving a smooth wake in the path of each bear. They had long teeth made from razor-sharp ice that glistened in the afternoon sun. They looked deadly.

Greenery could only stare, terrified and frozen to the spot, as both beasts approached. They came within a watch spring's width of his hiding place and completely failed to see him. They had clearly set all their malice upon Towelyn who was now standing sword drawn, facing them, several hundred metres away. Greenery hadn't realised he was holding his breath until his own sharp gasp for air made him jump.

'What's going on?' asked Night Light.

'I think Towelyn's going to fight them.'

'What! That's suicide! She'll be killed.'

'I don't think she has a choice. They're nearly on her.'

The first bear reached her and the attack was immediate. A heavy arm as wide as a telegraph pole and twice as dense struck out at her. She quickly stepped to one side and sliced through it with her long sword. The amputated club fell to the ground. She turned to fend off an attack from the second bear but the first had already replaced its lost limb and was coming around for a second strike. She sliced, ducked then parried, and in an amazingly graceful pirouette removed the two front arms from both bears at once. She had only a second before they came at her again, fully formed out of fresh snow. They had not slowed down one bit.

'They keep growing back!' Greenery shouted to Night Light.

'Yes. That's what they do.'

'But then, how can she beat them?'

'She can't, lad. No one can. She could slice those two into a million pieces and they'd still come back for more.'

'We have to do something.'

'Agreed, but what?'

'I don't know.'

Towelyn faced the nearest Snowlar Bear and charged towards it with her sword held out like a lance. She plunged her weapon deep between its eyes then used it to pole-vault onto the animal's wide back. As she ran along the length of the bear's body she dragged her sword through its torso from head to tail and sliced it clean in two. All this was still in vain. The second both halves were on the ground the bear rose from the surface of the snow as if it were melting in reverse. It slashed out even before it was fully formed and caught her clean across the face. She stumbled sideways but did not go down. Not until the second bear struck her from behind and plunged its teeth deep into her shoulder.

Greenery could hear the cry of pain sharp and clear. He felt his chest tightening with fear for his friend's life.

Somehow Towelyn found the fortitude to go on. She dropped to the ground out of the bear's grip and rolled. As she did so her sword came around and removed the head of the beast that had bitten her. It gave her a moment to get to her feet but it was not long enough. Her second attacker was upon her once more. This time its hard frozen claws raked at her back, drawing three deep gashes.

Another cry of pain reached Greenery and as he watched both bears engulf her completely he knew it was over. They set upon her for several seconds then backed away equidistantly from her prone shape. Their snow-white bodies were stained red with her blood.

Slowly, miraculously, she managed to stand up. But the Snowlar Bears did not attack. Instead they began to circle her, watching her intently as they started to build up speed. Faster and faster they went, gliding in that strange flowing way that moved the snow through their form like a wave. When they were nothing but an indistinct haze their shapes broke down completely so that Towelyn was now in the centre of a tornado of loose snow. There was no wind.

As the funnel of snow accelerated again Towelyn remained motionless in its centre, unwilling or unable to move. Greenery couldn't tell which. She didn't even lift her head up as her feet rose off the ground. She was still holding her sword but it looked heavy in her arms like a dead weight. When she was several metres from the ground the entire wintery tornado sped off towards the horizon carrying Towelyn far away from them.

Greenery burst from his hiding place screaming and shouting incoherently. He chased after them for a short distance, cursing and ready to kill. It was a futile attempt at rescue – the bears were long gone and he was powerless to help his friend. Exhausted and drained, he collapsed to his knees.

He was sobbing when Night Light gently put his arm around his shoulders and sat down next to him in the snow. There didn't seem like much else to do.

'Mrs Jackson, that is impossible. You couldn't have been in here last Wednesday because we aren't open on Wednesdays.'

Mrs Trestle, the chief pathologist at Littleton General, was also the head coroner. It was not a big town and so there was no great need for two people to fill both roles. She had been having this heated discussion now for several minutes and was starting to think that this Mrs Jackson was slightly deranged.

'I was here.'

'We were closed. We're closed every Wednesday. It's the only day of the week we are.'

'Well, it doesn't matter if you don't know what days you're open or not. I need to know who took my son to the funeral director's on the High Street.'

Mrs Trestle sighed. 'Mrs Jackson, I've told you this several times now. We never had your son's body; there is no record of a Greenery Jackson being brought here, ever. OK?'

'But I saw him! He was here!'

'Look, I can prove it to you. We have CCTV recording in the mortuary at all times. You say it was last Wednesday. Do you remember what time it was?'

'Of course I remember what time it was – it was five forty-five.'

'OK, then let's go and check, shall we?'

Standing in the security room of Littleton General and staring at a bank of monitors Gloria Jackson was starting to doubt her own sanity. She was actually relieved when her image appeared on screen and then her heart fell again as she saw the prone corpse of her son.

'I told you,' was all she managed to say in a quiet little voice.

She began to cry as a whole avalanche of emotions caught up with her.

The pathologist put her arm on Gloria's shoulder and spoke very tenderly.

'I'm sorry, Mrs Jackson, really. I promise you, we'll sort this out.'

They were just leaving the room when Ernie the security man called them back. He sounded almost panicked. He rewound the footage several seconds and all three of them stood open-mouthed as they watched the body of Greenery Jackson dissolve in front of them and a smug-looking cat take its place.

'Ernie, can we see the footage taken just outside of the lab door, please,' said Mrs Trestle.

Ernie pressed a few buttons and the required footage popped up on screen. From this angle you could see the cat pad through the door and jump into the arms of the old man who had accompanied Mrs Jackson. Ernie froze the footage just as Mr Johnson looked up – his face was fully visible. He was caught in the act of drinking a stripy liquid.

'He lied to me,' said Mrs Jackson.

Chapter Eleven

Picking up the Pieces

What's the matter with matter?
Why is mass such a mess?
Why is gravity so clingy?
What's the Galaxy's address?

Taken from *Wonderings from the Wanderer*
by The Mysterious Wandering Gump

The biting wind blew across the barren plains of Macadamia. Greenery and Night Light had trudged slowly through the snow back to The Eternal Abyss. So far there hadn't been any signs of any more Snowlar Bears.

Now they were sitting inside the dome, huddled together for warmth and sheltering from the constant icy wind. Both their spirits were broken. Neither one had spoken since their decision to head back. There didn't seem much to say.

Eventually Greenery broke the silence.

'Night Light.'

'Yes, lad?'

'When I was floating in space and that wormhole took me a long way away from here I saw your planet, well your . . . place, The Other Place . . . some of it. It's beautiful.'

'I know, lad, you told me. Don't you remember?'

'Did I? No I don't, I'm sorry. I was a little out of it when I got back. It was a bit . . . overwhelming, you know. It was just so beautiful.'

'That's what they say. Of course I've never seen it meself.'

'It is, it's incredible. But how is it possible? It defies all the rules of physics; an endless river of light floating through space. It shouldn't be able to be like that.'

'You still don't get this place, do you?'

'I honestly don't know.'

Night Light sighed slowly. He leant his head back to look up at the sky through the icy dome.

'Are you familiar with the concept of The Bulk?'

'No.'

'Well, a good few years ago a scientist, a scientist from your world actually, started telling everyone that space wasn't empty space. He said it was like a skin that we all live on. Kind of like a big springy mattress called Space–Time.'

'Are you talking about Albert Einstein?'

'That's the fella, yes. He used this idea to explain things like gravity. You place a bowling ball, which represents a star, onto a mattress and all the smaller balls roll towards it, the little balls being planets and the force moving them towards each other being gravity. Follow me so far?"

'I think so.'

'Good. Then some really clever chap called Edward Witten said that actually there are lots of mattresses, or membranes as he called them, all lined up next to each other like slices. Apparently this squishy-squashy mass is what we all live in and it is like a huge super universe called The Bulk.'

'OK, so how does that explain The Other Place?'

'Well, think of The River as the thread that holds all of those slices together. Does that make sense?'

'Kind of.'

'Good' . . .

. . . 'Night Light.'

'Yes.'

'Is it really infinite?'

'What?'

'The River.'

'I think it must be. It's an infinite universe, boy, and The River runs right through the heart of it.'

'Wow. And those Plates, the islands that float on it . . . how do they . . . what are they made of?'

'Well, sometimes a great scientist or a philosopher has an idea that's so profound it moves a whole species forward a little bit. When this happens a new Plate is formed.'

'Formed from what?'

'From The River. The River is made of potential energy.'

'Oh.'

Silence returned. Several minutes passed.

'Night Light.'

'Yes, lad.'

'What are we going to do?'

Night Light sighed much deeper than before. After a few moments' thought he turned to Greenery and looked him straight in the eyes.

'Well, you have the Tear. We could go back to Tracey, claim your key and you could go home.'

'But what about Towelyn?'

'She's a Djinditsu. If she can't look after herself then no one can.'

'No, I can't just leave her, Night Light, I can't!'

'But we don't even know where she is. Those things could have taken her anywhere.'

Greenery stood up. All of a sudden he seemed to be full of energy. As he spoke he paced back and forth with definite strides as if the motion were helping him think. The need for action had gripped him once more.

'Night Light.'

'Yes, lad.'

'If you drink the Tear you can see anything, anywhere, whenever you want to right?'

'Correct.'

'Well, what if you only wanted to see one thing once. How much would you have to drink then?'

'I don't know, why?'

'Because if I took a tiny little sip, then perhaps I could see where Towelyn was, we could find out and we could go and get her. Then there would still be enough left to claim the key back. They don't know how full this bottle should be. They'd never know.'

'It might work. But we'd still have to rescue her; we're not fighters, boy, and who knows she might be . . . well, you know.'

'She's not dead. Don't even think that. It would work, I know it would.'

The Tear of the Cyclops was resting in the pocket of Greenery's Yeti-hide exposure suit, which he still hadn't changed back into. He walked over to it now and wrestled the bottle free from its furry pouch.

Night Light stood up. He was about to argue with Greenery, to tell him to be careful, but there wasn't time. Almost before the Punster had got to his feet Greenery ripped the cork from the vial and took a tiny little sip.

He stopped pacing. He stood still like a statue and his eyes clouded over – only for a second or two, but it was still very creepy. When their true green returned Greenery looked around him. He seemed to be familiarising himself with his surroundings, as if he wasn't sure where he was.

'Did it work?'

At the sound of Night Light's voice his eyes came fully back into focus. They looked sharper somehow, brighter than they did before.

'Sort of.'

'What do you mean sort of?'

'Well, it worked. But I must have been thinking of the wrong thing. I saw the tax office in Tracey. That little floating man who sent us here? ... He's dead. Then I saw a man who seemed to be made of shiny stone and he was holding the key but he couldn't get it to work. He looked angry.'

They stood facing each other, trying to make sense of the vision. Greenery started pacing again only more slowly this time. He walked around the circumference of the hole and right back to Night Light. When he reached the little Punster he stopped short, looked up for a moment, then downed the rest of the Tear of the Cyclops.

This time his eyes clouded over for much longer and his entire body went into spasm, as if some electrical current were flowing through him. He took in several staccato breaths and then exhaled for what felt, to Night Light, like ages. When his breathing returned to normal his body relaxed a little. He smiled and opened his eyes, slowly. They sparkled like diamonds. His focus looked sharp and alert; he was aware of everything.

'Are . . . are you all right?'

The boy's brilliant gaze turned towards Night Light.

'Yeah . . . I'm really good.'

'Why did you do that?'

'Think about it. The person that made the deal with us is dead and I reckon the man with the key is the one who killed him. He's not going to honour some bargain we made, is he? So we might as well take advantage of the Tear because as far as I can see it's no other use to us now, is it?'

'I suppose not.'

'OK, then let's find Towelyn, shall we?'

Greenery closed his eyes. Calmness swept over him and he entered a trance-like state. All that Night Light could do was stand and wait.

In his mind's eye, Greenery's perspective rose through the top of his own head. He saw the rest of his body, then Night Light, the dome and then the whole of Macadamia, shrink away below him. There really was very little to see apart from ice and snow. Then he became aware of the edges of the region; he saw where the snow began to melt, turning to luscious pastures of multicoloured crops. As he continued to fly skywards the ground below him and everything on it shrank away as though he was being whisked backwards through an inverted telescope. Eventually, when his vision was high enough to make out the entire Faraday Plate, and several others whose names he didn't know, he stopped. He could see the oily spectrum of The River separating each island and was reminded again at how mind-boggling this place was. Suddenly his mind's camera rotated, readjusted itself to a location on a distant Plate and then focused. This was to be a close-up.

The clouds began whizzing past him as his vision headed downwards but there was no sensation of falling. As the land rose up to meet him more and more sights came into focus.

A huge lake or landlocked sea came into view. It could have easily swallowed any of America's great lakes. He seemed to be heading towards the shore of this lake. He came closer still and he could see a huge area where lake and land mingled, forming a massive swamp. From this height it looked a dark dingy green colour with patches of brown and grey. Then something caught his attention. He hadn't noticed it before simply because of the scale of it. It was too big to take in without re-evaluating your perspective.

A figure was lying in the swamp. It must have been around the size of a small mountain yet it was clearly a man's body lying prone, with one knee bent upwards. As he came closer he could see areas where fortifications had been added around the outlying areas, particularly around the head. Certain patches of skin looked as if they were rotting and putrefied and in one or two places the giant's interior was exposed to the elements.

Now he was close, he could no longer see the entire body. He seemed to be heading for the chest. When his point of view was right up against the waxy skin of the torso everything went dark and his vision penetrated the corpse. When he could see again he was in a narrow, moist corridor. The camera of his mind flew through these passageways like a bird within the confines of a labyrinth. After twisting and turning several times he shot straight through a metal wall and came to rest within a small chamber. Here Towelyn sat, shackled to the floor. She looked weak and tired. She was alive.

Greenery opened his eyes. It took him a moment or two to regain his sense of self and place but once again Night Light's voice brought him fully around.

'Well?'

Greenery smiled and at once Night Light knew his worst fears had not been realised. He told the small Punster everything he'd seen and tried to describe as best he could the swampy land he had found himself in.

'A giant?'

'Yep.'

'A dead giant?'

'Yes.'

'She's being kept locked up inside the body of a dead giant?'

'Yes she is. Do you know where that is or not?'

'Well, yeah, I think I do. I'm just surprised that it's real, that's all.'

'What do you mean?'

'Well, for ages people have said that the Violents had their base somewhere near Ben Nevis but nobody thought it was actually inside him. Eurgh, that's horrible! He died about forty-odd years ago. He was the last of the Titans. That's disgusting, that is. . . . I mean, yeaurch, they live inside a huge dead body. It's just . . . bleurgh. Actually inside . . .'

150

'Night Light!'

'What?

'Do you know where it is?'

'Oh . . . yeah, it's in Scumlumpia, but that's miles away. That's way back past Tracey. How did they get her there so fast?'

'I don't know, do I?'

'More to the point how are we going to get there?'

'Funny you should ask that. I think I have an idea.'

For the third time, Greenery let his vision wander. He had the same feeling of flying away from himself. This time he was expecting it though and felt much more in control.

Night Light stood and watched him. It was strange, he thought, how the boy looked so calm. Something had changed within him since he had drunk the Tear.

After a couple of minutes Greenery started to twitch slightly; he looked slightly puzzled and seemed to be searching for something. A moment or two later he was done. His eyes opened and this time his smile was radiant.

'I've found someone else and she's not too far away.'

'Who?'

'I need something to amplify my voice. Should I imagine something or can you help me?'

'I think I can help. How loud do you want to be?'

'Loud.'

'Right, better stand back a bit then.'

Greenery quickly changed out of his space suit and put his Yeti-hide outfit back on. As he followed Night Light out of the dome, he began to wonder what the little man could possibly turn into this time. If Greenery's plan for transportation was going to work he would need something very loud.

Night Light looked as if he was warming up for something, he was stretching and pacing. He looked up and smiled. 'I'd move back a bit more if I were you, sonny. This is going to be a big one.' Greenery shrugged and wandered away even further. Now he was really curious.

After another few minutes of preparing himself Night Light was ready. He stood still for a couple of seconds then . . . pop! . . . In place of a very short, bald man there was a massive red telephone. It must have been twenty metres per side at least. Greenery didn't know what he was expecting but this certainly wasn't it.

'What do I do now?' he shouted towards the shining red phone.

'Climb up on top, press the speaker-phone button and then talk into the microphone. Oh and I'd put my fingers in my ears if I were you.'

Night Light's voice came back loud and booming from somewhere within the mechanism of the thing.

'Just out of interest, what are you?'

'Oh, lad, I thought you would have worked this one out. I'm a Mega Phone, aren't I?'

'Course you are. Silly me.'

Greenery wandered over to the base of the Mega Phone chuckling to himself and piled up some snow to help him climb on top. He spotted the speaker-phone button straight away. It was a metre square, blue and furry. The inbuilt microphone was a relatively small slit in the plastic casing right next to it.

He stood on the speaker-phone button expecting to have to jump up and down but despite its fuzziness it depressed easily and smoothly. As soon as it clicked into place a slight hissing noise started behind him. He turned around to see the large speaker at the other end of the telephone.

'Well, here we go,' he said aloud to himself and put his fingers in his ears. He leant down to the microphone and shouted at the top of his voice.

'CECEPHELOPHOPUS CECEPHECOMEHEREMUST!'

The sound of the Mega Phone was phenomenal. Even with his fingers planted so firmly in his ears that his knuckles were in danger of being covered in wax it was still deafening.

When the mighty echo had finally stopped rumbling around the empty landscape he lowered his arms to the sound of a high-pitched ringing deep within his skull.

He jumped back down into the snow and was immediately joined by Night Light who looked very pleased with himself.

'Told you it was loud.'

'What?'

'I said, I told you it was loud.'

'I can't hear you!'

'Well, you don't have to shout at me. I can hear.'

'Who came here?'

'What do you mean, who came here?'

'That's what you said.'

'No I didn't.'

'Yes you did; you said someone came here.'

'Who?'

'What?'

'WHO?'

'I don't know you said it. You said someone came here.'

'No, you just said that. I said I can hear.'

'Hear what?'

'Nothing.'

'Maybe no one's coming then.'

They both stopped and stared. Each one looked more perplexed than the other.

Greenery tried again.

'What can you hear?'

Night Light spoke very slowly and clearly as if talking to an idiot.

'I can hear you asking me a lot of daft questions. What can you hear?'

'I can hear you talking to me like I'm stupid and a very high-pitched whistle.'

'How could I talk to you like you're a high-pitched whistle? How do you talk to a whistle.'

'Are you kidding me?'

'What?'

'Don't start that again. Look I can hear a whistle . . .'

They trudged back to the only available shelter bickering constantly. In the end this odd discussion was only concluded when Greenery sat on Night Light and covered him in snow. All of a sudden the Punster understood him completely.

An hour later they were interrupted by a clear precise trumpeting that rang through the sky like a tenor bell. Both of them craned their necks upwards to see Sheba preparing for a vertical, parachute landing. She was bright fire-engine red with gold stripes down the length of her body and tentacles. Cecephelophopi do heal quickly, thought Greenery.

As she touched down gently, small drifts of snow puffed out all around her, making it appear as if she were sitting in the centre of a many-pointed star. Her gold stripes caught the early-evening sun and she shone magnificently. Even though some of the larger scars were still slightly visible, Greenery was reminded how beautiful these amazing creatures were.

It took them a moment or two to climb up on her back. Greenery was happy to notice his school blazer was still wedged tightly through one of the straps that had been used to hold Sheba's travelling trunk in place. Night Light held onto the wormhole gun.

Greenery had watched Towelyn fly Sheba for a couple of days and was confident he could take control quite competently. With one last look at the land of Macadamia he pulled back on the reins and the Disco Beast took off into the cobalt sky.

Just as in his earlier vision Greenery saw the snow-capped hills give way to lush rolling pastures but still they climbed, higher and higher. When ice started to form on Sheba's hide Greenery decided they were probably high enough. He reached round, took the gun from Night Light and fired it straight ahead. The swirling vortex of a new wormhole opened up before them and the would-be rescuers flew across the bridge in Space–Time desperate to rescue their fallen friend.

Chapter Twelve

The Belly of the Beast

Did you ever stop to wonder, why?
Why the why is why it is,
Or why the where is quite nearby?
Did you ever stand and question when?
When did when become a now,
And when will soon become a then?
Taken from *Where? And When? A Guide to Space–Time*
by The Mysterious Wandering Gump

'Oh, Mrs Jackson, I wasn't expecting to see you today. I was under the impression it was Greenery's . . . the day of your son's . . . Well, won't you come in, please?'

Mr Johnson stood up to welcome Gloria Jackson into his office. She stood ramrod stiff, framed in the doorway like a soldier on guard duty. Although at first he had seemed a little taken aback, Mr Johnson's manner was now relaxed and polite. Gloria took a few steps towards him, her face set in a manner of grim determination.

'Now what can I do for you, my dear lady. As I said the other day, anything to ease your suffering in this time of need.'

Mr Johnson was definitely not prepared for the veracity or

indeed the force of the punch that Mrs Jackson so expertly connected with his face. Smack! His nose began gushing blood. As he rocked back on his heels he put his weight on his chair, which wheeled away and sent him tumbling to the floor in the corner of his office.

'Dow see here, Mrs Dackson. I dow you're grieving but dat is unaccepdable. Wads going od?'

'You lied to me.'

'Pardod?'

'You lied to me. You stood next to me and watched me weep over my dead son's body, knowing full well I was looking at some kind of . . . of . . . facsimile; and now you continue to lie to my face. Where is my son?' Her voice was scarily calm, like the sea before a storm.

'I swear to you I don'd dow whad you're dalking aboud.'

'Where is he!?!' she screamed, as she set upon the Headmaster.

Her nails were raking at his face as if she could claw the truth right out of his skin. She was completely frenzied and totally unstoppable until something with a vicelike grip reached out and grabbed both her wrists. She looked up and let out an ear-piercing scream.

The large wooden carving that always stood in the corner of Mr Johnson's office, the Native American that Greenery was so fond of, had left its spot. It was animated and alive. In her moment of terror Mrs Jackson looked into the staring expressionless eyes of the mannequin with total clarity and recognised the face of the waxy pathologist from the CCTV footage.

The wooden doll wasn't attacking her, it was simply holding

her firmly. It was incredibly strong. She screamed again just as Take-That the cat leapt from the top of the filing cabinet and landed squarely on her head. He dug his claws in deeply and painfully. Blood began trickling down Gloria's forehead, obscuring her vision.

Out of fear and surprise her legs gave way and she dropped to the floor. The carving was strong but stiff and clumsy. As she collapsed it fell over on top of her. Even with a crazed cat on her head Gloria Jackson realised this was the advantage she needed. She rolled over so that her body weight pressed down onto the Native American and managed to recover her footing so that she was crouching on the wooden man's chest. Then using all the muscles in her body she stood up and managed to free herself from the statue. It was very determined and did not want to let go. She reached up, wrenched the cat off her head and ran screaming from the office.

Take-That the cat landed calmly and somewhat stiffly on the desk staring straight down into the eyes of the crumpled old man on the floor who was drinking heavily from his flask of stripy liquid. He looked directly at Take-That the cat.

'I'm sorry. Please give me adother chance. I can fix dis, I probise.'

The air parted and a fluorescent-green Disco Beast with a schoolboy and a Punster on its back materialised at the speed of light.

'Eurgh! What's that smell?'

'That, my boy, is Scumlumpia. An area comprised mostly of thick, vile-smelling mud and made even less fragrant by the presence of a gargantuan rotting corpse. Look!'

Greenery looked down where Night Light was pointing and saw the putrid remains of Ben Nevis. The size of the thing was incredible. When he was alive and standing upright he could have stepped from Plate to Plate easily. No wonder the ancient Greeks of Earth believed these Titans used to hold up the planet. Maybe they did, thought Greenery.

'Wow, it stinks.'

'Yes it does. Now, where shall we land?'

'Well, I think the main entrance around the head is too well guarded.'

'We could always try the back door.'

'Have you seen where the back door is?' said Greenery, pointing down.

'What? Oh right! I see. Not the back door then.'

'I think it's best.'

'Well, where then?'

'In my vision I saw a hatch on the chest of the giant. That would also be a good flat place to land.'

'Let's do it, kiddo.'

They circled around the corpse a couple of times to make sure the coast was clear and, spotting the hatch, they then touched down on the chest plateau of Ben Nevis, close to the small entrance.

The Cecephelophopus touched down as gently as always but she seemed unhappy, as if touching the fleshy floor made her uncomfortable. Greenery knew what had affected her as soon as he climbed off her back. Standing firmly on the ground brought home the reality that this was a dead body. A person of incredible proportions but a person all the same. It sent a cold shiver up his spine. Looking at Night Light it was clear he had been affected too. The thought of climbing inside was not an attractive prospect to either of them. Night Light looked up at Greenery and shook his head in disgust, 'Come on, lad, let's get on with it. The quicker we find her the quicker we can leave.'

The short walk to the entrance seemed only to intensify their feelings of foreboding. There was something very wrong about entering a corpse. The sight of the hatch only added to this. It was basically a metre-square flap of skin that had been hacked out on three sides with a blunt, saw-toothed blade, leaving the edges frayed and raggedy. Patches of dried blood and areas of flesh were easily visible. The handle was a large soggy wound.

Greenery gingerly reached his hand in and pulled. Where the hinges should have been the stiff skin simply bent back easily with frequent use. Not knowing what to expect he looked down into the dark hole and was almost relieved to see a crude wooden staircase descending into the depths. He sighed and looked at his small companion.

'After you.'

'Oh thanks a lot,' said the Punster sarcastically.

The stairs creaked ominously as they carefully made their way down them. Greenery stepped off the last one and onto a soft, damp floor. It squelched slightly with his weight. The walls glowed faintly with some kind of phosphorescent fungus giving the whole area a blueish, green tinge.

'All right, clever clogs, which way now?'

Greenery closed his eyes and let the Tear show him the way. After a couple of seconds his eyes snapped open. 'This way.'

'Wait!'

'What?'

'We can't just go traipsing around this place can we?'

'What do you mean?'

'What if we get seen? We're behind enemy lines now, lad. This is serious.'

'Right, OK, good point. Well, I could imagine us up an invisibility cloak.'

'No you couldn't. There is nothing original about that; you'd never make one appear.'

'All right, smarty pants, can you change into anything that will help us?'

'Erm nope, don't think so.'

'Then what are we going t . . .'

'Wait . . . oh, no, sorry.'

'Come on, think.'

'I'm thinking,'

'Well, think harder.'

'Can I remind you that this was your idea,' said Night Light, crossing his arms, ' I'm standing here trying me best. I don't ask for much, but a little bit of respect wouldn't . . .'

'Stop talking.'

'Oh that's charming that is, thanks a lot.'

'I'm getting an idea, shhh!'

'Well, I was only saying . . .'

'Chameleon pills!'

'What?'

'Chameleon pills!!' shouted Greenery, forgetting where he was for a moment.

'Shhh, not so loud.'

Greenery spoke the words for a third time and the same smoky breath as before came out of his mouth. A moment or two later he was holding two strange tablets covered with a multicoloured camouflage pattern. Without hesitation he threw one into his mouth and started chewing. As he did so his skin and clothes began to change colour so that they matched the wall behind him exactly. When he moved there was a slight out-of-focus shift as the effect caught up with his background but when he stood still it was almost impossible to see him. Night Light looked impressed and popped his pill.

'Right, now we go this way. Follow me.'

It was slow going. The passage they were following sloped downwards steeply and was very slippery underfoot. After a while it split three ways. Greenery closed his eyes for a moment then continued down the right-hand passage with all the confidence in the world. As they progressed carefully the illumination changed from fungus to more formal-looking electrical lighting and they started to see the odd building. It was clear they were reaching the suburbs of the main city.

They were approaching a T-junction when they heard voices. A moment later two Violents came strolling round the corner. One was a disgusting pig man with huge tusks that curled out of his mouth and made him dribble constantly. The other was smaller and less spittle-covered. This didn't make him any more appealing, however, as he was basically a large blob of green slime. Greenery and Night Light just had time to throw themselves against the wall before he squelched right past them. Both stood stock-still, afraid even to breathe.

They passed by without a second glance and continued

162

completely oblivious to the trespassers in their midst. The chameleon pills, it seemed, were working.

Greenery and Night Light stepped away from the dripping wall, took a couple of deep breaths and continued with their journey. The twists and turns, junctions and intersections, became much more numerous. Fortunately Greenery had the knowledge of the Tear to guide them. Several times they came across the inhabitants of Ben Nevis and had to throw themselves out of the way but every time the Violents walked by without a second glance.

After walking for about an hour Greenery led the way round a sharp corner and stopped dead in his tracks. He was terrified by the sight that awaited him. Even when Night Light walked face-first into his bottom it didn't bring him back from his revulsion.

'Oi, big lad! What you doing?'

'Shhh! Look,' he whispered.

Night Light looked to see where Greenery was pointing and his mouth fell open.

'Oh no,' he said slowly.

The small passageway they were standing in opened up suddenly onto a massive chamber. It was the stomach of the deceased colossus. From this vantage point they could see the whole city centre.

The streets curved down into a huge bowl and up the other side, making a very evenly shaped valley. Within this bowl narrow streets and alleyways ran higgledy-piggledy everywhere. There were houses, shacks, shops and pubs built on every available piece of land. The ramshackle buildings looked as though they had been made out of whatever the Violents could scavenge, bits of wood, skeletons of strange animals, various types of cloth and countless other items. Some of the classier properties even had parts made of bricks and mortar.

In the centre of the stomach right at the bottom of the valley was a lake of acid. There was a dizzying haze over its vomit-yellow surface and every now and then it bubbled menacingly. The place was heaving with Violents.

There has never been a more disgusting collection of blood-thirsty, homicidal hotheads than the inhabitants of Ben Nevis and most of them were right here. They seemed to be at war; small battles were taking place all over town. This was not due, however, to some rippling social current of unrest. It was because they enjoyed fighting and were good at it.

'No, absolutely not. We cannot go through that,' Night Light said, backing away in fear.

Greenery closed his eyes for a moment. 'I don't think we have to . . . No, there's another way, follow me.'

They back-tracked for a while then Greenery took a sharp right down a very narrow passage. The walkways became smaller and smaller and the lighting became fungus-formed again. At one point the tunnel became so small they had to crawl on their hands and knees. Each wishing they didn't have to touch the fleshy floor with the bare skin of their hands.

Eventually the passageways got bigger once more and they returned to the busier parts of the city. It had been nearly two hours since they first entered the Titan. After another half-hour of slow-going carefulness and several more close calls Greenery stopped dead in his tracks.

'She's being held right around this corner,' he whispered.

'OK, what do we do?'

'Well, she's being held in a solid steel cube with a fifty-centimetre-thick reinforced-steel door. Outside are two guards armed with long, sharp, spiky things which I'm pretty sure are designed to make people die.'

'Oh right. Piece of cake then.'

'Er no. Not really.'

'Listen, lad, never underestimate the stupidity of your basic guard. They're employed to stand still for long periods of time and watch doors or walls. Thinking is not required.'

'Well, what do we do then?'

'Just get close enough to whisper this in one of their ears. Come here.'

Night Light motioned for Greenery to bend down to him, which he did.

'If my Snort-Horn looked like you I'd shave its bum and make it walk backwards.'

'You sure?'

'Trust me.'

'OK. I'll do it.'

Greenery wasn't too sure about the next part of his rescue mission. As effective as the chameleon pills were, they weren't fool-proof. He was suddenly very aware of how it would only take a tiny mistake to give the game away, leaving him vulnerable to attack from the long, sharp, spiky things.

He stuck his back against the wall and rounded the corner very carefully. This was the first time he had seen the two guards in the flesh, without using the power of the Cyclops Tear. They were both very big and very ugly. One looked like some kind of squid dressed in armour. Most of his tentacles touched the floor and seemed to act as legs but a couple were being used as arms and were holding his weapon. The other was a stereotypical version of a devil. He was red-skinned with horns on his head. He had cloven hooves and goat's legs. It was not as comical as it sounds. He was very large and very muscular.

As Greenery approached them he tried to make his breathing as silent as possible. He moved incredibly slowly so as to minimise the blurring effect of the pills. It worked and the colours of the corpse wall edged over his face with perfect clarity.

He was almost in position, right between the two of them, when Devil Man readjusted his weight and leaned back on the wall. If either of them turned around now he was sure they would see him, chameleon pills or not. The guard's hand brushed against Greenery's fuzzy hair and the boy almost cried out in fear. Instead he froze, not even daring to breathe. Terrified as he was he realised this was his chance. He took a long slow breath desperately trying to be silent until the time was right. He opened his mouth to speak,

'. . .' Phhrrrrrrrrrrrrp.

A combination of nerves and a strange new diet got the better of Greenery and he was interrupted by his own bowels. He farted right between the two guards.

The effect was almost immediate; in fact it was only beaten by the speed of the eggy smell.

'Was that you?'

'Me? No. It was you.'

'It wasn't me and there's only us here.'

'Are you calling me a liar?'

'Yeah. I think I am.'

Smack! Squiddy walloped Devil Man right in the face. It was one of those slow, relaxed punches that really, really hurt. As already implied, the natural state for a Violent is violence. It takes a massive amount of concentration at all times for them to stop themselves exploding into bloodshed. As they started hitting each other Greenery hit the deck. He fell to the floor, curled up in a tight ball and tried to stay out of the way.

After a minute or two when it was quiet and still again he uncurled from his defensive position and looked around for the two guards. They both lay on the floor unconscious. Squiddy was a couple of limbs lighter and the red guy with the horns and goat feet was now just the red guy with horn and goat foot. They did not look good.

'Night Light,' Greenery called around the corner. 'Night Light, come on.'

'Wow, you did it!' was all he said as he came trotting up to the scene of devastation. 'It worked then, hey? You said what I told you to?'

'What? Oh yes, er Snort-Horn, shave its bum. Worked like a charm, thanks.'

Standing together over the fallen guards, deep inside the giant, there passed a moment of stillness and quiet between Greenery and Night Light. It was filled with pride and deep camaraderie. There was no need for any words. These are the moments true friendships are built upon. It was only a second or two and passed without comment but was noticed by both.

'Right fifty-centimetre-thick, reinforced-steel door. Any suggestions?'

'Funny you should ask,' said Night Light. 'I have exactly the thing. Ever heard of a manhole?'

'Yeah, of course.'

'Well, let me show you the Man Hole.' Pop!

Where there had been solid wall there was now a hole, right through the steel cube. A hole the exact size and shape of Greenery. A man-shaped hole.

'You are incredible.'

'I know.'

Without any hesitation Greenery ducked through the Man Hole and found himself standing in front of Towelyn. She looked well. She was sitting calmly in the middle of the floor. She was not injured and was restrained only by a thin chain round her ankle.

Greenery was about to run over and hug her but something stopped him. Towelyn hadn't moved at all. She did not turn to look at him and had not seemed surprised to see a hole appear in the side of her cell.

'Something's wrong!'

Pop!

'What do you mean something's wrong? Come on, let's go. Towelyn, come on. Towelyn, Towelyn?'

Night Light noticed it now too. She still hadn't moved. He walked over to her, slowly, thinking she may be in some kind of deep shock. He reached out for her gently and called her name in a soft, soothing voice.

'Towelyn, come on now, love, it's time to leave. We've brought Sheba. Wouldn't you like to see her again?'

He brought his hand down on her shoulder to give her a reassuring pat but it never made contact. Instead his hand went straight through and disappeared into her body. The image in front of them was not their fearless warrior. It was a hologram!

Realising it was a trap, the two valiant friends turned and ran for the door. At exactly the same moment the floor beneath them opened up. It split cleanly down the middle. Greenery managed to dive towards one of the walls but there were no handholds. He could find no purchase and so down he fell along with Night Light. Down to whatever waited below.

Chapter Thirteen

Muscle and Blood and Skin and Bone

'Power corrupts,' so goes the verse
And absolute power is even worse.
But don't you think it's such a shame
That all this power gets the blame?
Perhaps we all should look instead
At the soft, corruptible human head.

Taken from *Homo Sapiens Are Only Human*
by The Mysterious Wandering Gump

At the exact moment Night Light had unwittingly sprung the trap, he had also severed the telepathic link between the hologram and the real Djinditsu. Locked in her cell, the empty body of the warrior shook violently. She would have fallen off the bed were it not for the heavy leather restraints.

The seizure stopped as quickly as it started and her eyes snapped open. Towelyn was once again within herself. As she lay there taking stock of her situation, some confused memories came flooding back.

She could remember the snow and the sky. She remembered pain and thinking she was going to die. She was proud that she had been brave and faced death head-on. Then there had been speed and spinning and cold and more pain as the bears ... No, that was wrong – they had become the wind and snow and had lashed at her body relentlessly. Then stillness. The image of a face with a cruel smile swam before her and again a sense of pride as she remembered that even though she could barely stand she had still tried to fight. That face laughed at her as she was grabbed by many hands. Two, she remembered in particular, were placed on her temples. And then distance. Only distance. Her memories faded with the image of herself, which was odd. She watched herself being dragged away still and unresisting.

Lying here now she knew only one thing. Wherever she was, she had to get out.

Greenery and Night Light were shooting through a very slippery, very slimy tube. The smell of decomposition was worse here than anywhere else they had been so far. Greenery didn't even want to think about what part of the body this was. Slowly the almost vertical tunnel seemed to level out. Greenery could see light ahead but it looked dim and faded somehow. He soon realised what was causing this effect.

Someone had placed a squishy, rubber-like film of some kind over the end of the tunnel. As they shot from the slimey exit they were immediately caught in its sticky clutches and came to a tangled heap in the middle of a small chamber.

Whilst they were still struggling with the gummy membrane one of many guards stepped forward and sealed the open end with a small machine. They were now trapped completely in its tight clingy grasp. The more they pushed against its sinewy strands the more it pushed back. Eventually they couldn't move at all. They were held fast and secure.

Clap!   Clap!   Clap!   Clap!   Clap!

A slow sarcastic applause brought their attention back into the room. The outer wall was surrounded by at least twenty guards, each more ugly and disgusting than the last. They were all armed with incredibly cruel-looking weapons. Blades and spikes and spears and pikes were all aimed directly at the captive duo. And there, right in the centre of the room, was a large fearsome-looking man made completely of smooth burgundy marble. It was he who was clapping so smugly.

'My, my, my, the infamous Greenery Jackson. You have caused me some considerable inconvenience, young man.'

His voice was cold and mocking and seemed disconcertingly loud in this enclosed space. What was most terrifying about him was his calmness.

'Allow me to introduce myself. My name is Ignatius Trump. Welcome to my humble home. It is considered quite rude where I come from to break into another man's private domicile, especially when you are considering taking something away without permission. I would, however, on this occasion, overlook your social misdemeanours if you were to help me with a small trifling little matter.'

At this point he bent down on one knee right in front of Greenery who tried desperately to back away. All he managed, though, was a small whimper.

'Tell me, do you recognise this, Mr Jackson?'

Shining in Ignatius Trump's hand as pristine and flawless as the last time Greenery had seen it, was the key. Even here in this miserable place it seemed as if some ethereal light was shining down on it. It gleamed.

'Now I know you want this. I also know what you were doing in Macadamia to get it. I surmised you would succeed and, being that you are here, I am going to assume I was right. Which means, Mr Jackson, that you can see anything, anywhere. A rare gift indeed. I was going to keep you alive because apparently I need you to make this key work. With the key I can return our glorious leader to power and we will once again rule . . . blah, blah, blah. However, a thought has lately occurred to me. If I were to use your unique gift to my own advantage then *I* could rule The Other Place, without the help of Lazarus Brown. Yes, if I were to utilise your skill to help me gain a weapon – a weapon like the Armies of Sorrow for example – then I would be truly unstoppable.'

He dropped the key on the floor as though it were nothing, just a piece of old rubbish, then he leaned even closer to Greenery and smiled. His teeth, so white and clean, also looked incredibly sharp. He pressed his face right up against the strange netting and spoke directly into Greenery's ear. His breath smelt like granite and his spittle on Greenery's face was stone cold.

'You will help me, Greenery Jackson. You will, or else I will bring down upon you and your companions unimaginable torments. Horrors of such brutality that I doubt you could stand to hear of just one of them, let alone experience them all. What say you, Mr Jackson?'

Night Light was squirming again. Greenery didn't know if his friend was acting out of fear or anger but it felt as though he was reaching for something. Now, however, was not the time to worry about Night Light. Even though he could barely move Greenery managed to turn his head and look Ignatius Trump right in the eyes.

'It doesn't work,' he muttered.

'I beg your pardon?' said Ignatius, standing up.

'I said it doesn't work,' Greenery managed in a much firmer voice.

'Nonsense, of course it works. You're here, aren't you?'

'Exactly, the Tear didn't show me where Towelyn was. It led me right into your trap instead. It doesn't work.'

'Ah but it does, Mr Jackson. It works perfectly. You see to all intents and purposes that was your friend. She's here, very close. Agonisingly close if you really want to know. And it only took a simple little piece of telepathy to put her consciousness into the shell of that hologram,' he laughed humourlessly.

'An old philosophical question that one, isn't it? What *is* really you? Your mind or your body? Well, as far as your gift is concerned it's the mind and that is exactly where it led you. So you see, Greenery Jackson, the Tear of the Cyclops works perfectly. And now you will make it work for me. Tell me where the Armies of Sorrow is.'

'Don't do it, lad. He'll kill us all anyway and then murder thousands. You can't tell him.'

'Silence!'

Ignatius' hand moved so fast it was almost invisible. He struck Night Light across the scalp so hard that Greenery thought he might have split his friend's skull.

'Night Light!' he called out in despair but it was no use – he was out cold.

174

'WHERE IS IT!?'

'I'll never tell you.'

For a big man Ignatius sure could move fast. The rock-hard blow to his head took Greenery completely by surprise. He thought his head would split open, the pain was so unbearable. A trickle of blood ran into his right eye obscuring his vision and the world seemed to spin as he struggled to stay conscious.

'WHERE IS IT? WHERE!!?'

The world was fading fast but Greenery heard the question even though it sounded fuzzy and distant.

'L, nvr, tll, you.'

The second blow broke his nose and almost dislocated his jaw. He passed out from the pain as much as the impact. Luckily he was out before he could suffer too much.

Ignatius Trump stopped with his arm in mid-air, realising his third strike would probably kill. He took a deep breath and regained his composure.

'No I think not. I need him alive.'

He turned to leave the room but stopped just on the threshold and turned to the nearest guard.

'Prepare the interrogation room . . .' He smiled. 'My favourite one.'

Towelyn's back was hurting where one of the Snowlar Bears had sunk its teeth into her and the other scratches and lacerations were equally sore. She was a Djinditsu though and had been taught from birth how to ignore pain.

She tested her bonds. She was strapped to a gurney with thick leather belts. There was one round each wrist, one round her ankles, her waist and her neck. She could also feel pressure on either side of her head as though she were wearing some kind of hat. In fact, she was wearing what looked like a small metal crown. It was the device that had until recently been keeping her connected to the decoy.

The restraints were strong and completely unmoveable but she had one remaining weapon. A weapon her ancestors had been grateful for time and time again, one that no captor would ever discover. Retractable claws. She extended the sharp nail on her index finger and began picking at the leather holding her wrist in place.

The belt was strong but her claws were sharp. It took only a few minutes to pick right through and free her left hand. Once that was loose it was simply a matter of undoing the other ties.

Now she was free to move about she threw her telepathic crown to the floor and looked around the room for the first time. It was tiny, not much bigger than the cot she had been strapped to. There were no other furnishings. Set into the nearest wall was a thick, heavy wooden door. It didn't give her much to work with.

She leant heavily on the wall and recoiled almost immediately. It was moist and fleshy, disgusting. But more to the point, it was soft. She pushed her claw experimentally deep into the pulpy matter and carefully made a small hole just big enough to spy through. As she put her eye against the makeshift peephole she nearly gagged. The stench was repulsive. Prepared for it the second time, she held her breath and looked through again. Just as she'd thought, there were guards, three of them, slouching in the corridor outside. She was pretty sure she could take them out but only if she could surprise them. The problem was that by the time she'd made a hole in the wall big enough to climb through they would be well aware of her presence. She moved to the adjacent wall and repeated the peephole procedure.

The room next door looked as though it was another cell. This one, however, was empty and the door was slightly ajar. Knowing this was her only chance she extended her other nine claws and began slashing her way through the wall. The pink wobbly matter felt repulsive under her nails but it took only a moment before she was through.

Buoyed up by her success she could feel her body coming alive again. The action of motion with a purpose was exactly the tonic she needed. Her senses were sharpening. She was ready for combat. Watching through the crack in the open door, she knew now that this trio of imbeciles would be no match for her.

The tallest of the three was also the skinniest. He was composed mostly of neck. His body was very close to the ground and all of his limbs were short and dumpy. He had a sword in one stunted arm and a shield strapped to his back. The second was short but strong-looking. His three legs formed a sturdy tripod and he had a long blade in each of his three hands. The third guard was closest to her. It was impossible to get any kind of idea of his capabilities. He was a mass of hair. No other features were at all discernable, apart from a ridiculous tin helmet that was too small to fit over his enormous bouffant.

Even while she was still mentally preparing herself for action her body was ready to explode like a lioness on the hunt. This was all instinctive to her now. It was who she was.

In one fluid motion she threw the door open and dived forwards into a roll. It was a move that took her past the reaches of the hairy one and right into the eyeline of the tall lanky guard. The rolling motion brought her elegantly back to her feet and even as she was rising, both hands, with claws extended, were slashing at his long exposed neck. The deep gashes across his throat were painful and dangerous but millimetres short of being fatal.

As he staggered backwards, wildly trying to stem the flow of blood from his open wounds, she wrenched the sword from his unresisting hand and in one liquid drive brought it around on Tripod. He had barely realised what was happening before one of his arms was lopped off and blood squirted across the narrow corridor. Another roll across the floor and over the newly detached limb brought Towelyn to her feet with another weapon. She expertly ducked a wild slash from Tripod that would have otherwise decapitated her, and with a small sideways lunge she brought both swords together in a scissor-like motion to remove one of his legs. Now that his sturdy base was gone the bulky guard dropped to the floor screaming. He was no longer a threat.

Finally she turned to point both blades straight at the hairy hat. He had not moved at all during the mêlée. She lunged forward and plunged her sword deep into the hairy depths. There was no resistance and no blood on the steel as she withdrew it. He was completely unaffected by the blow. It seemed he was pure hair.

'Which way is out? Nearest exit?'

'Why should I tell you?'

She swung her sword as fast as lightning and removed

twenty centimetres of fringe all across the base of the guard. He was now a lot shorter.

'The most direct route from here is the knee,' he blurted out.

'Knee?'

'Yes, end of this corridor turn right and straight up the main thigh thoroughfare. It'll bring you out on the highest peak of Ben Nevis.'

'This is Ben Nevis? We're inside him?'

'Yes.'

'You people really need a better hideout. Have you no self-respect?'

'I have actually. I hardly ever use the back door.'

'Gross.'

She swung the sword absent-mindedly and removed another few centimetres of height from the thing's main bulk.

'Oi!'

'It'll grow back. Now skedaddle before I give you a perm.'

With that the clump of hair sped away, gliding across the damp ground like a moulting ghost.

Towelyn leapt over the still-squirming ex-tripod, swapped one of her swords for Neck Man's shield in case she came under heavy fire, and sprinted to the end of the corridor. It looked like the guard had been telling the truth. On her right was a long dark passageway that ran diagonally upwards, straight and steep. As she began jogging it occurred to her that she was probably running through a vein or an artery. The thought gave her the creeps but this only intensified her determination to leave. She lowered her head and powered on upwards to freedom.

*

Greenery awoke suddenly and painfully thanks to a large bag of crystals thrust in his face. They smelt sharply of ammonia and almost made him choke with their acrid stink. He was welcomed back to the world by a skull-splitting headache and a relentless pain in his nose.

He looked into the eyes of the bearer of the smelling salts and went numb with fear. There was no mistaking that these were the eyes of a stone-cold killer. They looked at the world and at him without any trace of humanity. These ocular dead zones were set deeply into a face that stood out amongst the Violents for its normality, a handsome face with smooth olive skin. Had the 'man' not had two sets of arms, he would have been considered a catch in Littleton Bay.

The thought of home sharpened Greenery's terror. It was looking less and less likely that he would see his friends or his mum ever again. With startling resolve he managed to turn his fear into anger and tried to lash out at this new monster. He tried desperately to hurt him, to transfer his own pain onto the dead-eyed freak before him, but found he couldn't even move.

He was strapped to a metal trolley exactly like the one Towelyn had recently escaped from. Straps at his neck, waist, wrists and ankles held him firmly in place. By the sound of the grunting and groaning coming from nearby, Night Light was here too and was awake.

'You two boys are in deep, deep trouble,' said the guard in a creepy sing-song voice. He sounded as though he was having a great time. Without warning he grabbed Greenery's trolley with all four of his arms. He lifted the whole thing up as if it weighed nothing and propped it vertically against the wall giving Greenery a much clearer view of the inter-rogation room.

Night Light was here. He was not strapped to a table but was locked up inside a little cage at the opposite end of the long chamber. The bars of his cell were glowing and the whole cage was suspended from a track that ran across the ceiling.

In the centre of the room directly between the two of them was a large square cauldron containing a large amount of thick sticky-looking yellow tar. It was boiling and bubbling away with such ferocity that Greenery could feel the heat radi-ating from it even at this distance.

'Which one of you boys likes to swim then?' asked Four Arms.

He looked at them both in turn with those cold dead eyes and very slowly started to chant. As he did so he pointed alternately between the two.

> *'Tipsy, topsy, turvey, toil,*
> *Who's the one who's going to boil?*
> *Till he's done,*
> *We'll have some fun,*
> *And drown him in the roasting oil.'*

The slow mocking tone was bad enough but then he started to laugh. The laughter was dreadful. He howled like a beast and thumped his chest. The monumental satisfaction he got from this simple form of intimidation was appalling. He was clearly insane.

Without warning he picked up a metal rod that was resting against the side of the cauldron and thrust it deep into the liquid inside. After a few seconds he brought it out. The thick, viscous fluid clung to the rod like toffee. As he carried it over to Greenery several drops fell on the floor. They hissed and bubbled where they landed.

'This is gonna hurt, sunshine.'

He waved the stick frantically in front of his prisoner, causing a thin splash of liquid to flick off the end of the rod and spray across Greenery's chest. Luckily most of it landed on his Yeti-hide jacket but some landed on his thin cotton shirt and soaked through to the skin.

Night Light called out in anger and sympathy but there was nothing he could do. Greenery screamed and screamed. The pain was unbearable. It felt as though his entire body was on fire.

'Ouch,' the torturer mocked.

It was a long climb. Even though Towelyn was incredibly fit she found it tiring, especially as she had to fight her way past the odd Violent or two. They were mostly taken completely unawares and it only took a single strike to dispatch them. Even so the cumulative effect was exhausting. She was almost sorry now that she'd brought the heavy shield.

Finally she reached the kneecap. In front of her was an old rickety-looking wooden staircase that led up to a loose flap of skin. She pushed this aside and left the confines of the Titan behind her.

As she climbed out she was met with a starry sky. The wind on her face was invigorating and life-affirming. She felt so good she could almost ignore the ever-present stink of Scumlumpia. Almost.

Towelyn scanned the horizon. This stretch of The River passed a large ringed planet which was clearly visible in the Downstream sky. One of its moons shone reflected light down on the swamp, making it easier to see, but unfortunately the sights of this dreary place filled her with about as much enthusiasm as a pint of camel spit.

From this vantage point she could make out the entire scope of Ben Nevis, his odd posture, the fortifications around his head, the tattered remains of clothing ... and the large Cecephelophopus waiting patiently on his chest.

She looked again in baffled surprise. There it was, a mature Cecephelophopus simply waiting to be ridden. Towelyn had no idea what the stabling procedures were of the Violents but she was certain she couldn't waste this chance of escape.

The Disco Beast was a long way off so she had to move quickly before its owner came back to claim it.

The shield! The guard's shield she had stolen would make an excellent toboggan. She could slide down the angled thigh and be near the Disco Beast in minutes. She threw the armour on the floor and jumped on board.

The downward journey was nothing if not exhilarating. She found there were shallow channels, running through the fabric of the giant trousers. By sliding through these folds she was able to control which way she went. When one channel veered off too close to the edge she could skip grooves by leaning heavily in the desired direction and using a foot as a kind of rudder.

There were a couple of hairy moments when the channels were almost too deep to jump out of easily and she thought she would go sailing off the edge into oblivion. She managed, however, to escape disaster long enough to correct her course and finally came skidding to an abrupt stop at the base of the steep hill.

It was still a fairly long run to reach her goal but after a ride like that one she was pumped up with adrenalin and ready to go. She stood up, found her bearings and sprinted off at her full, lightning pace.

Greenery screamed. His skin was burning and had been for several seconds when a cold splash of water brought him back to his senses. The pain eased up considerably but still remained sharp enough to keep him terrified of the immediate future.

He looked up to see who had thrown the water and was surprised to see Ignatius Trump towering over him.

'Do forgive Hector, Mr Jackson. He does like his fun and I suppose he has illustrated a point very nicely for us. Did that hurt, Mr Jackson?'

'Yes.'

'Did that hurt a lot, Mr Jackson?'

'Yes,' answered Greenery, trying desperately not to cry.

'Would you please tell your friend as much.'

Greenery looked over at Night Light who was staring at him with tears in his eyes.

'That hurt a lot, Night Light.'

'I know, lad,' was all he managed in reply. His voice was barely a whisper. As he spoke it cracked with suppressed emotion.

'Good. I'm glad we all agree because you, Mr Light, are about to go swimming.'

'No.'

'Oh yes. That cage is surrounded by a compressed morphic-resonance field so no pesky shape-shifting for you. No, no. You . . . are going into the boiling pus-tar. I may dip you in all the way to your eyeballs or perhaps I'll stop at your ankles and just deep-fry your feet. I'll let you know when I decide, shall I?'

With that Ignatius walked over to a small control panel on the wall and pushed a button. The runners on the ceiling began humming loudly as they kicked into life. Slowly Night Light's cage began to move towards the smoking, bubbling, boiling cauldron.

Towelyn was close to the Cecephelophopus when she stopped suddenly. Something about it felt strange; nothing she could put her finger on just an odd feeling of familiarity. She took a couple of steps closer and strained her eyes. On the back of the animal was some webbing, the remains of a harness that had once held a travelling trunk perhaps. Suddenly the Disco Beast flashed a vibrant pink colour and, with the change, hundreds of small scars were clearly visible all over its hide. She could also make out a maroon blazer tangled in the webbing.

'Sheba!'

Towelyn sprinted.

Seconds later she was standing next to the Disco Beast, breathing heavily and gently stroking her soft pelt.

'What are you doing here, you beautiful, beautiful creature?'

Towelyn gently stroked and patted the animal. She was thinking fast, all the pieces slotting into place.

'Are you still linked? Did he call you?'

Click.

'But how would he know where? . . . The Tear!'

Click.

'And that means . . . if you're here . . .'

Clunk.

'Oh that stupid, stupid boy.'

She walked around Sheba so that her face was right up against the animal's gentle dish of an eye.

'Listen, girl, I need you to find him. He's here somewhere, isn't he? And I bet he's in trouble. Come on, girl, show me you can do it.'

She leapt up onto the back of the fluorescent-pink Disco Beast, grabbed the reins and accelerated away from Ben Nevis.

When they were approximately three kilometres clear of the rotting corpse they stopped dead. Turning slowly in mid-air the intelligent Disco Beast began to sense what her rider was planning.

As they pivoted through a hundred and eighty degrees her skin changed to a camouflage pattern of flaming orange and the deepest black of night. The front of her body morphed into a razor-sharp arrowhead and became hard like the shell of a sea creature. Sheba was ready for battle.

Nestled in behind the barb of the great arrow Towelyn dug her heels into the flank of the beast and yelled at the top of her voice, 'Cecephelophopus Cecephefindhimmust!'

'No, don't! Please! Please, don't do it!'

Night Light's cage was moving ever closer to the vat of boiling, sticky oil. He was almost directly over it. Greenery was desperately shouting and screaming, trying to get the marble troll to stop. The little Punster seemed to be in some kind of shock. He just stood still like a statue staring at the cauldron beneath him.

'Oh I'm sorry, I'm afraid I can't do that. You see I need you to tell me where the Armies of Sorrow is and unfortunately you haven't, so I'm going to boil your friend.'

'You can't, please, don't!'

The cage was now right over the top of the bubbling mess.

Ignatius walked back to the control panel and pressed another button. The cage started to descend.

Night Light's face was drawn and pale. Greenery knew that whatever the outcome of today he would be haunted by that look for the rest of his life.

'Stop!' he yelled. 'I'll do it, I'll do it.'

Ignatius pressed the stop button and the noise of the mechanism ceased. The room seemed very quiet. All that could be heard was the incessant bubbling coming from the yellow tar.

'I'm waiting.'

Greenery closed his eyes tight and focused all of his attention on the Armies of Sorrow.

Sheba and her passenger were travelling towards Ben Nevis at an immense speed. The Disco Beast had streamlined her entire body and had never looked more graceful. Towelyn was holding on for dear life and was just wondering if she had made a mistake when the moment of impact came.

The sharp tip of Sheba's front cone bore into the soft rotting flesh of the corpse like a chainsaw through jelly. With her jet propulsion system working at one hundred per cent and travelling at top speed, nothing within the makeup of the enormous cadaver could hold back the living bullet. Bone, sinew, muscle and fat, Sheba was truly unstoppable.

Greenery's eyes snapped open.

'There is a cave, on the shore of a Lake of Blood. In front of the cave sits an old man in tarnished armour. Next to the cave is a row of six slender trees. Each tree is made entirely of something precious – ruby, emerald, diamond, opal, silver and gold. A road runs to the entrance of the cave. It is a road of bones. Inside the cave on an altar of fire sits the Armies of Sorrow.'

The description came out in one long breath with no emotion. It seemed as though his voice was being poured through him from an outside source. The cage-carrying machinery was still and silent. Ignatius and Night Light were staring at him open-mouthed but still the tar bubbled away as a constant reminder of how close to death they were.

Greenery looked Ignatius right in the face and in a much quieter voice, one of a small frightened boy, simply asked:

'Will you please let my friend go now?'

Ignatius looked from one prisoner to the other then smiled. It was not a pleasant smile.

'Ah yes, I believe we did have a deal, didn't we? Now let me think: should I let you go? No. I don't think I will.'

Trump's fist moved with that same terrible speed as before and slammed into a large red button on the wall. The mechanical claw fixing the cage to the track opened with a snap. Night Light screamed.

It seemed to Greenery as if the next few seconds happened

in slow motion. Unable to move, he saw it all unfold right before him. The wall of the torture chamber exploded inwards in a giant soggy mass of flesh as a huge orange-and-black cone came bursting through it. The very tip of this cone hit Ignatius Trump in the centre of his back, sending him flying forwards, directly into Night Light's cage as it fell. The small prison was knocked clear of the vat of boiling oil and landed in a mangled heap in the corner. Ignatius Trump was not so lucky. He fell headfirst into the thick sticky, mess.

Whilst Greenery was still in shock, and even before the Disco Beast had stopped moving, a furry shadow dived off its back and freed him in a second. It wasn't until she screamed in his face, that Greenery realised it was Towelyn.

'Go, what are you waiting for? Move!'

She moved across the room like liquid, as she pulled a sword from the sheath on her back. With one stroke she broke the cage door and freed Night Light. Not even waiting to see if he was hurt she lifted him easily onto her shoulder and sprinted back towards Sheba. Greenery was just getting in place as she sat down beside him.

'Hold on to him for me. I've got to fly this thing. Yah!'

She urged the beast onwards. The acceleration of these animals was incredible. In an instant they went from stationary to vertical rocketing motion. As they ploughed upwards through the corpse, erupting from its stomach like a huge alien parasite, Greenery was sure he heard a strangled cry of rage from the parboiled leader of the Violents.

'You're dead, Greenery Jackson, you and your friends. Dead!'

Chapter Fourteen

Fight or Flight

If someone has a question that's burning deep inside them,
Isn't it a shame when the answer is denied them?
But maybe this knowledge isn't totally forbidden,
Perhaps it's just inside them, and is simply staying hidden.

> Taken from *The Codex Imaginarium*
> by the Mysterious Wandering Gump

Gloria Jackson was back on her favourite bench in front of the old abandoned theatre watching the sunset over Littleton Bay. The last time she had been here there had been a gaping emptiness inside her that longed for her son. Now that hole was full with a burning rage. That man, that school, they had her son or at least knew where he was. The scratches on her face and head left by Take-That the cat were stinging but that was nothing compared to the pain of not knowing whether her boy was dead or alive.

Mrs Jackson was disturbed from her thoughts by someone sitting down next to her. She turned to ask the stranger politely for some space and was surprised to see that it was Mr Johnson. He was looking at her calmly and kindly as if they were old friends, not people who had been fighting only hours earlier. He had a large plaster across his nose.

'It is nice here, isn't it? Calm. I can see why you like it. I do always find the sound of the ocean so soothing.'

Gloria studied him for a long time before speaking. He was still smiling. Not in a patronising or malicious way but genuinely smiling at her. His eyes looked soft and kind, if a little watery.

'Unless you're here to tell me where my son is, Mr Johnson, I don't think we have anything to say to each other, do you?'

He looked down at his feet and chuckled softly to himself.

'The truth of the matter is I don't know where your son is. Oh I know how he got there and I know what it's called but I don't know where that place is, not really.' He sighed deeply before continuing. 'I'm not an evil man, Mrs Jackson, though I'm sure right now you must think of me as such. I'm not. I am, however, a coward. I'm an old, old man, Gloria, and I don't want to die.

'When a man came to me twelve years ago and said he could hold back death with a potion of his own making, naturally I was intrigued. In return for immortality all I had to do was keep him safe and comfortable until the time was right for him to go home. Well, it seems that time is now.

'He was a very hard man to say no to. He had a certain power about him, a hypnotic quality that made doubting or denying him impossible. But then again you already knew that, didn't you, Mrs Jackson?'

'What?'

She looked at Mr Johnson, confused by his direct question.

His milky blue eyes were staring right into her own and seemed to suggest he knew more than he was letting on.

He tipped his head downwards and forwards as if to shift her attention that way. Sitting on the floor in front of the bench, and staring at her just as intently, was Take-That the cat.

Gloria found she couldn't look away from the creepy feline. There was something hypnotic and mesmerising about it. She felt as if she were falling deep into its eyes.

It was then that she noticed they were glowing, bright and sharp and green. In fact, it wasn't just its eyes; the whole cat was aglow with all sorts of iridescent colours. Strange undulating lights streamed from its body and several transmogrified into a dense gas. Gloria watched in amazement as its body started to break down, to evaporate right before her eyes into a glowing swirling cloud of mist and flashing lights.

The sea breeze that was blowing against her face didn't seem to be affecting this peculiar cloud at all. It began swirling around, forming a small spout like that of a tornado. Faster and faster it spun until the lights became one mass of colour. The mini-twister flashed from red, to blue to bright blinding white. Gloria had to lift her hand to shield her eyes from the overbearing brightness. When she lowered it again she almost fell off the bench with shock.

Standing in front of her, looking quite calm and composed, was a tall thin man wearing an elegant pinstripe suit. His mess of bright-orange hair stood out against the darkening horizon like a furry sunset.

'Lazarus!?'

'Hello, Gloria. Sorry about those scratches; I might have been a little overzealous before. I couldn't have you upsetting William here. I do rely on him for so much, don't I, William?'

Mr Johnson looked up at Gloria. 'He does, yes. Now, if you will excuse me, I believe you two have some catching up to do.' And with that he stood up, gave a small bow to Mrs Jackson, and left. Gloria watched him leave in stunned silence before turning back to Lazarus. A million thoughts all clamoured at once for her attention.

'But how did you . . . Where did . . . Lazarus, what the hell is going on here?'

'Yes, I imagine this must all be a bit confusing. Let me explain.'

'Where's Greenery?'

'Greenery? Oh I haven't the foggiest idea. He'll be in The Other Place somewhere running around and having all sorts of adventures, I don't doubt. That is, if he's still alive – it can be quite a dangerous sort of place – but I imagine he is. He's quite a resourceful little chap, isn't he?'

'What are you talking about, what other place? . . . You're a cat!!'

Lazarus Brown turned to look out to sea. He rested on the promenade railing and took in several large gulps of fresh salty air. He looked for all the world like a holidaymaker out for a stroll – except for one thing. William Johnson had been right about Lazarus when he said he was hard to resist. This incongruous-looking man had the confidence and charisma of a world leader. His aura was the size of a football stadium and he wore it like a summer jacket – effortlessly.

'Yes, the cat thing is a bit odd, isn't it. I'll explain why the disguise was necessary shortly but don't worry about it. It's just a question of multiphasic carbon manipulation across varying fluid polymers. Child's play really.'

'Oh,' was all she could manage.

'Here's the bad news though, old girl. I'm afraid I'm the villain, the bad guy, the boogie man if you will. You see I'm not from around here as you've probably worked out by now. I'm from another place, *The* Other Place, and I did some bad things while I was there. Very bad things. Things so bad in fact that they asked me to leave – well forced me to. I believe technically it was a war. I killed several thousand people, lost count actually, but I'm told it was a lot. Anyway my snivelling do-good brother created an ingenious little key that opened a doorway to here.

'As I was forced through said doorway I worked a little trickery of my own and managed to pull the key through with me. I am, after all, a genius you know. Fantastic, I thought, get home build up some new weapons, slaughter a few more races and take control for good. Unfortunately that sneaky little sod had engineered the key so that it would only work if operated by someone from both worlds. Sneaky, you see, because no one like that exists anywhere do they, or rather *didn't* exist anywhere.'

'I think I see where this is going.'

'Yes but it's a great story, so do shut up, there's a good woman. Well, there you were, young, buxom, beautiful. I knew that in order to make the key work I would need a progeny and you, my dear, dear sweet child, were the pick of the bunch in this little place you call home. It wasn't that bad; we had fun, didn't we?'

'I had the best three years of my life until you disappeared, leaving me alone with a newborn baby. I was in love with you.'

'Yes, well, I'm not the working kind. Babies and wives need money. I was pretty sure you could fend for yourself. Like I said, dear, I'm the villain. Do pay attention, there's a good girl.

'Anyway I did a little research. Who in this godforsaken place has the easiest most luxurious life? Turns out it's these cat things you're all so fond of. They practically rule you. Well, I thought, it seems a great way to spend my years in waiting, and will make an excellent disguise in case dear old brother sends anyone out here to finish me off. You know, just in case. Flash forward twelve years and here we all are.'

'So what happens now?'

'I'll be honest with you, old girl, I don't exactly know. Our stupid son has messed everything up. You see I was waiting for the right time to return, waiting for the Seven Stars of . . . no, I don't think I'll voice that thought. The Gump hears everything, even here.'

'What are you talking about?'

'The point is, that little git found the key and went straight through the door before I had a chance to go with him. Well, I'll have to kill him just for being so thick-headed. I do have an idea though. Now that the key is back in The Other Place there is a little trick I can do. But I need some blood.'

'Blood? Whose?'

'Yours actually.'

He laughed. It was harsh and humourless. It was laughter made of bitterness, of spite, and the evil of this man dripped through its tones like a story trickles through time. As it died away whatever spell he held over Gloria vanished. She stood up and ran. She managed two and a half steps before she froze in suspended animation.

Lazarus was singing. It was the strangest sound Gloria had ever heard. There were multiple tones and melodies within his song, each one overlapping the others to form strange harmonics that she could feel resonating throughout her body. The vibrations caused by his song had forced her into paralysis.

He walked over to her calmly, still singing his strange song. As he came into her line of sight she could see that he was holding some headphones. He placed them on her head. The last thing she remembered was his multi-tracked voice filling her world.

It was pitch-black when Sheba finally touched down. They were in a heavily wooded area. The ground was damp and it was getting cold.

'Where are we?' Greenery asked Towelyn.

'I don't know, but we're a long way from Scumlumpia. We should be safe here.'

'*Should* be,' Night Light muttered to himself.

He had barely spoken a word since they blasted their way out of Ben Nevis. Greenery was worried about him.

Towelyn produced a small pot of cream from one of her embarrassing pockets that Greenery didn't like to think about. When she handed it to him he noticed that it looked surprisingly bright in the cold moonlight.

'It's concentrated Dragon's milk, like the stuff I gave you in Big Tree only much more potent. Rub some on your nose, head and chest, then, if you don't mind, would you do my back for me? Those Snowlar Bears left their mark.'

Greenery did as he was told and felt the benefits almost straight away.

'Do you want some, Night Light?' he asked.

'No, thanks. I'm fine.'

It didn't take long before Towelyn had a fire going. Her camping and survival skills were, of course, excellent. Greenery and Night Light sat huddled together watching the flames dance as she hurriedly built them a shelter. He found it difficult, almost painful, to think back on the day's events. He couldn't believe he had woken up just that morning on a fluffy bed of clouds as he and the Vapours drifted over Macadamia. In just one day he had witnessed unimaginable cosmic beauty and terrible, landlocked horror. How sad, he thought, that one would always remind him of the other.

Even after the Dragon's milk, the burns on his chest were still hurting. He guessed they would for some time. His body ached from the labours of the day and his head still felt like it was being used as a percussion instrument. From the look of Night Light he was in pain too. He had cut himself quite badly as his cage flew across the cell and he kept clutching his head. Towelyn seemed unhurt and totally nonplussed by the day's events. All in the life of a fearless Djinditsu, thought Greenery.

With her shelter finished, Towelyn called the boys over. All three of them climbed in and snuggled up together on the pile of leaves that had been dried by the fire. Sheba took up a defensive position in front of the entrance in the form of a large boulder, her skin tone matching the surrounding rocks exactly. With this extra protection Greenery felt safe enough to drop off and was asleep before you could say sle . . .

Back within the bowels of Ben Nevis Ignatius Trump was steaming, literally. As the remnants of the sticky oil cooled, a thin haze of toxic-smelling steam rose gently off his marble skin. It's very hard to burn a man who's made of stone. It's almost impossible. His colour had changed though. The deep burgundy tone seemed redder and looked a little enflamed. The veins of white that ran throughout his body looked pink and puffy. He was in considerable pain. Several of his most caring disciples were nursing him back to health by fanning him and splashing cold water on the particularly sore patches.

'I hate that boy. I hate him.'

'Yes, Sir, I know you do.'

'What's your name, soldier?'

'Pentangle, Sir. I'm your valet. I have been for the past three years, Sir. We talk every day.'

'Oh yes that's right. Sorry, Pentangle.'

As the little minion bent over to fill his cup with more water, Ignatius Trump pulled a sword from a secret compartment in the arm of his chair and sliced Pentangle clean in two.

'That helped relieve my stress a little. Thank you, Pentangle. You!'

'Me, Sir?'

'Yes, you. What's your name?'

'Stuff, Sir.'

'Your name is Stuff?'

'Yes Sir.'

'What a ridiculous name!' He sighed deeply. 'Oh well. Stuff, you're my new valet. Go and prepare Embrillion for take-off. I think it's time we all went on a little journey. We'll leave first thing in the morning.'

Greenery woke from a deep sleep to the smell of something amazing. It was one of those smells that bypasses the nose completely and heads straight for the stomach. He realised he was starving.

He stuck his head out of the makeshift shelter which was still wonderfully warm and scanned the campsite. It was a glorious spot. They were on the rise of a small bluff, with a stunning woodland view. A rocky path nearby led to a fast-flowing honey-coloured river of goo. The trees were of the bizarre and beautiful kind so typical of Other Place flora and the rainbow-coloured foliage was dazzling in the morning sun. They seemed to be high up in a mountain range. The air had that crisp, high-altitude bite to it

Sheba was nowhere in sight but he knew she must be close by, probably disguised as a tree or something similar. Towelyn was cooking over an open fire. There were two large fish and three unfortunate-looking birds roasting over the flames on wooden skewers. Night Light was sitting as close to the food as possible without getting burnt. He was practically dribbling. His eyes never left breakfast for a moment. Not even when he called out to Greenery.

'Morning, sleepyhead. Thought we'd let you catch some more zeds; we've got a long day ahead of us. How you feeling?'

'That Dragony cream stuff is amazing; I feel loads better, thanks.'

This was true. A full night's sleep and the promise of a

good breakfast had really lifted his spirits. Waking up in such idyllic surroundings hadn't hurt either. Whatever the reason, it had clearly worked its magic on Night Light too. He seemed much more like his old self. I guess we all deal with troubles in our own way, thought Greenery.

'What we having then?' he asked, sitting down next to Night Light.

Towelyn pointed. 'Those are red herrings and that's wild goose. They are not easy to chase, let me tell you, so you better enjoy them.'

'They smell delicious.'

'They are,' said Night Light, inching even closer to the fire.

Breakfast was served on large porcelain leaves and they drank cold mountain honey water from cups made of bark. It was amazingly good.

Eventually the hearty breakfast was over and the conversation turned to a more serious note. Towelyn was restless. She paced up and down as she spoke.

'OK, it seems from what Night Light has told me that Ignatius Trump knows where the Armies of Sorrow is. Or at least has enough information to find it.'

'Yeah, look, I'm sorry I . . .'

'Greenery, it's OK. You don't have to apologise. You were in an impossible situation and you acted out of compassion. Never apologise for that.'

'Yeah but . . .'

'Listen, lad, you saved my life. You bought us enough time. Don't say sorry or feel bad. It's OK. No one blames you. Let it go. OK?'

'OK.'

'Good.' The little man slapped Greenery on the shoulder and gave it a reassuring squeeze.

'Night Light's right; you shouldn't feel bad. However, the question remains what do we do?'

'We find it,' said Greenery, 'we beat him to it and we destroy it.'

There was no sense of a question or doubt in his voice. It was a flat statement of fact that no one could argue with. Towelyn and Night Light exchanged a meaningful glance that lasted just a moment too long.

'What?'

'We were hoping you'd feel that way but, well it's only fair to tell you . . .' Night Light stopped unsure or unable to finish the sentence.

'What, Night Light? What are you trying to tell me?'

Night Light reached into his bag and brought out the key. Its golden surface reflected the morning light and shone like a second sun.

'If you want to go home right now . . . we'll understand.'

Greenery didn't move. He simply stared. Transfixed by the beauty of the key and the promise of what it meant. Home. He was beginning to think it was a place he'd never see again, yet here was his ticket right before him. He slowly reached out and gently took it from Night Light.

'It's real,' he gasped as he felt how solid it was in his hands. 'How?'

'That evil so-and-so dropped it. Didn't want it, did he? He had his mind on bigger things, like genocide. I managed to swipe it off the floor just before he knocked me out. Never underestimate the little guy.'

Greenery stood up and walked a short way off. He stood with his back to the fire, staring down at the key in his hand.

'No.'

'No, what?' Towelyn and Night Light asked in unison.

'I can't go home. Not yet. I stand by what I said a moment ago.' He turned back to face them. 'We have to stop him getting his hands on that weapon. If he does, thousands will die. I can't go back with that on my conscience.'

Night Light's smile lit up the camp almost as much as the key had. 'You're a good'n you are.'

'Thank you,' said Towelyn.

Greenery came back to sit by the fire. There was a different vibe about the camp now; it felt lighter again. Even Towelyn seemed more at ease. She stopped pacing and came to sit by Greenery.

'I tell you what,' said Night Light, 'that marble fella's gonna be right angry now. If we do this, chances are we're gonna end up against all of them Violents. The whole blinkin' lot of them.'

'We're already up against all of them,' said Greenery.

'But we've never faced them all at once,' said Towelyn. 'There are three of us and thousands of them. I can only fight so many.'

'How many can you fight?'

'What?'

'What's the most people you've fought at once and won?'

'I don't know. I've never kept count, ten maybe twelve if they were slow and untrained.'

'And are you exceptional or are all the Djinditsu as skilled as you?'

She snorted. 'Exceptional? Hardly! Some of the elders of my tribe could beat me in a heartbeat. I'm good for my age but I'm still training, Greenery. We train our whole lives.'

Greenery had that look about him again. Whenever his brain started working on an idea his whole face lit up. His eyes shone brighter and his body seemed to fizz with pent-up energy.

'How many Djinditsu are there, Towelyn?'

'Not as many as there used to be,' she said with genuine sadness in her voice.

'But roughly, numbers?'

'Several hundred.'

'Would they come, if they were called? Would they stand against the Violents?'

'Every single one. They would fight to the death to protect The River from the threat of evil.'

'Well, we could . . .'

'But we're so spread out, Greenery. Part of the reason for that is we've been looking for their base of operations for so long. Until you saw it with the Tear no one knew where it was. Most of the Djinditsu are at least several weeks' travel from here and I have no way of contacting them, let alone getting them to wherever they would need to be. It's a nice idea, Greenery, but forget it. We're alone.'

'You let me worry about getting them there. You just get us to the weapon in one piece. Anyway I think I have an idea.'

Scumlumpia is at its worst at dawn. This is the shift change. It's the time of day when the creatures of the night are scurrying home to their beds tired and hungry after a night of fighting for their lives, and the boys and girls of the daytime shift are waking up in a bad mood, hungry and ready for breakfast. The noise is atrocious – growls, snurts, screams, grumps, harumphs and wails. You actually have to shout to make yourself heard.

This is the time of day when the Slithy Toves do gyre and gimble in the wabe. They're one of the region's only tourist attractions.

Later, as the sun warms up the morning scum, a greenish-black mist ascends to cloud the swamp floor. The whole pit becomes a mess of murderous squirming.

Within this smoky carnage one animal stands alone, a creature whose very presence brings a terrified silence to the subordinates thrashing about on the swamp floor below – Embrillion, the carriage of choice for Ignatius Trump.

This typical gore-filled Scumlumpia morning preparations were underway for the journey ahead. Weapons, food and cases of a strong, bitter alcohol called Twerpentine were being stowed in the massive trunks strapped to Embrillion's worm-like back. Stuff, the new valet to Ignatius Trump, was overseeing the laborious work.

The fact that he was a large snail had been a huge disappointment to Stuff all his life. It's hard being cool when you leave a trail of slime behind you and are terrified of salt. Even painting his shell jet-black and covering it in shocking-pink tattoos hadn't helped with his severe lack of street cred. Eventually his desire to fit in had led him to the Violents where he had made his home amongst the other dejected misfits. The loading was not going well.

'Hurry up! Come on, come on! You there – stop messing

about with that man's head. Yes, I know it's detachable, but he needs it so he can work, doesn't he?

'Oi, you! The Twerps goes in the other box. Glass bottles cannot be transported safely in a case full of swords, can they?

'Stop! That man there . . . yes you. Don't kill that. It's called livestock for a reason. Just put it back in its cage and leave it alone . . . I don't care if it bit you . . . Well you've got fourteen more fingers, I don't think you'll miss just one.'

'Ah, Stuff, how goes it?'

It is incredible how quietly Ignatius Trump can move, considering he's three metres tall and made of stone. He had walked up behind Stuff without making a single sound, which was why the little valet screamed like a girl and dropped his list of provisions.

'Arrgh! Oh, er, well, Sir. We are just loading the last of the cargo on board now, Sir. The men are all waiting just inside Ben Nevis and are ready to embark. We could be on our way within ten minutes if you so desire, Sir.'

'Ten minutes?'

'Yes . . . Sir?'

'You have done well, Stuff. We will be off as soon as you give the all-clear.'

The dithering gastropod gave a huge sigh of relief before slithering off to finish the job in hand.

Ignatius stood still and surveyed the scene. It felt good watching the hustling mob, knowing that it was all under his command. Moving with a purpose was important. For so long he had felt trapped, like a weak, sickly little thing in a doctor's waiting room, waiting for Lazarus Brown to turn up and cure him. But now with the chance of finding the Armies of Sorrow he could take control once more, be the leader he had always wanted, and felt destined to be. With the ultimate weapon he would be the ultimate warrior and even Lazarus Brown would have to bow down before him.

'Sir!'

Ignatius turned to see Stuff grovelling before him.

'What?'

'We're ready when you are, Sir.'

He looked deep into the eyes of his valet. All he saw there was fear. Fear and loyalty. Just as he liked it.

'Excellent stuff, . . . Stuff. '

'Greenery!'

'What?'

'Come on, lad, we're ready when you are.'

'Oh right, sorry.' Greenery put down the stick he'd been using to investigate the massive weird insect he'd found. 'Where's Sheba?'

'See that bridge down there where Towelyn's standing?'

'Yes. Is she under that? Doesn't look like she'll fit?'

'She *is* that. Come on.'

They wandered down to the small humpback bridge. It wasn't until they were almost upon it that Greenery could see how Sheba had contorted herself into the desired shape. Her skin, the tone and texture of weathered pine, flickered for a moment to a bright lime-green as all three of them stepped onto her. A moment later she stretched, flexed and uncoiled smoothly, so that the trio ended up sitting comfortably on her back.

As the last of the Violents took their place on the back of the colossal worm the gangplanks were withdrawn and the tethers that held her huge head in place were cut. The grizzly juggernaut unfurled her mighty wings and gave a couple of experimental beats, creating a huge downdraft that knocked over several of the ground crew. A hush fell over the assembled masses as everyone waited for the word of command.

'Mush!' Greenery shouted with a sudden burst of energy.

'Onwards!' Ignatius Trump roared from his head-top throne.

At exactly six thirty-eight in the morning (Earth, Greenwich Mean Time) two creatures separated by a great distance yet joined by one goal took off into the air. One sailed high like a graceful shuttlecock, the other dragged itself skywards with heavy strokes of its massive wings.

The two parties flew off in opposite directions, even though they both had the same destination. Neither one knew where their journey would end but both had very different ways of finding out. The race to reach the Lake of Blood had begun.

Chapter Fifteen

Hide and Seek

DeoxyriboNucleic Acid,
Came from primordial soup.
Does mankind know to make them from it,
We used an ice-cream scoop?
> Taken from *A Practical Guide to Creating Existence*
> by the Mysterious Wandering Gump

As soon as they were high enough Greenery drew his worm-hole gun and fired it dead ahead. The spiralling rift appeared immediately and Sheba, who was quite familiar with the drill by now, barrelled on through without a moment's hesitation.

They came out of the other side expecting to be directly above the Lake of Blood. They were not.

Below them instead was a pack of wild animals. They were the size and shape of large robust dogs but were made entirely out of blood. As they charged across the barren landscape of Rockmoor they left a deep-red stain on the craggy wilderness.

'Blood Hounds,' shouted Night Light above the blustering wind. 'Where's the lake?'

'I don't know. Maybe the coincidence ring just mis-hit. I don't suppose it can be right every time.'

'I have a bad feeling about this,' said Towelyn.

'Oh well, on we go,' shouted Greenery, as he fired the gun again.

Another burst of light. Another flash. Another location. This time below them was a sprawling metropolis. The people seemed to be getting on with the hustle and bustle of their everyday lives. The entire city was made of twenty-four-carat gold. From this altitude the place shimmered in the morning sun and looked blindingly opulent.

'This is Eldorado,' announced Towelyn, 'I think there is something wrong with the coincidence ring. Two mis-hits in a row is odd.'

Greenery looked down at the ring on his finger. It didn't look any different from yesterday. Towelyn was right though; it did seem to be less accurate than usual.

'Let's try again,' she said.

This time they emerged from the wormhole above a forest of birch trees. They were obviously silver birches as each one was made of solid sterling silver.

'You're right, I think,' said Greenery. 'Something must be wrong. Let's set down and I'll try and find the Lake of Blood using the Tear.'

One textbook landing later they were standing in a small clearing surrounded by the solid metal trees. As the other two dismounted, Greenery made himself comfortable against a silver trunk, closed his eyes and tried to visualise the place they were looking for.

The vision came clearly and easily to him just as it had last time. There was the lake, the cave and the six precious trees. This time, however, the old man in tarnished armour, who lived near the cave, seemed to be the focus of his attention. He stood out against the background, making it hard to concentrate on any other detail. He was sitting on the floor outside his little ramshackle hut and was meditating. He was surrounded by a bright-blue aura. His eyes snapped open and it seemed to Greenery as though he looked straight at him – no, through him. He smiled and spoke one word quietly yet forcefully:

'No.'

Until now Greenery had never heard sound in his visions. His sight winked out like a television set turning off and he was back in the wood. If he had not been sitting, he would have fallen over from the shock of returning so quickly.

He tried again. This time it took all his effort to make the vision appear. When it finally came into focus all he could see was the old man. The harder he tried to focus on other details the closer his point of view came to the aged guard. His eyes seemed so sharp and piercing. Greenery felt as if they measured him, judged him for who he really was. It was quite a spooky feeling. The man in the tarnished armour was still smiling when he spoke again; this time, however, his voice was much more forceful.

'Pushy one, aren't we? I've told you once: NO!'

Even though the words were only from a vision in Greenery's head, they seemed to act upon him physically, throwing him out of his trance. He came to with such force that he actually screamed a little at the suddenness of the bright daylight.

'That looked interesting,' said Towelyn sardonically, standing a few feet away and leaning on a sturdy silver birch.

'What happened, lad?' asked Night Light. He was genuinely concerned.

'I don't know. That old guard seems to be blocking my sight. He knew I was watching him and wouldn't let me see where he was. I wonder if he's somehow blocking the coincidence ring's power as well.'

'He could be,' answered the Djinditsu. 'He must be there for a reason and one man wouldn't be much good against an invading army. Perhaps his main purpose is to stop invaders getting there in the first place.'

'So how do *we* get there then?'

'The old-fashioned way,' said Night Light who looked surprisingly happy.

'Which is?' asked Greenery.

'Local knowledge. Let's not start from here though. Let's get that ring of yours to take us as close as it can without old misery guts voodoo bloke interfering with its mojo. Then let's see what we can do with a friendly word and maybe a favour or two.'

With no other options at hand, the three of them climbed up onto the back of the Disco Beast (whose skin was showing an old black-and-white film), flew up into the air and, with a quick flash, were gone.

Ignatius Trump was not having much luck in his search for the Lake of Blood either. He was currently standing in the middle of the town of Escrow, a small place full of beautiful luxury mansions. Everybody in Escrow was either a property developer, an estate agent, or a builder. The town, however, was currently on fire. Most of its inhabitants had fled and those that hadn't were either dead or injured. Ignatius was holding the Town Elder in his hands and repeatedly asking him questions between rock-hard slaps to the face. The man was bleeding heavily and was almost unconscious.

This was the third place the Violents had visited that morning. Their particular way of searching for the Armies of Sorrow was to land randomly somewhere, terrify the locals and interrogate a claw-picked few for information. The chances were none of them had any idea about the Lake of Blood, the Road of Bones or any trees made of precious metals and jewels. It was, as detective methods go, about as useful as trying to find a lost painting by shouting out colours to random passers-by.

Ignatius dropped the now-unconscious man to the floor in disgust and sighed deeply.

'Stuff!'

'Yes, Sir.'

'Ah there you are, Stuff. What kept you?'

'My slow-wittedness and useless character no doubt, Sir.'

'Good answer!' He sighed again. 'Now see here, Stuff, as you know, I enjoy random violence as much as the next man, but this isn't working. We need an improved search method.'

'Well Sir, we could always fly to Libraria. I'm told they have the only accurate atlas of The River in existence. It keeps itself up to date, Sir, as The Other Place grows.'

'Really, Stuff, and how does it do that?'

'Well, Sir, Libraria is a tiny island off the coast of the Descartes Plate. The atlas lies in the cellar of the Central Archive and is plugged directly into the potential energy of The River. It updates itself automatically every time something new is formed.'

'Tell me this though, Stuff. How can a book accurately map an infinite location?'

'Oh, it's not a book, Sir.'

'Interesting! Well done, Stuff, you have earned yourself a place in my good books – excuse the pun.'

'I wasn't aware you made one, Sir.'

'Tell me, how do you know all this stuff, Stuff?'

'My father was born there, Sir; he is a native Librarian.'

'I see, and how long do you think it will take us to reach the Descartes Plate?'

'Several days I should think, Sir.'

'Well, don't just stand there then, Stuff. Round up the men. We are going to Libraria.'

Mr Johnson, the head teacher of St Augustine's Secondary School, lives at number 8 Ubiquity Drive. It's a modest little semi-detached with three bedrooms and a nicely sized back garden. Underneath the garage someone, possibly the crazed ex-dictator of an otherworldly location, has built a massive secret bunker. This is reached by a small trapdoor underneath the Flymo which leads to a spiral staircase that in turn leads to a cavernous workspace that was dug out using deflageration techniques which are almost unknown on planet Earth.

In a dark corner of the laboratory Gloria Jackson was hanging unconscious in mid-air. There were no visible means of suspension, which made her look like a human helium balloon. There were several tubes coming from various veins and one particular intravenous passageway that led across the lab to a workbench. A small but constant trickle of blood dripped from the end of this tube into a great glass labyrinth where it was boiled and filtered and tinkered with beyond all recognition.

Even the world's greatest doctors would have trouble recognising some of the apparatus and most people would be completely stumped. Bending over this myriad of glass piping, Lazarus Brown was working feverishly, as he had been ever since he had brought Mrs Jackson back here yesterday.

'Come on work, work,' he muttered to himself.

He was currently looking down a huge microscope at a sample of the plasma after it had been extensively fiddled with. It was barely recognisable as blood. It had lost all colour and didn't even look like a liquid anymore; it was thick and gloopy like jelly. As he examined it Lazarus prodded and poked it with a tiny pair of tweezers that were microscopically thin at the business end.

Suddenly his whole body tensed. He leant in closer to the microscope and froze for several seconds before revelling in a moment of ecstasy.

Upstairs in his living room Mr Johnson heard only the faintest echoes of celebration filter up from the secret laboratory below. He shifted in his chair and turned the volume up on *Hollyoaks*, feeling guiltier than he ever had before.

Back downstairs Lazarus finished his little celebratory dance and wandered over to the other side of his workshop. He took down a very similar-looking sample in a small glass jar. This one, however, was labelled Lazarus Brown. He then began the long process of mixing the two samples together to make a perfect DNA strain for one Greenery Frankincense Jackson.

Night Light was angry. It was quite unusual for the little man to lose his optimistic disposition but, after four whole days

214

of random wormhole landings and long questioning sessions with strangers who had no idea what any of them were talking about, his patience was wearing thin.

They had been zapping themselves all over The Other Place and no one had been any help whatsoever. Greenery was starting to think the coincidence ring was permanently broken.

Two days ago it had taken them to Libraria. Greenery would have felt much more confident about his invention had he known about the atlas. However, none of them had been there before and had no clue about the infinite map. The locals they spoke to hadn't thought to tell them about it either. It was very disheartening.

Now, they were out of ideas and had stopped for lunch on the outskirts of a picturesque little village located on the back of a fully grown Megawhale. As it swam majestically through the kaleidoscopic plasma of The River, Greenery despondently watched the towering cliff-face of a Plate cruise by on the horizon. Night Light was venting his anger by shouting wildly into the wind. Greenery couldn't tell what he was saying but, from some of the words he did pick out, he gathered it wasn't fit for polite conversation. Towelyn was sitting quietly eating something she had just killed. Morale was low.

The breeze coming from The River was quite chilly. Greenery went over to the Disco Beast to grab his school blazer for the first time in ages. As he picked it up from Sheba's back it felt heavier than it should. The extra weight, he realised, was coming from one of his pockets. He reached in and his hand closed around something cold and hard. He pulled it out. It was the snowless snow globe he had bought back in Big Tree. He'd forgotten all about his souvenir, although the memory of the ensuing kidnap was still frighteningly detailed. That seemed like a lifetime away now.

He put his blazer on and went to sit down with his back against a large barnacle. He sat there playing with the thing in his hand, not really paying it any attention when he suddenly stopped. He looked at it again – really looked.

There was a small ramshackle hut built at the entrance to a cave. Several trees that looked as if they were made of something shiny and artificial lined the decaying road that led up to this entrance. The whole scene was on the shoreline of a strange bright-red lake.

It was the Lake of Blood they had been desperately searching for! This had to be a sign; it had to mean something. He was just about to call the other two over when some movement within the globe caught his eye.

The guard came out of his hut. It was the old man in tarnished armour. He stood stock-still staring straight up at Greenery. Their eyes met and just as before, in the market place, Greenery felt as if he couldn't look away. He stared hard and felt like he was falling deeper and deeper into the old man's gaze. The little figure in the snow globe seemed to be growing, in fact the whole scene seemed to be growing – or was he, Greenery, getting smaller? It became harder to tell. As the miniature world filled his own, Greenery realised he was now walking up the last few metres of a long road of bones and was staring face to face with the old man who guarded the Armies of Sorrow.

The old man looked human. He could have been Mr Johnson's brother. His bright blue eyes were as sharp and as piercing as they had been when Greenery had tried to use the

216

power of the Cyclops Tear to see this place. He smiled and gestured for Greenery to sit on the floor next to the campfire in front of his raggle-taggle home. When the old man smiled, which he did often, his huge handlebar moustache rose and fell like a furry lifting bridge. He came and sat down at the fire, opposite Greenery. The tips of the flames flickered between their faces and realisation dawned.

'You're the man from the marketplace!'

'In the snow globe, yes.'

'No, the other man, the stallholder! That was you?'

'Yes, that was also me.'

'How?'

'If I told you that now, you would never understand. Things will become clear in time; they always do.'

'Yes but how could you . . .?'

'Greenery, why don't you ask The Mysterious Wandering Gump when you meet him? He'll be able to illuminate you.'

Greenery decided not to push the issue; he had become used to the bizarre and had more pressing matters to attend to anyway.

'Why am I here?'

'You're not here. You are sulking on the back of a Megawhale.'

'No, I mean what is the purpose of this conversation?'

The old man sat back and studied Greenery for some time before answering.

'I wanted to meet you. I know you want the weapon and I know why you want it, but I have to be absolutely sure you're the right person to find it.'

'Well, I'm trying to stop someone really bad getting his

hands on the Armies of Sorrow. If he does then hundreds maybe thousands will die as he tries to take control of The Other Place. Surely that's a good reason to find it.'

'But what will you do with it when you find it? Will you use it to kill the man who you claim will murder thousands? If you use it once you might use it again. And again. And again.'

'I don't want to use it. I want to destroy it. I just don't want Ignatius Trump to get his hands on it.'

'That's very noble of you, young man, but tell me: how did the most dangerous man in the whole of The Other Place learn the whereabouts of the most powerful weapon ever conceived?'

Greenery froze. This was the question he'd been dreading. It took all of his willpower to stop his voice from cracking as he answered the old man.

'I told him.'

'I see.'

'I told him where it was to save my own life and that of my friend.' Now that he had started talking Greenery couldn't stop. He felt he had to defend himself and his actions. 'I'm sorry, I really am, but I didn't have a choice. I was in a lot of pain and they were going to kill my friend in a really horrible way. But I think I can beat him, I think I can get an army too and I know we can win . . .'

The guard in the tarnished armour held up his hand for silence. He smiled again. A warm and friendly smile.

'Thank you for telling me the truth. On the Australopithecus Plate there is a place where three rivers converge on the small town of Triweir. Just outside Triweir is the start of the Road of Bones. Follow it. I'll be waiting for you, Greenery Jackson.'

There was no sensation of movement or even of waking up; Greenery suddenly found himself sitting on the cold windswept back of the giant Megawhale with the harsh breeze blowing in his face and the snow globe resting on his lap. He had absolutely no proof that the last few minutes had been anything other than a dream but he was convinced with every fibre of his being that it had been real. He stood up and called out to his friends.

'Towelyn, Night Light, come here I know where we're going!'

'... AND ANOTHER THING YOU CAN TAKE YOUR STUPID LAKE OF STUPID BLOOD AND SHOVE IT RIGHT UP YOUR ... What?'

'Calm down, Night Light. I said I know where we have to go. The old man just told me.'

'Greenery, are you feeling all right?' asked Towelyn as she wandered over to him.

'Yes I'm fine, listen ...' Greenery told them all about his experience and his conversation with the guard. Towelyn listened in silence but Night Light of course had to chip in with little comments and questions here and there. By the time Greenery had finished talking it was starting to get dark and it felt as if the Megawhale was getting ready to dive.

'What do you think?'

'Well, it's the best and only lead we have, so I say we should go and investigate regardless,' said Towelyn.

'I have complete faith in you, boy. If you say we go, we go. Good as gold. Come on, let's get a wriggle on.'

The three climbed up on Sheba's back and took off just as the Megawhale headed for the deep. As they began their journey to the Australopithecus Plate, Greenery looked behind to see one mighty fluke silhouetted against the setting sun. He turned and waved back, feeling more confident than he had in days.

Lazarus Brown was feeling more confident than he had in days. Who would have thought that manipulating and combining two DNA strains to make a genetic match for one precise person would be so difficult, even for a Technomancer like himself. But he was close now, agonisingly close.

He hadn't been outside once over the past few days. He'd had virtually no Whiskas or Go Cat, and the only company he'd had, had been the unconscious mother of his estranged love child.

He looked at her now, suspended in blissful ignorance of her current jeopardy. He had almost cared for her once. Even though he had only needed her for her offspring, he had felt something close to affection. But as soon as the irksome pest was born he found he lost interest in her. She was an expensive plaything, one that was far too costly for the meagre rewards she offered in return.

Then that stupid little brat had ruined everything by using the key prematurely. If he had only waited a few more months then the time would have been right. By the end of the year the Googoldome would be in alignment with the Seven Stars of Eden and only he knew how to harness their power. Then he could conquer The Other Place for good. Even The Mysterious Wandering Gump wouldn't be able to stop him this time.

Beep BeepBeep BeepBeep Beep

Lazarus was woken from his vengeful dreams by a small

tinny sound coming from his workbench. Here the two genetic soups he had been cooking up had been mixing and bonding together in the centrifuge. Now it would appear they were joined and ready for the final stage.

He carefully removed the mixture from its test tube and scooped it gently into the centre of a large Petri dish. To the casual observer it would have seemed odd placing a sample that small in a dish the size of a dog basket but Lazarus had his reasons.

Next he attached three chains round the edge of the heavy glass dish and winched the whole thing up and over to a large tank full of bright-blue, bubbling liquid. It was warm to the touch and smelt faintly of sulphur and marmite. As the Petri dish sank to the bottom of the tank the liquid clouded over to become a thick opaque aquamarine. The bubbling began in earnest.

Right, thought Lazarus, rubbing his hands together with the demeanour of a craftsman happy in his work, 'time for some Go Cat and a bowl of cream.'

Chapter Sixteen

Knowledge Is Power

I think therefore you are,
Is the truth of the matter.
You think therefore you eat
And that's why you're getting fatter.

Taken from *Unusual Truths* by
The Mysterious Wandering Gump

Libraria is a peaceful citadel made of shining white stone. Its lofty towers and intricate meandering lanes have been a cultural centre and a place of learning for centuries.

Every year hundreds of pilgrims make their way to the ancient schools and archives to become scholars and teachers. Most stay for a few years then return to their villages to pass on what they have learnt to the folks back home. Some, however, stay and become keepers of the ancient knowledge, leading a quiet life of dignified study. The greatest accolade of all, for a true Librarian, is to reach the title of Exalted Ring Binder. These lucky few have the honour of tending the ever-growing works of The Mysterious Wandering Gump which fill one whole wing of the Central Archive.

One day is pretty much like any other in Libraria and this

one seemed no different. The tinkling sound of falling water from one of the many fountains echoed through the streets. Below this was the gentle hum of serious and meaningful conversation and in the distance the sound of laughter came from some young Librarians playing in one of the public parks.

Suddenly a deafening scream shattered the delicate peace and a fierce downdraft filled the streets, throwing the town into chaos. Small children and the elderly were blown over and even the town's guardians were sent running for cover.

It was hard to make out through the dust clouds and flying debris what was causing the biting wind, but far above the tumbling detritus a huge monster was circling.

It dwarfed the citadel and with every beat of its wings a destructive gale was forced down upon the tiny town. There seemed to be things moving all over it.

Sitting on his throne carved into Embrillion's massive single horn, Ignatius Trump looked down at the chaos in Libraria.

'Well, it's far too small to land on,' he sighed. 'What a pity! I was rather looking forward to crushing the wretched little place.' He stood up and began pacing back and forth, clearly vexed about missing an opportunity to cause pain. 'I need that atlas!' His gait was steady but his mind was racing. After several furious thoughts he came to what was obviously a difficult decision.

'Pipistral!' he shouted towards the throng of waiting Violents, 'you know what to do.' Ignatius hated sending a minimum force; it meant very few people would die but he had no choice.

A woman almost as tall as Ignatius, though painfully thin,

stepped forward. 'Yes Sir, certainly, Sir.' Her voice sounded like chocolate dipped in a lie and she moved with an effortless grace that made her look smug and conceited.

Her face had the lupine features of a bat but she had no wings. She wore what looked like a large black cloak that upon closer inspection revealed itself to be a loose appendage of skin and fine bone.

She turned and shouted towards the back of Embrillion. Her Parabat sisters were never too far away.

'Radial, Spyro, Hubris, Sharon, it's our time to shine, girls.'

The four women that came forward looked almost identical to their leader. The only thing to distinguish them from each other was their bright primary-coloured clothing. They all moved with the same air of self-loving arrogance.

With barely a moment's pause to exchange knowing looks, the five women stepped off the side of Embrillion and began the descent to the helpless little island far below.

Just after gaining terminal velocity, Pipistral spread her arms out wide. All of the others in her team followed suit. As she arched her back dramatically her cloak-like appendage began flapping in the rushing wind. With a sharp lunge forward the fine bones that radiated out from her vertebrae extended. The cloak flipped upwards and inflated to many times its original size. She was now hanging from an organic parachute that was attached at her shoulders and the base of her spine. Her sisters had also opened their chutes successfully and were heading right for the centre of town.

The five Parabats landed elegantly in the central square of Libraria. They stood straight and tall as the scared citizens stared at them wondering what would happen next. The anorexic creatures sauntered around the square as if weighing up the situation. All five looked ready for a fight.

Pipistral, the leader spoke to the town:

'We want your atlas. Give it to us and we will go away and leave you fine people in peace. Deny us and you will all die.' She smiled. Her sharp fangs poked out from under her top lip, just enough to be threatening.

'Never!'

A wispy-haired old man, wearing a light-blue robe and sandals ran out from the crowd. He was pointing a long thin spear straight at Pipistral's heart. At the same time several other old gentlemen emerged through the crowd. There were ten of them in total, each one wearing the same blue robes and carrying an identical spear. Their combined age must have been close to a thousand. This was the town guard.

The Parabat sisters looked at each other in disbelief. They were clearly amused by the so-called threat.

'Bring it on, old man,' scoffed Pipistral, taunting the guard by beckoning him closer.

The fight did not last long. The home guard of Libraria were woefully outmatched. The men in blue were used to guarding books in a place where books were considered sacred. The most action they had seen in years was chasing a young misguided graffiti artist.

The sisters, on the other hand, were a combat-trained elite fighting unit. They had been battle-hardened over an extended campaign under one of the most ruthless leaders in the history of The Other Place.

They fought in a series of lightning-fast jerky movements. It was possible to see the start and end position of each manoeuvre but the action in-between was just too quick for the eye to follow.

Twelve point eight seconds later it was over. Five of the old men lay on the floor either groaning in pain or unconscious. The other five were each held by a Parabat and a small, very sharp knife was pressed against each of their throats. Again Pipistral was the spokesperson.

'Tell us where the atlas is or one after one these men die. Slowly and painfully.' There was no threat in her voice, just a simple statement of fact. Unfortunately it was met with complete silence from the square. Nobody dared move or speak. Fear can do funny things to people.

'Tell us!'

Nothing . . . Silence.

'Very well.' She grabbed her hostage firmly and pulled him towards her body with one arm; the other was flexed and about to plunge the knife deep into his throat . . .

'Wait!'

She froze. The point of her knife was piercing the wrinkled skin, causing a small drop of blood to trickle down the old guard's neck.

'I'll show you where The Atlas is.'

The town turned as one and parted to see Humboldt Stuff standing at the back of the square. He was well known around Libraria. His battered shell and sad old face had been one of the constant sights in the Central Archive for the past fifty years or so.

'At last! Someone with a bit of sense. Lead the way, Librarian, but don't try anything stupid. We still have our hostages.'

'Of course. Follow me, ladies.'

The eleven-strong group moved through the streets slowly and quietly. They had to move slowly; after all, they were being led by a large snail. The rest of the town followed at a safe distance, still terrified yet unable to look away from the unfolding drama.

As they entered the Central Archive, even the sisters were impressed. Its grand scale and imposing architecture was designed to make the most self-assured person feel small and insignificant. It was a grandiose structure of white coral sand-stone, shining glass and the purest green jade.

The Atlas was kept in a small web-encrusted catacomb below the public halls of the main building. It took them some time to reach it, and it was a tight squeeze fitting everyone inside the small space.

Sitting on a small pedestal in the middle of the room was a very large book. Its burgundy leather cover looked old and dusty. Emblazoned across the front of it, etched in gold, were the words: *Geographical Elements of the Infinite River.*

Pipistral stopped dead and pulled her hostage closer to her.

'What's going on here, Librarian? Is this some kind of trick. I was told The Atlas wasn't a book.'

'Oh it's not a book,' said Stuff.

'It *looks* like a book.'

'Yes, well looks can be deceiving.' He slithered over to the large tome and opened the front cover.

All five of the Parabats took a step back in surprise. The inside of the book was some kind of doorway or passage. A set of sturdy stone steps led down into the dark recesses of the peculiar volume. Pipistral walked all around the small pedestal to make sure this wasn't a trick or an optical illusion, but it was quite clear from all angles that the stairway led into the book and nowhere else.

'Lead the way, old man.'

Humboldt went first followed by the Parabats, and then by the majority of the town who were now more curious than ever. Most of them had waited their whole lives to see inside The Atlas.

At the bottom of the stairs was a simple-looking wooden door. The old snail opened it and ushered everybody through. They entered what appeared to be a gothic cathedral, so vast that the walls and ceiling were at the edge of sight. At the opposite end of the medieval immensity a strange pale light shone down through an enormous stained-glass window, giving the whole repository a heavenly feel. This cavernous space was full of row after row of shelves, each one too long to measure. They reached all the way up to the towering ceiling and were filled with filing cabinets.

Humboldt Stuff reached out to the nearest drawer and pulled hard. It opened easily and then opened some more and then some more. The drawer was impossibly long, and full of folders. There were thousands of them in this one cabinet alone.

'Every drawer here is full of these folders,' said Humbolt. 'Every single folder opens up to reveal a different staircase which leads down to an archive at least as big and just as full as this one. Every drawer within those secondary levels contains hundreds of thousands of pages of the great map. Oh and an entrance to an even larger third level and so on and so on. So every drawer you see here represents millions of depositories just like this one. I hope you know what page number you want because it'll take you a long, long time to go through all of them.'

'And how do I find out what page number I want? There must be a way or else all this information is useless.'

'There is a way.'

Pipistral put one arm on her hip and looked at the slimy archivist with new respect in her eyes.

'And what will this information cost me?'

'Nothing much, simply the fair exchange of knowledge. I want three questions answered and of course the safe release of everyone here.'

The Parabat bared her teeth in frustration and looked at Humboldt Stuff as though she was going to kill him, but it was clear she had no choice.

'Very well,' she snarled, 'ask your questions, old man.'

'Do you belong to a group of people calling themselves the Violents?'

'We do.'

'Are you aware of someone in your group who looks similar to me and has pink tattoos on his shell.'

'You mean Stuff. Yes.'

'He kept his name,' Humboldt muttered to himself in an anguished mixture of pain and pride. He managed to fight back bitter tears, then in a voice as soft as spider silk he asked his third question:

'Is he alive?'

The map thief tilted her head to one side and paused before answering. She looked deep into Humboldt Stuff's eyes and answered very slowly.

'Yes. He is.'

The relief on the face of the Librarian was visible and immediate. He looked as if the weight of the Big Tree itself had been lifted from his shoulders.

'Thank you, thank you very much.'

'Enough, old man, I'm not here to make friends. Tell me how I find my page number.'

'I don't know.'

'What do you mean, you don't know?'

'I'm a paper technician. I clean and repair the books. I'm not a Keeper of the Knowledge. I don't know.'

The Parabat's head rolled backwards and she let out a cry of agonised rage that echoed round the capacious church. In one lightning-fast second she sliced the throat of Humboldt Stuff.

'Kill them all!' she screeched as she turned on the watching crowd.

The townsfolk screamed and ran, most people tried to squeeze back up the narrow staircase and exit The Atlas but some scattered throughout the cathedral. The Parabats were a second away from making their first kill when a high-pitched voice broke through the panic and brought the vast room to a standstill.

'Tofindthepageyouwantyouhavetoaskthemap!'

The voice belonged to a tiny bespectacled Froglodite wearing an orange robe that clashed with his green skin. He was a Keeper of the Knowledge. With all eyes on him he continued much more slowly and calmly:

'Go to the altar at the head of the church, kneel in the light that shines through the stained-glass window and ask the map. It will bring your page to you.'

'You, Librarian,' Pipistral pointed at the Froglodite, 'have saved the lives of your town, now go. All of you get out!'

Angry and embarrassed at being tricked by Humboldt Stuff, the leader of the Parabat sisters didn't want to stay any longer than necessary. She stormed from the heavenly space, up the stairs and out of The Atlas. Once everyone else had left the book she slammed it shut and carried it back through the Central Archive.

Her team assembled in the town square, extended the thin hollow bones in their backs and flicked their parachutes upwards. Next they tilted back their heads and screamed.

The noise was deafening. It was like the siren of a perverted emergency vehicle in a minor key. Somehow the sounds they were making or the air they were expelling, or perhaps both, were inflating their parachutes. When each one was full, the ungodly wailing stopped and the sisters floated silently up to the waiting juggernaut above.

Inside the ascending Atlas the body of the day's only casualty was still lying where it had fallen. The corpse of Humboldt Stuff looked up at the towering shelves through glassy eyes. The smile on his face would last an eternity.

'Excuse me, Lady Pipistral, Ignatius has asked me to take The Atlas to him. Congratulations on a successful mission.'

'Why thank you, Stuff. Here you go.'

He took the dusty book from her and headed back to Ignatius.

'Hey, Stuff!'

'Yes.'

'Your dad says hi.'

*

Greenery gasped in awe as Sheba flew over Triweir in a low graceful arc. It was without doubt the most wonderful place he had ever seen.

The three great rivers that flow across the massive Australopithecus Plate, the Gamgees, the Aslan and the Ahab converged on this spot in a perfectly symmetrical 'Y' shape. What had once been a minor sinkhole in the centre of the watery letter, had been carved out, by the trinity of rivers, to form a massive circular basin.

The triplet of mighty waterways merged as they fell down the enormous natural well, becoming a torrential cataract that billowed spray upwards for hundreds of metres.

The town itself sat on a disc of rock perfectly centred above the round chasm. It was kept in its elevated place by a tripod of natural land bridges that had been left behind by the generous flow of the otherwise unforgiving water. Several rainbows glimmered in the evening light, caught in the mist from the surrounding torrents.

The rock surface around and throughout the town was covered in thick lush foliage that matched the colours of the rainbows above.

Breathtaking! thought Greenery as Sheba performed a reverse swoop parachute landing in the centre of town. Even though she was flying perfectly Greenery was worried about the Disco Beast. He had never seen her show so many different colours so fast. It was as if she were trying to display everything in her armoury at once.

Towelyn gently soothed and stroked her as she dismounted the Cecephelophopus' back.

'Is she OK?' asked Greenery.

'Oh yes, she's fine. They appreciate beauty that's all; she's just excited.'

'Come on, slow-pokes!' The Punster jumped down off the animal's back. It wasn't clear who was more excited, Sheba or Night Light. 'We'll be well looked after here, had a friend from Triweir once, used to rave about the place. As I remember he couldn't wait to get back. I'll sort us out some lodgings.'

He began rummaging through his bag, humming tunelessly to himself. After only a second or two he pulled out three leaves from the forest of sterling-silver birch trees they had passed through nearly a week ago.

'These should do the trick. Follow me,' and with that he set off across the square to a very hospitable-looking inn called The Three Falls.

It took only a moment for the expert businessman to sort them out with room and board. The innkeeper was only too happy to accommodate them for the night, and offer them unlimited food and drink. Greenery couldn't help wondering how much Night Light had overpaid by.

The food, however, when it came, was delicious and welcome. It was something large and meaty with no legs, accompanied by some gloriously greasy roast vegetables he didn't recognise. Greenery fully intended to have seconds but was full after his first plate. Night Light, even with his diminutive size, tucked away three whole portions and let out a huge burp to conclude.

The three friends talked and laughed the night away over a few warm Yaba roots and some whiskeywine for Night Light. A lot of whiskeywine. Too much whiskeywine, as it turned out.

By the time Greenery climbed into his ridiculously comfortable bed he was already sleepy. It felt good to be here. To be heading for the Armies of Sorrow with the consent of its guardian made him certain he was doing the right thing. He fell asleep feeling very, very content.

The bright morning sun shone down on the clean waters of Littleton Bay. Lazarus Brown stood and marvelled at the beauty of it.

He was an odd man, Lazarus Brown. He would maim and kill to get what he wanted and his ambition for power was like a hunger that drove him onwards regardless of all consequences. But he couldn't resist a good sunrise, and this *was* a good one.

The warlord leant on the promenade rails and watched the burning globe of hydrogen and helium until it was well above the horizon. He was lost in his thoughts. Seeing Gloria again after all these years had stirred up some old, for want of a better word, emotions. It was true he had left her after the birth but only because he had felt himself becoming attached to her, mentally. Removing himself from her poisonous humanity was another advantage of the cat disguise. But now he could see her again with fresh eyes he realised he had forgotten how pleasing she was to look at. How nice the sound of her voice was and how she made him – he shivered at even the thought of the word – *feel*.

A rusty alarm from a mechanical contraption brought him back to reality. He sighed deeply as he silenced it and began to wander slowly back to Ubiquity Drive.

That sound meant his project would be entering its last

growth phase. He could almost go home. But what to do with Gloria? Sweet, trusting Gloria. Perhaps his new toy could help out there as well, when it was finished. He sighed deeply and trudged on back to his laboratory.

Morning in Triweir was accompanied by a fanfare of birds. Hundreds of them flocked to the falls and the luscious vegetation to feed. As loud as it was, it was also enchanting. Greenery was sure he'd never heard birds sing in harmony with each other before or sing counterpoint to one another. The luscious music that woke him filled him with a sense of purpose. He flew down the stairs two at a time and positively ran to the dining room. He could smell freshly baked bread and something that smelled a lot like bacon.

'Good morning, everyone, and how are we today?'

Towelyn was standing with her back to the wall, eating a bowl of something that looked like porridge. Greenery could tell it wasn't because it was purple, and moving. Trying hard but failing to suppress a chuckle, she inclined her head towards the table. She put her finger to her lips and silently mouthed.

'Shhhh.'

Night Light was sitting with his head in his hands, staring at his almost bacon sandwich and swaying slightly. He had a scarf wrapped around his head to cover his ears and some dark gauze in front of his eyes.

'What's wrong with him?'

'Too much whiskeywine, I think.'

Greenery looked at Night Light again and started giggling. He went for a chair at the breakfast table but, instead of sitting, he lay across it with his head dangling towards the floor.

'Hey, Mr Punster, look. What do you think I am? Go on, guess . . . I'm a hangover. Get it? A hang over!'

Towelyn laughed so hard she snorted some of her breakfast out of her nose and down her fleecy front. Night Light groaned softly, picked up a spent piece of crust and threw it feebly at Greenery. He missed.

After that, breakfast continued on a more sedate level. When they had finished they got directions from the innkeeper to the start of the Road of Bones. On the way Greenery and Towelyn discussed the plan of action for the day. Night Light chipped in now and again with a quiet moan or a self-pitying hiccough.

The mighty hole carved into the rock by the waterfalls of Triweir is almost a perfect circle. The circumference is only interrupted on one side. Here the combined waters of the three rivers become the River Gormenghast and continue to flow Ebbwards, making a steep-sided narrow gorge. It was along the bottom of this gulley that the Road of Bones ran.

Standing on the edge of the cliff, Greenery looked down onto an almost vertical stairway carved into the rock face. Laid on the top of each step was an immaculately sculpted piece of bone. The steps were roughly two metres wide.

An animal capable of producing a bone of that size would have to be massive, thought Greenery. Remembering some of the things he'd seen on his travels he guessed that would be less of a problem here than it would be back home.

The gully was very deep and there were hundreds of steps. Even though they were all as well crafted as the top one, the flight of stairs was still very winding and treacherous-looking. It was a long way to fall.

They had decided to walk down the steps rather than take the Cecephelophopus express because it was impossible to see the bottom of the ravine. It looked very tight, and very craggy. They weren't sure if there would be enough space for Sheba to land or even if it was wide enough for her to fit.

The idea of following the road from the air wasn't an option either. The vegetation was so overgrown and the forest either side so thick that, within a couple of hundred metres from the town, the valley and the road were invisible from above. They had no option but to walk.

Greenery gave Sheba a friendly pat and told her he'd see her soon. He had no idea how much the Disco Beast understood what he said but she did seem to realise they were parting. One of her soft fury tentacles reached out and playfully ruffled his hair. As she did so, she flashed an image of waving hands all over her body before returning to a newspaper-print motif.

'Come on, Greenery,' called out Towelyn, 'we have a long way to go.'

Chapter Seventeen

As Above – So Below

If you travelled round the world
On a magic flying carpet,
Do you understand, the reason why
You'd end up where you started?
Now a universal truth,
Even though it sounds insane,
Is that if you travelled inwards
It would also be the same.

Taken from *The Lexicon of Creation* by
The Mysterious Wandering Gump

Towelyn, Night Light and Greenery stood at the bottom of
the winding staircase, soaking wet and slightly shaken. The
spray from the mighty waterfalls had drenched them all on
the way down. Greenery had slipped more than once and it
was only due to Towelyn's quick reflexes that he was still in
one piece.

It was a long, long way to the top of the deep ravine and
very little light managed to navigate its way down to the
valley floor. The Road of Bones continued along the dark and
miserable bank of the river, winding through the harsh rock

like a minor tributary of the main watercourse. The three friends sighed in unison and set off through the gloom.

They walked all morning. The scenery changed very little. The trees, so very far above, grew thicker and darker and the rapids settled down to the sedate pace of a mature river. As they did so, large red flowers started to decorate the fluvial landscape. They were roughly the size of tennis balls and were growing straight out of the water itself. Even though they were quite pretty there was something menacing about them. They looked wet and sticky. Every flower was surrounded by a swarm of tiny insects that were clearly attracted to its pollen.

As the day wore on and the enthusiastic morning turned into a lazy afternoon Greenery couldn't stop thinking about Ignatius Trump. He knew the monster was also looking for the Armies of Sorrow. He wondered how far the crazy troll had got in his search for the ultimate weapon and what would happen if he found it first, let alone managed to use it.

Greenery was so lost in his thoughts it took him a few steps to realise that they had left the security of the river bank and were walking on a sturdy wooden pontoon that floated on the wide waters of the river. The bones were laid out on top of it, making it as stable as the rest of the path. It was beautifully crafted and there were even bowls carved into the edges of the osseous matter at regular intervals. Towelyn said they were probably filled with oil in the past and set on fire so that the road could be used at night. Night Light was very apologetic when he threw up in one.

Now he came to look at his surroundings again Greenery noticed the flowers he'd spotted earlier in the day had grown in volume and number. They ranged in size considerably and the bigger they got the bigger the insects were that flocked to their scent.

In fact, there were so many large flies now that it was almost unbearable; thousands of them buzzed everywhere. Their iridescent colours flashed brightly as they flew through the random shards of unfiltered sunlight.

The instant these chunky insects landed on a large bud its petals would snap shut and the plant would devour them. The carnivorous blooms only ate the flesh, however, not the blood. This waste material would drip from the bottom of each flower and dye the surrounding water a light shade of pink.

'I thought insects' blood was green,' said Greenery, feeling a little peaky.

'Could be. I dunno, do I? Theirs is obviously red, innit? I wouldn't worry about it, sunshine,' replied Night Light, who seemed much happier now he'd emptied his stomach.

Eventually there were so many flowers eating so many insects that the water itself became dark red. It gave Greenery the shivers to think about some ancient people travelling this road in the dark, their way lit only by occasional fires that shone down on a river of blood.

After what seemed like forever the road emerged from the stagnant swamp and back onto dry land. The air felt fresh and clean again as the bony path rose above the thick sweet blood of a million deaths.

They clambered up the last few metres of the steep hill and stopped dead when they reached the pinnacle.

'Well, I'll be!' mumbled Night Light.

The bizarre view was staggering.

There really was a lake of blood. It was lined with towering cliffs that circled the entire valley like an impenetrable fortress.

The crimson lake looked glorious as small waves rippled its deep-red surface, but most astonishing of all was the colossal flower that grew from its centre. It towered above them and plugged the wide valley so successfully that only a thin line of bright yellow sunlight could escape unmolested around its circumference. It reminded Greenery of the corona of a solar eclipse.

The whole spectacle was given an amber glow as tinted light broke through the translucent petals stemming the valley, petals so fine that dark veins could be seen within them. They pulsed menacingly, adding a strange throb to the peculiar light.

The silhouettes of large flying creatures were projected down onto the organic screen of the gigantic flower from above. They looked like large birds but Greenery suspected they were giant versions of the insects they had already seen.

'It's the Amaranthus-megabigius,' said Night Light, 'the flower from the Big Tree.'

'It can't be!' said Towelyn.

'It is. Look at it.'

'What's so surprising about that?' asked Greenery.

'The Big Tree has only ever flowered once and that flower was sucked away by gravity storms,' said the Djinditsu.

'Gravity storms?'

'Some stretches of The River flow very close to large celestial bodies causing strange shifts in gravity.'

'Anyway,' said Night Light, 'everybody thought it had been sucked out into space. I'm just surprised to see it, that's all. I can't believe it's taken root and spawned all these other little flowers. We might have a new Big Tree one day.'

Suddenly one of the huge insects landed in the centre of the massive flower and the Amaranthus-megabigius snapped shut with a definite squelch, loud enough to echo round the valley for a second or two. In that instant unfiltered sunlight flooded everything with a bright golden warmth. It didn't last long. Just long enough for the carnivorous plant to complete its kill. Almost before the echo died away the floral roof folded back down and returned the whole scene to a dim tangerine dusk.

A moment later it started to rain blood. The dark claret fell from the flower onto the pristine surface of the lake turning it into a dappled minefield of tiny explosions. Like its smaller offspring this huge flower had no need of the animal's fluids and excreted them as a waste product.

Greenery tore himself away from the spectacular sight of the Amaranthus-megabigius and turned to face the wide-open plain before them. The Road of Bones cut across it, splitting the otherwise uninterrupted surface in two. There were small pink elephants grazing on the long green grass and on the other side, far off in the distance, was the entrance to a small cave with six expensive-looking trees close by.

'We're here,' shouted Greenery, 'we're here, we're here! Come on!'

With that he sprinted off down the wide path towards the distant cave. Night Light and Towelyn needed a moment longer.

'It's beautiful,' she said.

'It is.'

'I've travelled, you know – the Djinditsu see a lot of things – but this is . . .'

'I know, love, it really is.'

'Yep.'

'Yep . . .' Night Light sighed. 'Come on, we'd better catch up to the big fella before he gets himself in trouble again.'

It took them almost another hour to reach the cave. As they made their final approach the Road of Bones became more dishevelled. Some slabs were partially buried in the dry earth while others were sticking out of the ground at perverse angles. Eventually the walkway disappeared completely only to be replaced by a worn, dirt track that forked before leading to the hut and the cave.

The old man in tarnished armour was nowhere to be seen.

'Hello!' shouted Greenery. 'Hello, Mr . . . guard . . . man, I'm here!'

There was no answer.

'Hello!'

Towelyn looked away and tactfully checked her weapons. Night Light coughed pointedly.

'Ah-hem.'

Greenery sighed. 'What?'

'This bloke you saw in armour. You said it was the man from inside your snow globe, right?'

'Yes.'

'Well, is he there now?'

'What? I don't know.'

'Well, you could always have a look.'

'Oh yeah, good thinking.'

Greenery brought out the heavy glass sphere. He looked deep into the bubble and nearly dropped it with shock.

'What is it?' asked Towelyn.

'Look.'

Night Light and Towelyn peered into the souvenir.

'It's us!' whispered Night Light in amazement.

He was right. Standing inside the snow globe and looking down at something were three tiny versions of themselves. Greenery raised his left hand above his head and watched in wonder as his tiny self did the same. He turned and looked up, almost expecting to see a *giant* version of himself mapped out across the sky. Instead all he saw was the strange pulsing petals of the massive flower.

He looked back into the globe. This time there was a fourth figure standing behind his mini self.

'May I help you?'

'Aaaargh!'

He spun around to confront the stranger, had the Violents got here already? Was it a sneak attack?

Towelyn had obviously had the same thought. By the time Greenery turned she already had a blade pressed up against the throat of the sneaky stranger.

'Ah it's you, my boy. Welcome, welcome. Would you mind telling your hirsute friend here to release me? I'm rather partial to my head and was hoping to keep it for a few more years yet.' It was the man in tarnished armour.

'Oh yes of course, sorry. Towelyn, it's all right, you can let go of him. He's on our side. This is the guard I was telling you about. Night Light, come and meet . . . Where's Night Light?'

Pop!

A miniscule potato wedge lying on the floor blossomed upwards to become an embarrassed-looking Punster.

'. . . Jumping out and scaring people, shouldn't be allowed, stupid . . .'

'Night Light!' reprimanded Greenery. 'Be nice.'

'Yeah, but he scared me,' said Night Light, looking up at the guard for the first time. His whole demeanour changed in a heartbeat. 'Oh God! It's you! I mean I didn't realise, I'm sorry, Sir, I . . .'

'I DONT BELIEVE we've met. My name is Delphinius. How do you do?'

'Er . . . hello.'

'That was a microchip, wasn't it. Unless I'm mistaken, you're a Punster, yes?

'Yes?' said Night Light, trying desperately to read the old man's face, which was a picture of pure innocence.

'Where were you just now?' asked Greenery, completely unaware of the odd moment that passed between Delphinius and his friend.

'Oh forgive an old man's suspicion, dear boy. I was . . . elsewhere. I had to make sure it was really you . . . and it is. You have the snow globe. Welcome! Tell me, where are your allies? They are following you, yes?'

'What allies?'

'You've come to fight the Violents. They are an army of two thousand – you must have people with you. Yes?'

'No. There's just us three.'

The old man's smile faded as fast as it had appeared. His drawbridge moustache sagged and his eyes lost some of their sparkle.

'One Djinditsu and a Pun Monster? You travel in good company, my young friend, but you are no match for the Violents. I have a gift of sight, I see many things. I have seen them on their journey and they are ruthless.' Delphinius looked as though he had aged fifty years in the last minute. He sat down by the fire with a vacant expression on his face. 'We're all dead.'

'No, it's OK. I have a plan. I think we can get ourselves an army of our own, maybe not as big but definitely a match for the Violents.'

'Listen to me, my eager young friend, this is an isolated spot, chosen on purpose to hide the awful power of the Armies of Sorrow. The Violents have found it and are on their way. You cannot get an army of your own here before they arrive tomorrow.'

'Tomorrow? They're going to get here tomorrow?' asked Night Light.

'Yes, early.'

'Then why don't we move the weapon now? We can destroy it before they even get here.'

'I wish it was that simple. This lake is tidal, you can only enter the cave at low tide and that is not until tomorrow afternoon. So relax, enjoy your food and you can be a hero tomorrow. It's going to be a big day. We're all going to die.'

'I'll eat your food and I'll drink your drink but I can't rest. And you're wrong. I think we *can* get an army of our own.'

'Greenery,' said Towelyn, 'you're talking about calling the Djinditsu, aren't you? What did you have in mind?'

He smiled his knowing smile. 'All of you stand back.'

As the others moved away, Greenery closed his eyes and

started muttering to himself. At the same time he began, without realising it, to rub the coincidence ring. It made him look as though he was praying.

Slowly the mist of creation began to form in the air near his mouth. This time, however, it split into two different clouds. One drifted a metre or two to his right and the other the same distance off to his left. Once in position they began to take shape. It only took a minute but when it was done there were two very strange, very solid-looking objects where there had been nothing only moments ago.

The one to Greenery's right was roughly the size of a cylindrical phone box and it looked a little like a cage. Its thick copper bars came to a conical point at the top and there was a series of powerful-looking wires around its circumference that connected at the base.

The object on Greenery's left was similar in design to the first, only lower and wider. Unlike its counterpart it had no roof and the thick black bars combined with the open circular shape made it look like some kind of bizarre wrestling ring.

'Nice,' said Night Light, 'but what is it?'

'I guess you'd call it a physical thought transporter,' said Greenery, shrugging slightly.

'How does it work?' asked Towelyn.

'Well, first you think of a simple message and you hold that in your head. Then you step inside and think about everyone that you want to pass that message on to. This machine will send you to all of them at once. If they agree to come back with you, you reach out, take their hand and it brings them back here.'

'Sounds simple.'

'Trust me, Night Light, it's not.'

'Greenery, I hate to burst your bubble but I don't know all of the Djinditsu personally. I can't send a message to all of them if I don't know them, can I?'

'Ah, no. But the ones you bring back will know others that you don't and they in turn will know others and so on and so on. It should work but it might take us a while to get everybody here so I think we should start as soon as possible, don't you?'

'I suppose so.'

'I've got a feeling this is going to be right good,' said Night Light to Delphinius who was staring with his mouth wide open.

'Er, what shall I do,' he asked, looking a little bewildered.

'Why don't you build up the fire and get more pink elephant milk,' said Greenery. 'We're going to have a lot of thirsty troops.'

'Right,' he said without moving an inch.

Towelyn took a deep breath and, following Greenery's instructions, stepped inside the tall, conical device.

'Just think of every Djinditsu you can and hold the message in your head, OK?'

'OK.'

He closed the door and pressed a small blue button on the side of the contraption. It started to make a deep pulsing noise, which quickly rose in volume and speed. Radiant sparks began to travel and flash all along the wires attached to the cage.

When the entire machine was glowing bright electric blue, Greenery pressed a second button. It was big and red with the word 'charge' embossed in dark-green letters across its front.

The effect was immediate. Hundreds of tiny flares jumped from the glowing bars and zapped Towelyn in a nanosecond. As they did so her body exploded in a shower of sparks. It was so bright that the three spectators had to cover their eyes. When they looked again even Greenery, who had invented the machine, had trouble believing his eyes.

Towelyn was still standing in the centre of the cage, sort of, only now she was made entirely of glowing particles of electricity. She looked like a living bolt of lightning. She looked straight at them and giggled. 'It tickles.'

The throbbing base note accelerated again and Towelyn began to dissolve. A bright-blue beam emanating from her electric body shot through the top of the thought transporter and cannoned skywards. As it did so it pulled Towelyn with it, unravelling what was left of her like a loose cord on a knitted jumper. The higher it went the more of her it took with it.

With disturbingly perfect timing the Amaranthus-megabigius closed up its petals for the night revealing an evening sky of smoky dusk. Every one of the smaller flowers folded up in unison, giving Towelyn a floral salute as she flew further and higher.

'That was strange,' said Night Light pointedly, shooting a sideways look at Delphinius.

'Yes it was, wasn't it?' said the guard, looking a little guilty.

Once it was in mid-air the fizzing current gathered itself into a large blue sphere. It hung there for a moment, motionless, before exploding like an incredible firework and sending bright-blue sparks of electric Towelyn whizzing off to the horizon in every direction at once. From start to finish the whole process took only a couple of minutes.

Back on the ground the only noise was a metallic pinging as the machine cooled. Greenery, Night Light and Delphinius stood in silence.

After a while Night Light spoke ... 'Wow!' was all he managed.

'Yeah, I know.'

'Wow.'

'Yeah.'

'I mean, wow!'

'I know.'

'Er ...' interrupted Delphinius, 'what do we do now?'

'Now?' said Greenery. 'We wait.'

Ox Hide and Lint were settling down for the night under a grove of Eye Pods. These dense overhanging trees provided excellent shelter as well as added security. When the ever-searching Eyes of the plant spotted anyone approaching, the Pod would play a loud burst of random music.

Lint was arranging the sleeping mats while Ox Hide was seeing to the fire. It had been a long and hard day for the two brothers. A property dispute in Green Witch had turned nasty and they had been called in, to settle the ensuing riot.

Ox Hide was the older of the two and was big and powerful; his younger brother had a wiry strength and was fast with a blade.

The quiet of the clear starry night was shattered instantly when a fizzing blue asteroid came smashing down from the heavens and turned the camp to chaos. Dust and debris went flying everywhere and the two brothers were sent diving for cover accompanied by a rich and varied soundtrack.

When the air cleared and they could see again. Ox Hide and Lint were left facing a glowing electric-blue figure that looked very familiar.

'Towelyn?' asked Lint. 'Is that you?'

'Not exactly no . . . well yes, sort of. Listen, it's not easy to think like this; my brain is in several places at once. I have a message for you. The followers of Lazarus Brown have discovered the location of the Armies of Sorrow. If you want to help keep The River free from tyranny, you must come with me now and together we can win.'

She reached out with both hands, prompting the brothers to take one each.

'I don't suppose we have much choice really, do we?' said Lint, looking at his big brother.

'Well, if you can't trust your little sister,' said Ox Hide, reaching for his battleaxe, 'then who can you trust?'

The two Djinditsu stepped forward and took their sister's hands in their own. As soon as they touched her, the sparkly, star-like material that she was composed of spread down their arms, transforming the two boys into electric matter as it went. The brothers looked at each other and laughed. 'It tickles!' they said together.

The instant the transformation was complete the three siblings rocketed skywards like a trio of superheroes. As they left a blue streak across the sky, the Eye Pods started to play themselves to sleep with some mellow jazz. They didn't like company.

Back at the Lake of Blood, Greenery was watching the sky. The Amaranthus was still closed so the bright stars were clearly visible. His neck was just starting to ache when a thin blue line traced across the ether. When it was directly overhead it turned sharply and headed straight down. It smashed onto the landing platform that looked so much like a wrestling ring and crackled with pent-up energy.

The three glowing figures standing on the pad seemed a little shaken up; they swayed slightly from side to side, stunned into frazzled silence. Towelyn let go of her brothers' hands and the sparks slowly fizzled out. They both returned to normal. Towelyn herself did not.

Still glowing just as bright, she stepped off the platform and walked over to Greenery.

'That was really strange. I didn't think I'd be back so soon though.'

'Erm . . . you're already back.'

'What?'

'In fact, I think you might be the last.'

Greenery pointed over Towelyn's shoulder at a friendly-looking group of Djinditsu. Her brothers, she noticed, had joined them and were hugging and back-slapping friends and family they had not seen for some time. Standing a little way off from the crowd, looking slightly confused, was another shining, electric Towelyn.

'If there are so many of them, why is there only one of me?'

'All the other Towelyns sort of smooshed together.'

'What do you mean smooshed?'

'They just kind of blobbed back together. It was quite nice really.'

'OK, well here goes.'

She turned on her heel and walked straight up to the other her, who smiled. They hugged each other and as soon as they touched they smooshed together. The effect was like two soap bubbles meeting; they simply became one.

Once they had been reunited the sparkly glowing effect fizzled out in the same way it had with Lint and Ox Hide. Towelyn was complete again.

She turned back to Greenery and smiled as her friends and family rushed around her. The back-slapping and hugging began again.

'Excuse me, everybody!' shouted Night Light, standing on top of a large rock so as not to get lost in the noisy crowd. 'We've got a lot more people to bring here and not much time so if you wouldn't mind stepping this way we'll warm this baby up and you can all have a go at whooshing off to invite your friends back here.'

It didn't take long for Night Light and Greenery to get the Djinditsu organised into a production line. On one side of the small camp they were queuing up for blast-off and on the other side the new arrivals were stepping off the platform and joining the back of the line. It was very efficient.

Towelyn was helping the returned messengers through the smooshing process and Delphinius was on hand to offer them a warm cup of pink elephant milk.

As the night rolled on the machine hummed constantly. The hidden valley of the Lake of Blood was full of electric-blue flashing as if a lightning storm were raging within. Even before dawn there were only a few Djinditsu left in the queue and the messengers that went out returned with only a handful of new warriors. There were fewer and fewer out there to find. The last messenger returned with only one new warrior and Greenery realised they were all here.

The Djinditsu had been called and they had come.

Greenery had his army.

Chapter Eighteen

Bloodbath

So, you tell me you're you
And you tell me I'm me,
But who else did you think I could possibly be?
I have always been me,
Though for you that's not true.
Every time you are born you become someone new.
Taken from *A Beginner's Guide to Reincarnation* by
The Mysterious Wandering Gump

'Wake up! . . . Hello? Wake up, boy. . . . I said, wake up!'

A cold hard slap across the face was a harsh welcome to the world but it brought him round instantly. He opened his eyes. Everything looked fuzzy. He felt dim and sluggish. He tried to think, to remember where he was, but he could recall nothing. He tried to move but found he couldn't. Slowly, fighting off panic and with great effort, he managed to bring the world into focus.

He was in a dimly lit room with no windows. There was lots of strange equipment spread out everywhere and an odd bubbling noise coming from behind him.

Directly in front of him, staring at him as though he were

a bug under a microscope, was the man who had just hit him. He spoke:

'Welcome to number 8 Ubiquity Drive. You may have noticed that you cannot move. That, I am sorry to say, is my fault. You will find you can do nothing without my say-so. Let me just repeat that for you. You cannot do anything unless I allow it. Your mind, brain and body are completely under my control. Is that understood?'

The hostage tried to lash out, to hit, to shout, to scream defiance in the face of his captor but he could not move.

'Good, I'm glad that's understood. In a moment I'm going to give you a little freedom and allow you some independent movement but I will take it away from you the second you abuse this privilege in any way. I think that's fair, don't you? You may nod if you agree.'

The boy felt the muscles in his neck relax. Out of pure defiance and as the only possible outlet for any revolt he tried to shake his head. He strained his muscles as hard as he could until the pain was unbearable, but his head simply wouldn't turn. There was nothing he could do. He resigned himself to his fate and nodded.

Lazarus Brown smiled. 'Good, I'm glad we agree. I'm not a monster. If you do as I say we'll get on fine. Now you must be a little confused. You can ask me one question. Think hard. Don't waste it. . . . Have you thought of it? You may nod.'

The boy nodded again.

'Very well. You may speak.'

'Who am I?'

'Who am I?'

'What do you mean?'

'What?'

'You just said *who am I?*'

'I don't think I did.'

'Yes you did. You stopped with your cup halfway to your lips and you said *who am I*. Your voice went all funny and you looked all weird. You feeling all right, mate?'

'I think so. Maybe it's stress. I can't stand this waiting. Come on, let's go and find Towelyn.'

Greenery and Night Light put their cups of pink elephant milk down next to the little sink in Delphinius' hut. He had let them use his bed to try and get some sleep but they had both found they were far too anxious to get any kind of rest.

Greenery poked his head out of the little doorway that led to the waiting battlefield. The Amaranthus-megabigius had opened up its petals again and covered the valley. Standing in the dim tangerine light were just over three hundred Djinditsu warriors.

They had formed themselves into several battle groups. Each fighting unit was a mixture of the different castes that made up the Djinditsu population.

On the front line of each battalion were the large powerful-looking males. These alpha types were by far the strongest of the combatants. They looked serious and tense. Their weapon of choice was something heavy, designed to do maximum damage like a battleaxe or a mace.

The second group of fighters had long delicate-looking swords. Every individual was thin, toned and wiry. They looked fast and deadly.

Behind them came the archers. As a group they were taller,

on average, than the other Djinditsu. Even so their long power-
bows stretched way above their heads and they had various
types of arrows in their quivers. Some bolts had painful-looking
barbs; some were more streamlined for distant flight and some
were short and stubby – these were designed for their close-
range armour-piercing capabilities. Greenery had no doubt as
to the accuracy of the archers.

At the head of each battalion was a single grey-haired
Djinditsu. These older generals were not a caste in themselves
but seemed to be drawn from the elite of each skill set. Every
one of them, however, had the same thing in common; they
wore their scars like medals. Their years of experience clearly
put them in another league to the foot soldiers, and the respect
the younger warriors had for them was palpable.

Greenery was full of admiration for his troops, which was
how he thought of them, and he couldn't believe their confidence. There were small patches of quiet conversation and
the odd outbreak of laughter here and there, but on the whole
they stood in silence simply waiting for the battle to begin.
Greenery was well aware how outnumbered they would be
when the Violents arrived.

He spotted Towelyn within the ranks of the closest fighting
unit and trotted over to her. The other Djinditsu moved respect-
fully out of his way to let him and Night Light pass.

'Good morning, Greenery. What's that you're wearing?'

Towelyn pointed at Greenery's new vest. It looked like a
waistcoat made of the finest chain mail imaginable.

'Oh do you like it? It's something I invented last night
as everyone was arriving. It's Karma Armour. When
you're wearing it no harm will come to you as long as your

intentions are morally right. I'm quite proud of it. I just hope it works.'

'Yes, that would be useful.'

'How do you think everyone is doing? I can't believe how calm they all look.'

'Greenery, this is the fight we were born for, literally. We have been trained from birth to be warriors for one reason only, to defend The Other Place. We failed when we let Lazarus Brown rise to power but we were taken by surprise and were heavily outgunned. Now we have a chance to stop the same thing happening again. We would all gladly give our lives for the honour of saving The River.'

'Wow, that's well impressive, Towelyn. I wish I felt like that.'

'What do you mean, lad? You're here, aren't you? Surely you *do* feel like that?' said Night Light.

'No, I'm sorry but I don't.'

'Then why *are* you here, Greenery?' Towelyn asked in a concerned voice.

He shrugged before answering.

'Guilt.'

'THEY'RE HERE!'

The cry came from several voices at once. Three hundred and forty-two pairs of eyes looked up in unison as the sky burst into flames.

'Wake up! Hello, Greenery. Wake up. It's me, it's your mum . . . Greenery . . . Greenery!'

He opened his eyes. He was in the same dimly lit room as before only now there was a strange lady in front of him looking extremely happy. She was crying and talking a lot. She seemed completely overjoyed to see him. He pretended to listen to her, but as she pulled him close all he could do was try and remember what the man had told him earlier.

He was a clone of this lady's son and he must pretend his name was Greenery, Greenery Jackson. He had returned from somewhere. The Other Place? Was that it? Yes, he had returned from The Other Place but had lost his memory and the man whose name was Lazarus had found him wandering on the beach.

The lady was still crying. The clone felt bad for her but he had to play along with these lies or the man, Lazarus, would hurt him for a long time. Lazarus had taught him what pain was earlier, and the thought of it still terrified him.

Silence brought the clone's attention back to the lady. She had finished talking and was looking at him expectantly. He had been so caught up trying to get his story straight that he hadn't heard a word she'd said. It was OK though. Lazarus had told him what the first words out of his mouth should be, regardless of what the lady said to him.

'I love you, Mum.'

'RUN!'

'Night Light, I think I just heard my mum's voice.'

'Greenery, this is a very stressful situation. Please don't make it any worse for me by going insane.'

'What?'

'Run!'

Flaming pieces of debris rained down upon Greenery and the waiting army as the monstrous head of Embrillion burst through the burning flower that covered the valley.

'Come on!' shouted Night Light as he grabbed Greenery's hand and fled for cover.

The rest of the fiery roof exploded inwards in a shower of hell as the body of the monstrous leviathan ploughed on through. With her wings fully spread, Embrillion almost filled the canyon but managed somehow to angle her body into a tight downwards arc and touched down upon the crimson lake like the world's ugliest swan. She skidded across the surface of the blood water for hundreds of metres, destroying most of the floral swamp and the Road of Bones.

Greenery and Night Light made it to the shelter of the small cliffs near Delphinius' hut just in time. A huge piece of Amaranthus shrapnel came crashing down upon them. They were protected from the red-hot ember by the overhanging rock, but only just. They had to keep running or succumb to the scorching heat.

'Greenery! Over here!' It was Towelyn – standing near the entrance to the cave and beckoning him frantically. She was surrounded by a contingent of the old grey generals. They had decided to stand guard at this tactical hotspot to supply some well-needed extra defence.

In the distance a massive bass rumble sounded and the Violents' war cry echoed across the valley. They were pouring off the back of Embrillion and heading towards the Djinditsu with alarming speed.

Greenery picked up Night Light, put his head down and sprinted to Towelyn. He reached her just as the first wave of warriors breached the rise at the top of the grassy plain. On and on they ran, screaming and bellowing like demented animals. They continued undeterred as a volley of arrows rained down upon them.

'What do we do?'

'Greenery, keep calm. This is what we expected. We're ready for this. Go into the cave. If the tide of blood isn't low enough to reach the Armies of Sorrow just yet, it soon will be. Go and destroy that weapon.'

He looked at her panting and panicking, then managed to pull himself together.

'OK.'

The roaring wave that was the front line of the attacking Violents crashed into the wall of Djinditsu with the sound of thunder. Like a battalion of reapers the alpha males hacked away at the Violent tide with their big heavy weapons and a terrifying animal ferocity. Their strength was incredible and even the bloodiest injuries seemed to go unnoticed.

'Go!'

Greenery darted through the small entrance and headed into the beckoning cave. The sounds of the battle chased after him as he ran into the darkness with his hands covering his ears.

'Greenery, listen to me: we have to get out of here.'

The clone looked at her like she was crazy.

'I know you think he's nice because he helped you on the beach but he is not a nice man. He can do things, strange things, and he's evil, Greenery, evil.'

Gloria Jackson was clearly terrified. She was pawing at her counterfeit son. Grabbing his arms and trying to pull him out of the basement. She was whispering with such intensity that her voice had the nerve-jangling effect of a scream.

The new Greenery desperately wanted to go with her. She seemed nice and kind and she looked at him like he was a person not an experiment. He wanted to tell her he wasn't her son but he was scared. Scared of what Lazarus would do to him and scared that she wouldn't look at him in the same way anymore.

'Come on, son. We have to go. He's coming.'

He nodded. She took his hand. It felt warm and comforting. The only other time he had felt physical contact in his life was when the man had beaten him. He had been twenty minutes old.

She began to lead him towards the only exit. They were within touching distance of the handle when the door flew open and Lazarus Brown came billowing into the room. He was wearing a long black cape over his suit that made him look like a stage magician. He was smiling when he entered and seemed genuinely surprised to catch them both in an escape attempt. His face fell. He closed the door behind him slowly but forcefully. The loud click as the latch sprang into place made Gloria jump. Even though she was afraid she placed herself between her imitation son and the intruding aggressor. This did not go unnoticed by the clone, who longed to help her more than ever.

'Leaving so soon?' said Lazarus in a voice as heavy as lead.

'Please move out of the way, Lazarus. We want to go home.'

He did not move.

Her voice cracked with fear and she fought back tears as she asked him again.

'Lazarus, please let us go. We just want to leave. We won't tell anyone where you are . . . or *what* you are.'

He did not move.

'But I found your son. I helped you. You shouldn't fear me.'

He took a step towards her.

'I can be good. I've shown you. I can be nice.'

He took another step closer.

'I can also be bad, Gloria. I can hurt you.'

His face was centimetres from hers.

'Why don't you want me?'

He was staring at her so intently it almost hurt. The eyes are said to be the windows to the soul. These windows had a very unpleasant view.

She turned away, unable to bear the horrific truth of the man she had once loved.

'You're not human.'

He bit his bottom lip to prevent himself from snarling in her face. His body stiffened as he fought with himself. He was trying not to kill her where she stood, and it took him a silent moment to wrestle his murderous instincts back into submission.

Gloria's heart was beating so hard she thought it was going to rip her chest wide open. With monumental self-control Lazarus managed to smile. It had all the warmth of a snowman's carbon grin.

'No, Gloria, you're right, I'm not human, which means that, unfortunately for you, I can do this.'

He flicked his finger towards the clone. It was a simple gesture, a tiny movement, hardly worthy of comment, were it not for the horrendous consequences.

The clone began to scream. Agonising pain raced through his entire body. He felt as if he were being eaten from the inside.

'Stop!' yelled Gloria.

Lazarus flicked his finger and the clone screamed again, flick, scream, flick, scream, flick . . . flick . . . flick . . .

'Stop it! Stop please!'

Lazarus lowered his finger. The clone collapsed in a wretched heap on the floor, crying and moaning. Gloria bent down and gathered him to her bosom, caressing him gently and soothing his tortured body. With tears streaming down her face she spat at the feet of Lazarus Brown.

'I'll do what you want, you son of a bi . . .' she stopped herself. 'I'll follow you anywhere, whatever you want, just please don't hurt my son anymore.'

'Excellent, old girl, that's the spirit! Right, I think a trip to the theatre is in order, don't you? Follow me.'

The real Greenery leant heavily on the cave wall and winced in pain. He'd run deep into the cave until the sounds of battle had faded. Now he stood panting and wheezing in the semi-darkness, clutching at the stitch in his side and listening to the blood from the retreating tide drip slowly from the roof.

A sound in the distance brought fresh fear. Someone or something was coming. Greenery could hear footsteps approaching quickly and the heavy panting of someone breathing hard. He looked for somewhere to hide; there was nowhere. He looked for a weapon; there was nothing. He reached into his pocket and pulled out the heavy snow globe, raised it above his head and braced himself.

The footsteps were still approaching, getting louder constantly. Greenery was about to swing his makeshift weapon when a small shadow barrelled round the corner and ran head first into his kneecap.

'Ow! Blood and thunder what kind of a stupid place to stand is that? Ah don't hit me! What you doing? It's me.'

'Night Light. You scared me to death. I thought you were one of them.'

'Yeah well, I'm not. What did you nearly hit me with anyway?'

'The snow globe. Look.'

Greenery held it out as he tried to apologise to the Punster.

'I am sorry, Night Light, I really thought you were one . . .'

'Greenery, shut up! . . . Look.'

Even in the almost pitch-black cave the snow globe was clearly visible. The scene inside was lit by a distant sun and the reflected glow of many fires. Through this strange glass portal they could see the entire battle.

The Djinditsu were still in a tight formation and so far seemed to be winning. They fought with an almost supernatural skill. The speed of their reactions made it seem as though they were able to read the future. Most adept at this and fighting several assailants at once were the Grey Generals. Each one, surrounded by a circle of dead or dying enemies, fought with a radiant peace that gave them a terrifying edge. Towelyn was right: they were born for this.

'Looks fierce, eh?'

'Yeah.'

'Come on, lad, we need to get to that weapon.'

'Yeah you're right. Let's go.'

Greenery put the globe back in his pocket and they continued down the twisting passageway through the rock. The sound of blood dripping from the ceiling was met by the occasional groan from Night Light as he stepped in a puddle of the stuff.

The light from the entrance was blocked out by the many twists and turns of the downward path but it was not quite pitch-black. If anything, it was getting lighter. Greenery was just about to ask Night Light if he knew why, when it became all too clear.

They rounded another corner and were met with bright blinding light. It was so fierce it hurt to look straight at it and both Greenery and Night Light ducked back into shadow to shield themselves from its glare.

'What is that?'

'Beats me, kiddo.'

'You got any bright ideas up your sleeve, a handy little pun that might help us out?'

'You know it's funny you should say that because I think I have just the thing.'

He winked at Greenery and then popped out of existence to be replaced by a small black torch. Greenery picked it up and examined it. Apart from its strange dark lens it looked like any other torch. He turned it on and shone it into the semi-darkness behind him. Nothing happened. He shrugged. Knowing Night Light, this would probably help out, but how, was anybody's guess. He shone the torch into the light and almost laughed out loud as a beam of darkness filled the space, protecting his eyes and making it easy to navigate.

'Oh my God! I get it! You're a night light, Night Light. Brilliant!'

The small black torch vibrated gently in his hand as it chuckled to itself.

Now that Greenery could see, he could make out what was causing the dazzling light. It was diamonds. Thousands of fist-sized diamonds covered the walls and ceiling, each one glowing with a pure white light from its centre. Greenery shone his night light over a patch of them and could see the energy coming from something moving in the heart of each diamond. Something small but almost human-shaped.

'Troll eggs,' said the night light.

'Troll eggs? Wow.'

'They'll incubate down here for centuries. They probably get nutrients or something from their daily soak in all that blood.'

As Greenery stared in wonder at the constellation of new life before him, the noise of the battle above suddenly penetrated his subterranean world. It was very loud, which meant it was very close. He guessed something had broken through the main ranks of the Djinditsu and was fighting with the Grey Generals at the cave entrance.

Whatever it was it kept screaming, though it didn't sound as if it was in pain. These were screams of manic, animal fury. As Greenery listened, the metallic clash of many weapons thinned out gradually, as if one at a time they dropped out of the fray. This could only mean one thing. The Generals were losing. Eventually silence returned, only this time there was no comfort in it. Instead it was a huge ominous hole that sucked at the ears. Greenery stood in silence waiting for a clue, waiting to see if his life was in danger or not.

A terrible scream of hatred and fury echoed down the dark winding chamber followed instantly by the sound of something big scuttling.

Something had taken out ten of the greatest warriors The Other Place had ever known and was now charging towards Greenery. Something with lots of legs and sharp teeth was coming to kill him.

He ran. There was nowhere to go but further into the cave. As he sprinted, the random beam of the dark torch on the bright walls created a strobe effect. He couldn't see what was in front of him and didn't want to know what was fast approaching behind.

He rounded another corner and as the path dipped steeply he was met with a dead end. He had caught up with the retreating red tide. A few metres away on the other side of a large puddle the roof of the cave dipped down into the dark red waters. There was nowhere to go.

Another hateful scream from the pursuing death forced him into action. There was nothing else for it. He placed Night Light on a small shelf in the rock, out of harm's way, then he took a deep breath and plunged headfirst into the crimson abyss.

The visibility underneath the surface of the insect blood was absolute zero. His only option was to feel the surface of the roof and move forward by a combination of pulling himself along and kicking frantically. He was desperately hoping the path would rise again and he would find breathable air once more. A splash in the tide behind him sent shockwaves pulsing through his body. Something big and fast was in the claret with him.

Every muscle in his body strained to move faster. He pulled manically at the rock ceiling trying desperately to avoid drowning or being ripped to pieces. Suddenly something sharp and warm brushed against his leg. Whatever was chasing him didn't seem too nimble in the water and clearly couldn't see any better than he could. It was close though and still incredibly dangerous.

Greenery was running low on air, very low. He couldn't have made it back now even if he wanted to. He pulled himself onwards as every fibre in his body cried out for oxygen. He thought his chest was going to explode but still he forced himself forward.

Then as he groped along the rock ceiling he felt a cool breeze on his fingers. He was just about to break the surface and take a life-giving breath when a spindly claw closed around his trainer and pulled him downwards. In a blind panic he kicked out with his other leg and felt the adrenalin-fuelled blow connect with a satisfying crunch. The thing let go and grabbed its wounded face in a defensive manner. Greenery reached up and pulled himself free of the bloody purgatory. He waded up the tiny beach gasping and dripping. His head was spinning from lack of oxygen and he started to see lights in front of his eyes. He blinked back delirium and managed to focus.

Not five metres away, sitting on a pedestal of fire was the Armies of Sorrow. It looked like a stylish water pistol for the Wii generation. It was white all over with a large ergonomic handle. There were blue lights running the length of its wide elliptical barrel and chrome detailing on the stock and trigger.

The creature in the lake was not as badly injured as Greenery had hoped. With another blood-curdling scream it leapt from the crimson plasma and ran towards him. It was an insipid light-blue colour all over its wiry body. Underneath its vaguely human torso it had eight spindly legs tipped by fierce-looking talons. It barrelled towards Greenery with razor-sharp teeth dripping saliva and its mouth wide open ready to bite.

Greenery stumbled forwards. As he collapsed to the floor he reached out and managed to grab the weapon from the pedestal. As the blue spider-like creature pounced he rolled onto his back and fired the Armies of Sorrow.

A wide vibrant beam hit the creature full in the chest sending it flying back to the shoreline and onto the floor.

Greenery didn't wait to see what effect the terrible weapon would have on the screaming demon. If it hadn't worked he was still in danger; if it had, it meant the monster was about to kill itself and he didn't want to stick around to see that. He clambered to his feet, took a deep breath and fled back under the shrinking tide of blood.

Chapter Nineteen

Infected with Life

Love it, live it, enjoy it, please.
Your life is a gift that is given with ease.
But if you're not careful the forces of hell,
Will infect your mind as a place to dwell.

Taken from *The Origins of Action*
by the Mysterious Wandering Gump.

'Ah, this is the place.' said Lazarus.

Gloria Jackson looked up at the old abandoned theatre on Littleton Bay seafront. It was one of her favourite places; it had a strange ghostly charm to it.

'Why here?' she asked the Technomancer who was telekinetically removing planks from the boarded-up stage door.

'The place we are going to, Gloria, relies heavily on human imagination. The theatre is a place of fantasy and belief. Here the boundaries between the worlds are thinner than you can possibly imagine.'

'We're going to another world? You didn't say anything about that. Please, Lazarus . . .'

'Gloria!' he raised his finger threateningly towards the

pretend Greenery. 'Do not disappoint me. Need I remind you of the consequences?'

'No.'

'Good.'

The last plank of wood floated past Lazarus as he spoke and landed on the neat stack at his feet. He waved his arms about in an overly dramatic gesture and the stage door burst open.

It was dark and terribly dusty inside the abandoned theatre. All the signs were distorted by years of grime but somehow Lazarus seemed to know where he was going. He led them out onto the stage – the curtain was up. He clicked his fingers and several broken spotlights shone down upon them.

'OK, "Greenery", it's time, do your job.'

'I . . . I don't know what you want me to do.'

'Yes you do. Don't be difficult.'

'I don't, I'm sorry. Please don't hurt me.'

Lazarus took a step towards the clone, turned and gave Gloria the most obsequious smile imaginable before gently placing a hand on the boy's shoulder.

'Now listen, son,' he said in a smarmy overly paternal voice, 'this is what you were made for. Don't think about it. Just do what feels right.'

'OK, I'll try.'

'Good boy.'

The clone turned to face the extinct audience; he seemed awkward and unsure of himself. After a moment of reflection he looked up at Gloria who smiled encouragingly and then he began to sing. His voice was much higher than Lazarus' but it carried those same magic tones that seemed to resonate within the fabric of the universe. As he sang, his eyes turned black. The darkest black of night, only punctuated with small twinkling lights like stars in distant space. He tilted his head to the side then began patting the air in front of him as if searching for something. He smiled when he found what he was looking for.

Greenery was covered from head to toe in thick sticky blood as he and Night Light came sprinting out of the cave.

'I've got it!' he shouted, clutching the weapon proudly in front of him, then stopped dead in his tracks as he saw the devastation before him.

At least a third of the Violents lay dying or dead on the floor and there were far too many Djinditsu in the same state, groaning or still. The skirmish continued unabated, only now there seemed to be pockets of fighting spread far and wide as opposed to one huge battle royal.

Embrillion had taken off again and was circling high above. Now that most of the Amaranthus-megabigius had been burnt away there was very little hindering her path and someone was throwing Flaming Tar-Bombs down from her back. They exploded on impact, causing liquid fire to splash and burn the battling Djinditsu, who were losing on two fronts.

'Come on, lad, don't stop. We've still got to destroy that thing. Come on! Greenery! Greenery?'

Night Light looked up at Greenery. He had fallen into some kind of trance. He was standing stock-still and his eyes had turned black. The darkest black of night, only punctuated with small twinkling lights like stars in distant space.

Night Light turned, ready to kill whoever was doing this

to his friend but could see no one to blame, no cause to rally against. He was helpless.

The terrible weapon fell from Greenery's hand like a piece of rubbish, discarded and forgotten. Next he began patting his own body. His movements were jerky and unnatural as though his hands were being controlled by an outside source. Soon enough whatever was searching him found what it was looking for. It thrust his right hand deep into his pocket and brought out Captain Calefaction's most prized possession.

Something alien looked out through Greenery's eyes at the gold and turquoise key which shone as magnificently as ever. The Greenery thing stroked it gently, as if it were a delicate animal, then promptly flicked the switch on its side.

The key burst from his hand immediately and sailed high into the air. It hovered for a second or two like a plane stalling out at the peak of a dangerous climb then crashed back to earth like a metal meteorite, embedding itself deep into the soft turf below.

Night Light watched on, still unsure what to do, as the key began to spin feverishly. It seemed to grab hold of the sod as it spun, somehow dragging the earth around it and with it, making solid ground move and act like liquid. After a moment or two a large part of the grassy plain was spiralling madly. It looked like someone had pulled the plug from a bath deep under the ground and all the land was being sucked down the resulting hole.

Night Light was so mesmerised by the spinning key he didn't notice a Parabat land silently behind him. She grabbed him roughly and threw him aside like a child's toy. She grabbed the Armies of Sorrow, inflated her hood with her banshee-like wail, and sailed off to Embrillion circling far above.

The clone stopped singing. His eyes turned back to their original green and his arms came to rest by his side. He turned to face Lazarus Brown.

'It's done.'

Greenery's eyes turned back to their original green and his arms came to rest by his side. He blinked a couple of times then shook his head and staggered slightly. He looked around as if unsure where he was, then seemed to remember and began desperately looking for the Armies of Sorrow. He noticed the Parabat floating high above and could just make out a bright white dot with blue lights on its side resting in her arms. Confused, angrier than ever and still dripping with blood he looked around for his friend.

'Night Light! Night Light!'

A groan from nearby alerted him to the Punster. He was lying on his back clutching at his side and was having trouble breathing. Greenery ran over to him.

'Are you OK?'

'Yeah I think so. Just winded that's all. What happened to you?'

I don't know. I think I was brainwashed or something. But listen, Night Light, they've got the weapon. The Violents have got the Armies of Sorrow!'

'What!'

'We need to get up there, onto that big ugly flying thing. Can you think of anything?'

'Course I can, lad. Stand back.'

Night Light changed quickly into his Bye Plane guise and shouted to Greenery to jump on board.

'Can you make it all the way up there?'

'I can if we're quick and you don't move about too much.'

They trundled over the rough ground driven on by the old-fashioned propeller, slowly at first but gaining speed and momentum all the time. The Parabat was just climbing aboard Embrillion as the small plane became airborne.

A cry went up from someone aboard the massive flying worm and several Violents pointed towards the small aircraft. They jeered and shouted as they started to fire Tar-Bombs with deadly accuracy. The first would have certainly hit them but Night Light saw it coming and swerved defiantly. This move unfortunately took them into the path of another bomb which missed only by millimetres, due more to good luck than skill. Seconds later another volley of flaming explosives came sailing towards them. Night Light tried to climb above their reach, but there were just too many of them and he wasn't fast enough. A flaming ball of red-hot sticky tar clipped his left wing. He cried out in pain and spiralled out of control. They began to fall immediately.

Their evasive manoeuvres had taken them way above their target and it was a clumsy downward glide to the relative safety of the monster's back. They crashed into the makeshift runway at a fairly obtuse angle and skidded along the bumpy spine for several metres, taking out most of the remaining Violents with them. They came to a tangled halt at the feet of Ignatius Trump.

Night Light returned to his true form but looked weak and in pain. His arm was badly burnt and he had no strength left in him. He looked up at Greenery with a pleading look. The boy nodded and waited for his friend to change again, then bent down to put the night light in his pocket for what little safety it offered.

'Well, well, well, Greenery Jackson. I believe I owe you some pain. Yes, last time we met I was left in some discomfort. I think it's time to return the favour.'

Ignatius towered above Greenery with a manic look on his face. He was flushed and excited. It appeared as though he had been enjoying the battle very much, but then again death was his life. He was holding the Armies of Sorrow and aiming it right at Greenery's heart.

'Or maybe I'll just kill you.'

Ignatius Trump pulled the trigger and fired the Armies of Sorrow.

Lazarus Brown paced back and forth impatiently across the dusty stage. 'Where is it? it should be here by now?' he said, lifting his hands to the gods.

'Erm, what should?' Gloria asked tentatively, so as not to anger the Technomancer.

'The doorway of course, you stupid woman, the gateway!'

'Oh,' was all that she managed in response.

Just then a single mote of dust, drifting gently through the beam of an enchanted spotlight hit something solid and tiny, in mid-air. Whatever it was caught the light and fractured into a thousand spectroscopic beams, before ballooning outwards to form a spiralling Catherine wheel. A vertical spiral galaxy trapped within the confines of an old abandoned theatre.

'About time too.'

Greenery ducked and rolled. He knew the murderous troll wouldn't hesitate to kill him and had begun to dodge the shot even before it was fired. His options were limited though. The further from the weapon the blue suicide ray travelled, the wider it became. He had to stay close.

Ignatius roared with manic glee and began firing the weapon at Greenery over and over again. Greenery put all of his trust in the Karma Armour and moved randomly across Embrillion's back. He wasn't thinking about dodging anything; he was just focusing on moving. It worked! Five shots missed him by millimetres, but how long could he keep this up for? He was out of options. Suddenly a terrible, guttural retching behind him made him look round.

Something was wrong with the Violents. They had all stopped fighting and were simply staring. All apart from one. The strange insectoid man standing closest to Greenery was making awful pain-filled sounds and it was disturbingly obvious why.

He had drunk the flaming liquid from a Tar-Bomb and was vomiting his insides up while they were still on fire. Several of the other clan members took this as a golden opportunity and threw themselves onto the flames, rolling around in the burning flesh to make sure they roasted quickly. Others began hacking away at themselves with their own weapons and a couple simply stepped off the edge of the flying monster. It was as close to a vision of hell as any schoolboy should ever have to witness.

Greenery felt an urge, a strange impulse and dropped to the floor just as another blue suicide ray flew over his head.

'Sir! Sir! What are you doing? You're killing your own men!'

'Get out of my way, Stuff; they're all replaceable. The boy must die!'

Ignatius fired again but was so angry and wild that Greenery didn't even have to move. The shot missed him by miles.

'Stop it, Sir, please!' yelled Stuff.

'Move, worm!'

Ignatius turned the weapon on his valet and pulled the trigger again. With unbelievably fast reflexes, especially for a snail, Stuff lashed out. Fear and desperation combined to give him a strength he didn't know he possessed – he walloped his villainous leader with *Geographical Elements of the Infinite River*.

Ignatius was caught completely off guard and the blow from the big atlas sent him flailing backwards awkwardly. The suicide beam flew from the gun at a wild angle and missed Stuff altogether. Unfortunately it headed straight for Greenery. It spread out wide and low as it approached him and he knew he only had one option. Ignatius lost his balance, tripped and fell over the edge, Greenery turned and jumped. The Armies of Sorrow, Ignatius Trump and Greenery Frankincense Jackson fell from the back of the flying beast.

'No! I don't want to go. I'm scared.'

'Gloria, I won't ask you again.'

'Please don't make me.'

'Very well, you leave me no choice.' Lazarus Brown flicked his finger. Flick.

'No!'

Flick.

'Stop it!' she begged.

The clone was screaming over and over again, writhing around on the floor in uncontrollable agony.

Flick.

'Please! You're killing him!'

Flick.

'All right!!' screamed Mrs Jackson. 'All right, I'm going.' She took a deep breath, said, 'I love you, Greenery,' and stepped off the front of the stage. She was instantly sucked through the singularity at the centre of the spiralling vortex.

'Good work. Right, you next, clone.'

The clone didn't need telling twice. He would have done anything to avoid more suffering. He picked himself up off the floor and practically ran into the rift.

Lazarus Brown looked around at the dusty old auditorium and waved theatrically at an imaginary audience.

'Goodbye, you filthy stinking rathole of a planet,' he said before bowing and stepping into the heart of the event horizon.

Down on the battlefield Towelyn had been staring up at the fight between Greenery and Ignatius. She gasped as first one then the other sailed off the back of Embrillion and into open space. She held her breath, her chest tight with fear, as she watched them fall towards certain death. There was nothing she could do.

As they fell, something unnoticed before detached itself from the undercarriage of the enormous beast and began speeding towards the falling figures. As it flew it changed in form and colour until it became the familiar shape of a tartan Cecephelophopus.

'Sheba!'

It was still going to be a close call. The Disco Beast was a long way off and Greenery was falling fast. Towelyn felt the earth tremble as the marble dictator slammed into the rocky terrain but at the last minute Sheba swooped beneath Greenery and caught him only metres from the ground.

Towelyn let out a sigh of relief. She pulled her sword from her fallen enemy and ran back towards the cave. She had a feeling this wasn't over yet.

Greenery dug his face deep into the furry hide of the Cecephelophopus and screamed. It was a cry of relief and of pent-up fear but overall it was of overwhelming joy. He was still alive.

He looked down and saw the Armies of Sorrow not too far below him. It was intact and resting in a bush. The growing vortex made earlier by the golden key was incredibly close by and pulling at the world, trying to suck everything inside its dark centre.

On the other side of the strange portal was Ignatius Trump. He did not look good. He had been dashed against the rocky outcrops near the cave entrance. His left arm was completely smashed, there was nothing left below the elbow, one foot was gone and he had a huge chip in his forehead. Regrettably, though, he had survived. With unrelenting hatred and the slow determination of a mountain glacier he began to move.

Greenery jumped off the back of Sheba and carefully plucked the Armies of Sorrow from the prickly shrub.

The spiralling ground was still reaching out with strange

gravitational forces. Flashes of white light burst from it sporadically, accompanied by loud electrical fizzing, and a constant hurricane whipped noisily around its circumference.

'Give me the weapon, boy!' shouted Ignatius over the howling, crackling rift.

The manic tyrant was only metres away. Greenery was now trapped between the edge of the portal, the spiky bush behind him, and Ignatius, who had managed to stand and, even though he was walking on one jagged stump, was now getting closer with every ponderous step. There was a scary inevitability to his heavy limp and his good arm was outstretched as if he could pull Greenery towards him and crush the life from him in his stony grip.

'Give it to me!'

'Never!'

Greenery turned the Armies of Sorrow towards Ignatius Trump.

'You can't shoot me, boy, you can't! You might hit some of your furry friends. Hell, you'd probably hit them all!'

Greenery felt as though he'd been stabbed in the gut. Ignatius was right. Behind him the battle between the Violents and the Djinditsu was still raging. If Greenery fired now the suicide beam would take them all out. Ignatius took another step closer.

'Back off! I will shoot!'

'No you won't.'

Step.

'Greenery! Shoot him. It's now or never. Shoot him!' It was Towelyn. She was running towards them both, waving her arms and shouting like crazy. She was directly in the firing line.

Step.

'What a terrible dilemma, Mr Jackson. Kill me, kill your friends. Save your precious Djinditsu and you'll have thousands more deaths on your conscience. What a pickle you're in, Mr Jackson.' Trump's voice was harsh and cold. His eyes shone with manic obsession as he mercilessly teased Greenery.

Step.

'Greenery!' Towelyn was closer now. 'Shoot him!'

'I can't!'

Step.

'Greenery.' A quiet voice, close by, drifted effortlessly above the deafening wail of the black hole. It belonged to Delphinius, though he was nowhere in sight.

'Trust me, Greenery. It's all right – you can fire.'

Step.

Greenery aimed the Armies of Sorrow at Ignatius Trump and pulled the trigger. At exactly the same moment a massive bolt of white lightning leapt from the agitated vortex and left a timid-looking figure standing between the two enemies.

'MUM!'

'Greenery?'

The weapon fired. A wide ray of light radiated from the oval barrel and began to spread. Greenery watched in horror as the suicide beam passed through his mum. It travelled further, washing over Ignatius then Towelyn. It spread wider and wider until eventually it filled the entire battlefield and doused everybody in a strange green light.

Green? When Ignatius had fired the weapon it had definitely produced a blue light.

The metallic clashing of weapons slowly came to a halt.

The cries of anger and hatred subsided until the only sound was the wailing from the rift in space–time. Everybody turned to stare at Greenery. It was exactly like it had been on the back of Embrillion. He couldn't bear it. On top of everything else he had been through, would he now have to witness the self-mutilation and slaughter of all these creatures, of the innocent and noble Djinditsu, of Towelyn, of his own mother?

Out on the battlefield someone moved: one of the big alpha male Djinditsu dropped his weapon. The repulsive feathered thing he had been fighting dropped hers. Slowly at first but spreading like an avalanche, soldiers from both sides threw their weapons down and began . . . talking. Some sat on the floor; others began wandering around aimlessly while a few simply stared up at the golden sky.

'I don't understand?' said Greenery.

'You changed it,' said Delphinius.

Greenery didn't see where he had come from. 'That's why I knew you were the right . . . no, the only person who could be allowed to find the Armies of Sorrow. You infected it with life.'

'How?'

'You have a gift, Greenery, a vision of the world that too few people share. A hunger for knowledge that permeates everything you do. The weapon fires emotion and you didn't want anyone to die when you pulled that trigger.'

'Greenery? What's going on here? Where are we?'

'Mum, what are you . . .?'

BOOM!!

The vortex spat a sizzling bolt of white-hot lightning directly between Greenery's feet. He was blown into the air and caught by the pull of the gravity well. At exactly the same time another blinding bolt hit the Armies of Sorrow. It exploded into a thousand harmless pieces of trash.

In the nanosecond before he was sucked through the rift he caught sight of a wild-haired salesman in a cloak grabbing his mum roughly. And then he was gone, sucked through time and space away from armour-clad preachers and wondrous creatures, from giant plants and Bedazzlephants, from Towelyn, from Sheba, from his mum.

Chapter Twenty

A New Perspective

There was a time when I was mighty.
There was a time when I was bold.
There was a time when I was feared,
Truly awesome to behold.
But now my light is fading
And now my light is dim.
One day my light must be passed on,
I'll pass it on to him.

Taken from *The Passing of the Watcher*
by the Mysterious Wandering Gump

Greenery opened his eyes. Everything was a bit fuzzy. A golden cherub hovered above him. Its compassionate gaze looked down on him with a strange beatific smile that seemed to say everything would be all right. He blinked and managed to focus. The angel was still there, only now he could see more clearly he noticed it was covered in dust and some of the gold leaf was peeling off its pitiful wings. He sat up and looked around the old Victorian auditorium. There was a large red stain on the stage, left by his blood-soaked clothes as he'd skidded to a halt. After a while he picked his bruised body up off the dusty floor and began the long walk home. Inside he was numb, it was too painful and confusing to feel anything so instead he felt nothing.

He showered, he got changed and then he ate. As he munched his way through uninspiring beans on toast he heard a thump from upstairs followed by angry swearing. The boy tensed and grabbed a weapon – the bread knife from the kitchen. Heavy footsteps from above crossed the ceiling and came to the top of the stairs. Slowly they thudded down each one in turn and then stopped at the bottom. A small dark shadow rounded the corner into Greenery Jackson's kitchen.

'Where the devil are we, lad, and what in high heaven is that you're eating? I'm starving.'

Greenery threw the knife aside and rushed towards Night Light. He knelt down and hugged the little Punster with all his heart.

'Hey, hey, easy now, son, it's all right. What's the matter? What's wrong with you, lad?'

'We're home, Night Light. Well, I'm home. But I think I saw Lazarus Brown and he's back in The Other Place and he's got my mum and I'll never get her back because I haven't got the key and I don't know what to do. I don't even know if she's alive. He could have killed her when I left or he could, he could . . .'

'Greenery, Greenery, calm down. Take a deep breath. Close your eyes and look for her.'

'What?'

'Use the Tear of the Cyclops.'

'Will it work here?'

'It should do.'

Greenery did as he was told. It took him a few minutes to concentrate; he was wound up too tight to focus but he got there in the end.

His eyes snapped open.

'She's alive but she doesn't look happy.'

'She's alive, Greenery; that's enough for now.'

'How do we get back though? I have to save her.'

'Greenery, The Other Place is closer than you can possibly imagine. That's the deal with an infinite universe; it's only infinite from the inside.'

'But we are inside it.'

'Yeah, we are but you have the Tear, you can *see* it from the outside, and if you can do that, you're one step closer to breaking down the barriers.'

'Night Light, what are you talking about?'

'Remember when we were sitting by the Eternal Abyss and I told you about the idea of The Bulk?'

'Yeah, vaguely, the one about Einstein and the squishy mattress.'

'Right. Well, I want you to imagine you can chop a piece off that universe. Can you picture it?'

Greenery closed his eyes and imagined.

'Yes.'

'Right now this is confusing but stay with me. That little piece in your hands is also infinite.'

'What? How?'

'Because a small piece of infinity is always infinite. That's the very definition of the word.'

'Night Light, I don't understand.'

'That's all right, lad. How can you? You're human. But you

will, when you've seen it. Look at something, anything, then use the power of the Tear to see the smallest possible piece of it.

Greenery shrugged and decided to look at the back of his hand. It seemed as good as anything. He concentrated and stared. The perspective of his mind's eye flew away from him exactly as it had in Macadamia; only this time instead of flying up, it was zooming in.

He saw the back of his hand, the pores and hair follicles growing to the size of football stadiums; he penetrated the epidermis and barrelled on through to the subcutaneous layer. In this small region of flesh his vision focused again. Now he could see complex molecules and long chains of carbon atoms fizzing with energetic impulses.

Zoom. One massive carbon atom filled his vision. Its electrons disappeared and reappeared with dizzying speed around its heart, the nucleus, a tight cluster of six protons and six neutrons.

Zoom. He sailed through the vast and open expanse between the orbit of an electron and a positively charged proton.

Zoom. Deep inside the proton he saw tiny quarks held together by long chains of gluons and here, at the edge of known science, his mind focused again.

Zoom. Inside the quark was a bewildering array of vibrating strings, the elementary particles that all things are made of. They resonated with a melodic tone so perfect in its nature that it almost brought Greenery to tears.

Zoom. One string now filled his vision. Unlike the others its ends were joined together to make a perfect circle. A so-called 'hypothetical' graviton. Inside its oscillating structure Greenery could see clouds of spiralling galaxies, massive nebula, and great cosmic reaches.

Zoom. Running through the middle of this great universe was a fine bright ribbon of light. Greenery had seen it before, and was the only person in creation that could recognise it from this perspective. It was The Infinite River and it stretched forever onwards connecting all of the other countless gravitons, all of the other universes together.

Night Light watched as slowly Greenery's confused expression gave way to focused attention, then surprise, then jaw-dropping wonder, as the truth was revealed.

'Oh my God,' he whispered.

'Exactly,' Night Light nodded slowly. 'Listen, lad, we have only just touched upon the surface of the impossible. I'm going to show you such wonders. I'm going to take you by the hand and I'm going to lead you back to The River.'

'But how, Night Light? How do you know all this?'

'Let's say I'm on a training programme. I've known from the start we would end up here. My employer told me.'

'And who's your employer?'

'He came to me a long time ago and told me I was going to meet someone very special, that I was ideally placed in space and time to help that person. He said that he would teach me things, unbelievable things, and he did and they are glorious. He said that this person would be the first to travel independently between worlds . . . can't wait for that one . . . and he said this person was important for the future survival of creation. That person is you, Greenery. It's no coincidence that we met. My employer knew that would happen and trained me years ago to be your guide. It took me a little time to realise you were the one I had been waiting for. It wasn't until I realised your key was *the* key and then events were already in motion. But he knew.'

'Who knew?' croaked Greenery, unable to speak above a whisper.

'Oh didn't I mention it before?' said Night Light with a sardonic smile and a twinkle in his eye. 'I work for The Mysterious Wandering Gump.'

Not the End.